THE LAST V[IKING]

About the Author

Ronnie Wheeler was born in Birmingham's Dudley Road Hospital in 1940. At the age of two, he was adopted by a canal boatman and his wife and his name was changed to Ron Dawson. He was raised on the giant Kingstanding council housing estate. He began work as a butcher's boy and for the next nine years had a succession of jobs, ranging from building site labourer, window cleaner, soft-drinks delivery man, and power-press operator to door-to-door salesman. A motorcycle accident led him to train as a teacher of maladjusted children. He went on to gain the degrees of BA., M.Sc., and PhD., mainly by part-time study. He became a Research and Chartered Psychologist, and an Associate Fellow of the British Psychological Society. He has worked as a LEA and OFSTED Inspector, and was Principal Lecturer for post-graduate awards and Head of Special Needs and Habilitation in what is now the University of Winchester. He has numerous academic and research based publications, many focused upon behavioural and emotional difficulties. His Teacher Information Pack (Tips), which was published by Macmillan Education, embraced the whole range of Special Educational Needs and was described as an 'Opus Magnum' in a professional psychological journal review. He also wrote a regular satirical column, 'The Dawson File', for Special Children magazine. 'The Last Viking', his first novel, was first published in Canada by Trafford Publishing in 2006. His second novel, 'The Worm that Flies in the Night : A Diary of Incestuous Love and Serial Murder,' was published by Mulberry Tree Books in 2009. He is also the creator and author of 'The Amazing Adventures of Scary Bones the Skelton Series,' which are also published by Mulberry Tree Books.

A CLP catalogue record of this book is available from the British Library.

First published in Canada in 2006 by Trafford Publishing.
This edition first published in Great Britain in 2009 by
Mulberry Tree Publishing.
Mulberry House
Dorset DT11 0NT, UK

Cover design courtesy of Infinite Wisdom Productions Ltd,
'Mind over Media', Film and Television, Birmingham, UK.
www.iwisdom.co.uk
Artwork by Richard Jordan.

Printed and bound in the UK by
Imprintdigital, Upton Pyne, Exeter EX5 5HY

ISBN 978-0-9561732-3-2

MTBooks
Mulberry Tree Books
Mulberry House
Winterborne Stickland
Dorset DT11 0NT
www.mulberrytreebooks.co.uk

THE LAST
VIKING

RON DAWSON

⌘⌘⌘⌘⌘⌘⌘⌘⌘⌘⌘⌘⌘

THE LAST VIKING

This is the last testament of a man I used to know. His name was Ronnie Wheeler. He finished writing it on the thirteenth of May, two thousand and one. He sent a copy to me which I received on the seventeenth of May. On the eighteenth of May he was found to have died in his home. I believe he was murdered. He was truly the last of the Vikings and this is his story told in his own words.

Ron Dawson

⌘⌘⌘⌘⌘⌘⌘⌘⌘⌘⌘⌘⌘

RONNIE WHEELERS STORY

The Prologue

This is the inside and untold story of the world's greatest robbery which happened over forty years ago. In telling it to you now, I have signed my own death warrant. Had I told it any earlier, it would also have served as the death warrant for many good friends, and perhaps their close families too. Now, after all these years, I am sure that I endanger only myself and perhaps one other. Despite this, I know that she will approve of what I have done and face the consequent sentence of death as compliantly as I.

Unlike me, however, she does not deserve to die at the hidden bidding of an unrelenting and unforgiving British establishment, for her crime was merely to have been there, to have been with us on that day, the sixth of June 1954. I truly hope that she will be allowed to live the remaining years of her life unharmed and in peace, but my life and the story I tell here has taught me that British justice conspires to conceal far greater crimes than either hers or mine. So, like me, she will almost certainly die as a result of what I have written here, but I know that, like me, she will die with triumph in her heart and a final curse for our tormentors on her lips.

The final casting off of my unacknowledged cloak of cowardice began just six days ago on the seventh of May. On that day I went to the funeral of a close friend of mine at Birmingham's Perry Barr Crematorium. He was a mate with whom I had enjoyed my youth, had been to war with, had fought and killed with, laughed and cried with and, now I recognise, a mate whose friendship protected me both in times of danger and of foolishness. He enriched my life through his undemanding support and his constant pitch for a better life. For the past long forty-seven years of our lives we were not able to live as friends do and should. Our mutually sustaining friendship was maintained only by furtive phone calls and occasional meetings which put the lives of both ourselves and our families at risk. His birth name was Michael Tibbetts but he was known to all who loved and loathed him as 'Big Mick'.

Mick was a big man. Not in a physical sense for, although he was just about six feet tall, he weighed no more than twelve and a half stone.

Not big, you'll agree, by big man standards, but he was rated big by his presence, his demeanour, call it what you will. He was a big man to those of us who knew him. He looked hard and was hard, hard as a rhino's bollocks. A mean bastard to those who crossed him but someone who was totally dependable to those whom he chose to befriend, which were few beyond his own family circle. I, and most of the others who grew up with him, believed that Mick's family name of Tibbetts gave a partial explanation as to why he became so hard and mean.

In his early years at school he was a lanky, spindly kid whom the others would torment by calling him 'Tibbles'. Mick hated it and consequently he would attack his tormentors, be they one or six. At first he nearly always came off worst in the resultant violence, but the constant scrapping and fighting toughened and fortified him. The sinews strengthened, the muscles hardened, and his face and body lost their sensitivity to maliciously inflicted pain. He learned to take the pain, and so he was able to keep getting up, to keep coming back. The more he did so, the more he learned how to dish it out, how to hurt others, how to disable them, how to make them crawl. He became a hardened, mean street-fighter and so he began to win, and then never to lose, no matter how big or how many the opposition.

From then on no-one, including me, ever called him 'Tibbles', although as closer mates in later years I could get away with it in a well-timed jest. Mick was big in our eyes and no one who met him ever questioned why he was known as Big Mick. It fitted him like a Saville Row suit. He also became the best friend I ever had.

The crem preacher knew none of this. He knew nothing of Mick, but still he spieled on and on, probably the same spiel he used everyday for any dead flesh he had never met or known as a living soul. What was amazing is that he was able to do it without touching upon or even hinting at what the real Mick was about or at the magnificent achievement he had been part of. When he'd finished, we, his disbelieving mourners, stood to sing some platitudinous hymn none of us knew or even recognised. In consequence, our pitiful bleatings were unable to fulfil even the hymn's true purpose of drowning out the quiet hum of the electric motor driving the coffin's conveyor belt.

As we hoarsely whimpered our mournful tune, the coffin, with Big

Mick in it, moved slowly but surely forward, pushing through the tiny purple curtains into the void and the unseen flames beyond taking, if the preacher was to be believed, Mick, with all his sins, to sainthood. I stared at those closed, unmoving curtains long after Mick had gone, as if hoping for an encore with the coffin re-emerging and Mick stepping out again large as life.

My mind obstinately tried not to accept it, but there was no way out. This big man, this big friend, was finally gone, taking with him his part of our secret and his part of the story. Soon he would be no more than a small jar of budgie grit to be scattered wherever his missus, Mavis, decided. I learned yesterday that she plans to get a friend to scatter his remains in the sea off Saints Bay on the south coast of Guernsey. I hope some kindly soul will do the same for me when I'm put to the flame and reduced to the handful of earthly ashes that eliminates all human distinction and aspiration. And the thought of both Mick and me being back in Saints Bay will be, despite all their malicious power, a final 'up yours' to secret George and the whole bloody British establishment.

So lost was I in these thoughts that when my mind returned to the here and now, the dutiful congregation had left and I was alone in the chapel. I moved out to the porticoed porch at its front. Outside small groups of mourners were chatting quietly and sedately. It was a grey morning and a light drizzle added to the bleakness. My worn out translucent eyes moved from group to group, person to person, consciously deciphering each grey wrinkled face, each bent and distorted body, searching desperately for the gleam of a familiar eye, the reminiscence of a triumphant smile or arrogant strut, an echo of shared laughter or tale, but there was none.

Nor were there any there who had been with us on that fateful day in June, all those years ago, when we pulled off what is still the greatest robbery of all time. This epic achievement of ours has been kept from public awareness by an establishment desperate to protect its power and to wreak revenge on any who threaten its way of life or despoil its version of humanity. I knew that now, with Mick gone, I was the last, the last of those who could tell the story from our side of the fence. If any of the others were still alive, they would have been there like me, or at least they would have sent something to mark that they knew, and remembered.

I moved over to the meagre but expensive and discreet line of wreaths. There were no gaudy wreaths proclaiming 'Mick' in giant letters of flowers, or 'Not Forgotten', or all the other sort of sentimental over the top crap that marked the funerals of the Krays and other pretentious London dickheads. I paced the line, stooping at each wreath to read every condolence slowly and deliberately, again searching for a hint or trace of a name from the past and again found none. Rising from the last I became aware of Mavis, Mick's widow, standing alone beside me.

'Hello Mavis.'

'Hello Ronnie.' She paused for a moment. 'I knew you'd come if you were still alive and heard the news.'

'Yes, I'm still alive, beat the old bugger at something at last.'

Mavis smiled. She knew that I felt this loss as much as she. 'After all these years, I could still tell it was you. You've still got that cocky way about you,' she said with a glimpse of a smile. She opened her handbag, took out a small tissue packet and handed it me.

'I'm glad you had the guts to come. Mick always said you would. He wanted you to have this.'

For its size it was heavy. I started to unwrap it.

'Keep it down,' she whispered, furtively looking around.

I drew it within the curtained drapes of my top-coat to open it. I saw that it was a gold chain necklace and medallion. The medallion showed the emblem of a Nazi swastika framed by a victory laurel crested by a stylised Roman eagle. I had seen it once before. I turned it over. It was the same one all right. On the back an inscription in German read 'SS Gruppenfuhrer Adrian Mordaunt, Fur Dienste an den Fuhrer.' (Adrian Mordaunt, for services to the Fuhrer). It was the last thing I'd expected to see, a total surprise, but even so I couldn't help smiling at this confirmation from the grave of Mick's life-long addiction to sticking two fingers up to authority. Mavis was scrutinising my reaction.

'How did the cheeky bastard spirit this away?' I asked. Mavis managed a tributary smile but didn't attempt an answer.

'Put it away,' she whispered more urgently, her eyes still flitting around. 'They'll see the bloody thing!' I slipped it quickly into a waistcoat pocket.

'There's probably half a dozen of the bastards watching us right now.' Mavis rarely swore but she was probably right.

'You shouldn't have come,' she went on quietly, 'I'm glad you did, but any one of this lot could be one of them, the drivers, the ushers, even the bloody Vicar. You can never tell, you're taking one hell of a chance.'

'I expect you're right,' I replied, 'but I thought, "sod it". After more than forty years, I just thought "Sod it" and sod them.'

She ignored my response and spoke quietly. 'I had a visit from George within a day of Mick passing on, you know.'

'George? Secret George? I haven't heard from that little turd for ages. I thought he must be dead or pensioned off or something. I can't bloody believe it.'

'It was him all right. He said he wanted to offer me his condolences and to remind me that the deal still held good. 'Till death us do part,' he said as he left, and he still means it.'

'The bastard, the little bastard!' I spat the words out. 'After all this time and after what they've done, you'd have thought they'd have let it drop by now.' I looked around in anger, wanting to lash out at somebody, something, anything.

Mavis could still recognise all the signs, and so to calm me she said, 'Mick would have been glad that you came,' and we both fell silent.

To break the impasse I asked her if any of the others had been in touch. She shook her head.

'No, for the past few years Mick was always saying that there was only you and him left now.' Her sad eyes turned to look right into mine. 'He was probably right, too, you know.'

Tears began to trickle down her worn face; she was finding it difficult to speak.

'It's a bloody shame that nobody will ever really know what us lot did, it's a bloody shame, it just ain't right what they did to us. I know you pulled off the deal Ronnie and that we all agreed it, but I sometimes think we'd all have been better off to have done our time. At least we'd all have gone down in history like Tony wanted and still had something of a life when we got out.' She wiped her tears with her hand. 'You know what George did? He squeezed the life out of Mick, out of everyone of us, and even out of what we did.'

At this Mavis broke down completely, her frail body shaking and convulsing as she cried. While I'm wondering what to do or say, one of the women mourners spots that Mavis is in a state. She comes across, puts an arm around Mavis's shuddering body, gives me a witch's eye over her shoulder and leads her away. For a brief moment Mavis turned and looked back at me. Her eyes, her whole frail body was silently pleading with me, pleading as if it were for her own life.

'I'll see what I can do,' I said. It was a phrase from the past but it seemed to do the trick. Mavis braved a weak smile, nodded, and was soon lost among a gaggle of other mourners. I turned and headed back to where Kevin 'Moggsie' Morgan, my driver, was waiting with the car. I could feel the tears welling up. I was breaking up too.

'You all right, Ronnie?' Moggsie asked as he opened the door and helped me in. I nodded and Mogs knew me well enough not to pursue the matter. He got into the driver's seat and asked, 'Straight home, is it?'

I sat silent for a moment or two, memories rushing and tumbling into my mind. 'Yeah, I just need cheering up. No, wait a minute. Tell you what, take me on a tour around some of the old places, see if we can recognise any of 'em still.'

Moggsie started the motor and we moved off.

'Yeah,' I says. 'Why not? Cut along Witton Lane first, then up Electric Avenue, down Deykens and past the Villa ground, up to Six Ways, down Newtown Row, past the Bartons and the Hipp, then go up town, just tour about a bit but make sure that we go past the old Castaways Club and then out Edgbaston way, see if the old Tower Ballroom is......' In the rear view mirror I could see Moggsie shaking his head.

'I've got the idea,' he says. 'All the old haunts, right?'

'Yeah, you've got it.'

I settled back in the broad cream leather seats of the Jaguar. There was no need to tell Moggsie where to take me, we'd done this sort of trip on many occasions, it was just that we were starting out from somewhere different. Perry Barr crem was not usually on our itinerary, it was that that threw me, that and thoughts of the funeral.

I drew the Nazi medallion and chain from my waistcoat and spread it out carefully across my knees so that I could have a closer look at it. It was the same one all right, and it still looked as good as new, just as it had all those years ago, solid gold weighing five to six ounces. Give those Nazi bastards their due, they could make good stuff. Every time I looked at it or touched it I couldn't help smiling and silently repeating, 'the cheeky bugger.'

Holding this direct link with the past and seeing what was left of the old haunts brought every moment of those eventful and dramatic days back to me. In the mirror Moggsie must have seen me alternating between tears and smiles as the black and the golden times carrouselled around my mind, and he probably wondered what the bloody hell I was thinking about. These life clinging memories flooded and saturated my mind. But as each memory ebbed and flowed, my last words to Mavis echoed repeatedly like a menacing siren call deep in a sea mist, 'I'll see what I can do..... I'll see what I can do....'

'Silly old prat,' I thought to myself. 'What the hell can you do for anyone now? Just look at yourself.' I looked at my grey, ashen, weary face in the rear mirror and looked away in anguish to the anonymity of the outside world. There was a time, many years ago, that when I spoke those same words, they really meant something. People took them very seriously, so much so I had to be careful not use them too loosely or else some poor innocent bastard would get a hard kicking rather than it be seen for me to back down or lose face. Now they sounded ridiculous, a bragger's bluff fooling no-one but the no-hope punter with a losing hand. Perhaps Mavis was right, George had slowly squeezed the life out of all of us for all these years. It only needed one more turn of the tourniquet and me and Mavis would be gone too. George and the establishment would have finally triumphed then as we two also lay silent in death, their treacherous secrets hidden for all time.

Some two hours later the crunch of the Jag's wide tyres pushing through familiar gravel broke through my melancholic reminiscing. We were on the long drive leading up to the house. Moggsie stopped at the front steps, came round, opened the door and helped me out, me, who once upon a time could be out of a dodgy motor and a hundred yards up the road before the local plod could even get his whistle out.

'Thanks, Moggsie,' I said as I levered myself slowly up the steps to the house. 'I can manage on my own now, go on, take the rest of the day off, practice playing that bloody trombone of yours or something, yeah, play at least one burst of "Rock around the Clock" for Mick.'

'Blimey, Ronnie,' he replied jokingly, 'he must have been some mate. I'll do him two verses for good measure!'

I nodded, opened the door and went in. The house was empty and quiet. I had given Janet and David, my resident helpers, the day off too. I poured myself a large dose of Hennessey's best, fell into a chair, and turned on the telly to ease my mind and paper over my thoughts. It was not to be. On that same day, Ronnie Biggs, last of the inept Great Train Robbers, returned to Britain to give himself up to the full weight or mercy of the British judicial system. He is claiming that he now wants to die in the land of his birth, the land he loves and has pined for during nearly forty years of being on the run and of living in exile. The real truth of the matter, however, is that he is hoping to end his predestined days peacefully and painlessly in one of Her Majesty's freebie penal institutions rather than die in long slow tortuous agony in some Brazilian hell-hole of a hospital. He probably could have afforded a decent hospital over there but he is desperate that the piteous remains of his once considerable fortune passes to the runts he has fathered rather than be squandered on futile attempts to preserve his spent body.

'Fair enough,' you might say, 'a brave, brave man, puts family before himself, so give the poor bloke a break.' The publicity surrounding his return shows that you are not alone in these sentiments for this thieving bastard, and I say this as a former thieving bastard myself. On his grovelling return he was greeted as a sort of national celebrity, if not a national hero. Along with the half dozen or so coppers waiting to arrest him there were several hundred Joe Publics cheering, shouting and screaming at his every stunted move. There were reporters from TV and radio stations, newspapers, glossy magazines, all hoping for a word, a picture, even a glimpse from this dying crook, and all ready and willing to pay handsomely for the privilege. It made me sick. And very, very angry.

It's been the same ever since Biggsie and his mates pulled off the so-called Great Train Robbery back in nineteen sixty-three. They were soon collared by the law and got over three hundred years in jail sentences between the twelve of them less than a year later. As a tribute to the ineffectiveness of our prison system in the face of an organised team, some of them were out and about before the screws had time to pocket the cell keys. Most of those who escaped, however, were dozy bastards and were caught soon afterwards. One of the last to be caught was Charlie Wilson whose run of luck in ducking and diving ran out in nineteen sixty-eight when the law finally caught up with him in Canada.

But Ronnie Biggs managed to get himself a one-way ticket to Brazil. The establishment cockroaches traced him there and had the neck to arrest him in Rio, but, true to form, the Brazilians told them to fuck off; Biggsie was there with his money and they didn't care where he'd got it from as long as he spent it with them. So Ronnie gets to living the high life in Rio, chased, it seems, by beautiful women and the world media wanting to give him even more money to look or speak in their direction. He became a world-wide celebrity, there were pictures, articles, books, even bloody films, and all from doing one poxy train robbery!

Watching his return on the early evening news had little effect upon me at first. I watched unmoved as this grey, broken figure of a man was respectfully helped out of a privately chartered aeroplane, probably paid for by some moralistic tabloid newspaper. He was then helped into a publicly chartered Black Maria, undoubtedly paid for by Her Majesty's taxpayers, who would have been much better off if he'd been left to rot in Brazil. The desire of the British establishment for retribution, however, knows no costs, particularly as the money doesn't come out of their own back pockets.

But the news just wouldn't let it drop. No way. It goes on about the 'Great Train Robbery', on and on until eventually the hype, the reporting, the whole Ronnie Biggs thing, him being presented as the greatest, the most wonderful, god all fucking mighty, he's the main man shit, gnawed its way through my gut and into my being.

Suddenly I was up on my feet, with no pitiful struggle or condescendingly conspicuous help. I had flipped. I was angry and shouting at the telly. 'Great fucking Train Robbery? The bastards only nicked two and a half million! What's that, a bloody gnat's bollock to what we took!' The Brinks-Matt job gets a mention. I'm a bit more respectful here because it's held that they nicked twenty-five million or more, forgetting the odd shilling or two, and largely got away with it. But I'm still angry, so I shout at the telly again, 'Hardly worth getting out of bleeding bed for!' By now I'm in a right frenzy, shouting and screaming uselessly like a frustrated bailiff's mark long after the bit about Biggsie and the train robbery has finished.

I eventually realise I am left shouting pathetically at some marble chewing BBC prat chuntering on about foot and mouth disease and noticeably ignoring me and my rantings. I sank helplessly back into my chair still rumbling on. 'All this fucking publicity for small timers. Small timers, the lot of them. Take those two vicious bastards, the Krays, look at their fucking funerals, you'd have thought they were bleeding royalty instead of two vicious no-hopers who never had the nowse or guts to pull off a real job. Beating up fucking has-beens and nicking old ladies' handbags, that's all that they were good for, nothing but a pair of useless bollocks! Not fit to polish Mick's boots, yet look at his funeral today, nobody noticed, nobody cared, no press, no TV, no fuck all and yet our do was bigger than all that lot put together.' My anger broke into almost pitiful chokes. 'Mavis was right, it's not right, it ain't fair, it just ain't fair, it's bloody criminal.' The finality of Mick's death had finally got through to me.

I was still in this turmoil when the phone rang. I picked it up angrily and shouted, 'Hello!'

'Hello Ronnie,' a formal quiet voice droned, 'just a courtesy call to let you know that your presence at Mr. Tibbetts' funeral today has been noted and recorded. The good news, however, is that given the prevailing circumstances, we shall not be.....'

'What do you mean?' I yelled at the voice, 'given the prevailing fucking circumstances? You mean because all the other bastards are dead and buried, and there's only fucking me and poor Mavis left!'

'As I was saying,' the voice calmly continued, 'given the prevailing circumstances we shall not be taking any further action in this instance.' Before I could speak, the phone clicked and went dead. I threw it across the room and stormed around in a frenzy, kicking and shouting like a crazy man.

'Bastards, bastards, but that's it, deal or no deal, they're not going to tell me what I can and what I can't do anymore, I'm not fucking useless! I'm not fucking helpless. Killing me don't matter any more, I'm going to die soon anyway, my time's near enough up. There is something I can do, even at my age, and I'm going to bloody well do it. I'm going to do it for Mavis and Mick, for Marge and all the rest, you can't get at them any more. And I'm going to do it to shit on you lot. You've just made your biggest mistake George, you couldn't leave it alone, you just had to let me know you were still there, still watching, still threatening, still squeezing and shitting on who you like, when you like. Well I'm going to let you know I'm still here too. The deal's off and it's your turn to be shit on. I'm going to let the whole fucking world know the whole fucking story from beginning to end.'

I was mad, mad with anger and frustration, and when I'm mad I often fall to using strong language, and when I'm frustrated I often resort to extreme violence.

I calmed myself, poured another large shot of Hennessey's, and began to write this, our story. The story of Mick, Mavis and Marg, Ernie, Tony, Ikey and Barney and a bunch of other good mates who, had they have been born of a higher caste, might have ranked amongst the greatest of Britons. Where I was personally involved, the story is told exactly as I remember it. Where I wasn't so involved, it's pieced together from what the others told me or what I worked out for myself at the time or sometime later. Hand on heart, mother's death bed and all that shit, it is the truth as best I can tell it.

1 Call to Arms

My story starts back in the second week of January, nineteen fifty-four. The whole of Britain was in the grip of a prolonged ice-cold winter. In Birmingham, freezing winds and deep snow intensified the hardships of a forgotten city still recovering from six years of terrible war, loss and national neglect.

To revive flailing souls desperate to hold on to something of the good life, the Aston Hippodrome was offering 'Heat-wave', a nightly variety show with a daring strip-tease 'finale'. The finale was a procession of 'artistic tableaux' featuring shivering overweight nudes who, by law, were not allowed to move whilst under the gaze of a mesmerised audience of dissatisfied men and submissive wives. So the nudes stood statuesque behind transparent veils drawn across vast gilded picture frames in lamentable attempts to replicate gaudy paintings of some tropical paradise. Their artistic positionings were elevated to the sublime by the Hippodrome's depleted orchestra playing 'We're having a heat-wave, a tropical heat-wave' with little gusto or musical appreciation. Meanwhile, in the Bartons Arms Pub opposite, coal and coke fires, warm beer and a low regard for the law offered solace to less dispirited souls.

It was a Friday night, villains' night out. Despite the bitter weather, the 'Gents Only' Bar in the Bartons had attracted all of the usual crowd with surprisingly few absentees. The bar was exclusively ours. As usual, the Landlord, Ray Clayton, had reserved the bar for a 'Private Function' for the 'Aston Villains', which meant our mob, claiming that we were his personal friends and associates. He did this to protect us from our own loose chat and ear wigging intruders, and in return we looked after him handsomely. He reserved the bar in this way for us every Friday night and when need demanded.

As every one of the regular interns had either served in the War or had done their time in National Service, Ray's 'Private Function' had become an imaginary soldier somewhat akin to the mythical 'Tommy Atkins'. Many's the time that, when pulled by the local law for questioning about some job or other, the chief suspect would claim, 'but officer, I was with Private Function all night!' The law were rarely amused but most had enough nowse to realise that it meant they were beating a dead dog. If in ignorance a particular copper persisted with a charge, a sufficient number of the regular 'Villains' would swear on the Holy Bible and their own mother's death-bed that the suspect had been with them in the 'Gents Only' at the time of the said crime, and probably also vouch to the suspect's honesty and integrity for good measure.

So, as usual, the blokes in the 'Gents Only' that Friday night were all life villains, minor or major. Whilst for some, villainy was their one and only occupation, for many it was an addictive and lucrative sideline which brought some excitement, hope and lucre to assuage the despair of their daily drudgery in wage slavery. What united them was their irrepressible need to get out and do something, anything, to escape the place allocated to them by an oppressive class-based society. Born into the overflowing gutters of the lowest caste, the only escape route readily available to them lay along the yellow-brick road of crime which stretched out to their personal rainbow, pointing the way to the elusive pot of gold they sought so desperately.

Fifteen years before, without consulting them, their country had gone to war. They were taken from their homes and loved ones to defend their 'way of life' and protect the rich bastards that benefited from it. They were taught how to fight and how to kill and sent to places where their newly acquired skills of wreaking death and destruction could be practised and made perfect. Unfortunately, when the fighting stopped and killing people became illegal again, their country tipped them back into the Birmingham gutters they had come from to fend for themselves armed only with these limited skills.

At that time there was little demand on the Brummie job market for trained killers, be they ex-tank drivers, machine gunners, artillery experts or the like. There were plenty of jobs going, of course, but not for these particular skills and consequently the sort of jobs these men could attract did not pay the sort of money that could attract them or support the sort of life style they craved. But unlike most of the subservient masses of those years, they could not and would not accept their lot. So they turned to crime.

The early nineteen fifties was a time of widespread shortage and deprivation although at the same time everybody was getting better off by the day. It seemed like anything you could get your hands on you could sell at a handsome, if not criminal, profit. Many of the lads, including Mick and me, started off by selling on stuff some other aspiring entrepreneur had acquired illegal title to. Sometimes we might be second, third or even fourth in this distribution chain, each stage down the line producing less and less of the cake to take home. You didn't need much of the old grey matter to suss out that the way to riches was to be number one in the chain, to be the fountain head, because at this point, apart from a few minor expenses, the goods all came free. Anything you got for lifted stuff was all yours, twenty-two carat bunce, one hundred per cent profit.

As an example of how easy it was, Mick and me once requisitioned a lorry-load of vacuum cleaners on a Monday afternoon and we'd sold the lot on by the Thursday afternoon of the same week. We more or less did the same with a load of Swiss-made sewing machines a couple of weeks later. If there was a problem at this stage, particularly when you were first starting up as an independent, it was getting to know where and when a particular valuable consignment was to be stored, moved, or inadvertently left unattended.

Mick and me sorted this problem out by setting up a couple of separate legit front businesses. Mick set up in industrial and commercial cleaning while I bought a couple of ex-WD wagons at a knock down price to set up a short haul transport business. These met our needs in two ways. Firstly, they both entailed visiting manufacturers, wholesalers, importers and the like, which gave us direct knowledge about the whereabouts of poorly-protected valuable stock, and secondly, they helped to explain our rapidly improving financial situation to any inquisitive busybody.

We also found that as we became widely known to those in the know as traders of dubious distinction, the vital information necessary for our more lucrative ventures came to us unsolicited, although we always paid handsomely for good information. Soon we were getting a regular flow of tip-offs for the most profitable commodity of all, cash. Cash meant no selling on, no third parties; it was just pure unadulterated bunce!

At that time in the fifties, most working people got paid weekly in cash sealed in little brown paper envelopes, and usually on a Friday afternoon. This inevitably meant that around mid-day each Friday the wages of hundreds of workers were collected in bulk readies from the Banks. More often than not, the cash was picked up by some young office girl or useless old tosser and touted around Brum in the back of cars, on buses, and even on push bikes or shank's pony. These pay rolls were just asking to be taken and, as Mick, me and many others used to say, 'refusal often offends,' and so, rather than cause any offence, we took them on a regular basis.

A successful Friday morning's or afternoon's work inevitably called for a celebration that same evening, and this was usually undertaken in the Bartons. I've known blokes nick all the wages money due for a local factory on a Friday afternoon and that night they would be out buying a drink for some poor tosser who was going to be skint till next week because some villains had nicked his factory's wages! They would stand in the Bar, drinking each other's health and mournfully questioning what the world was coming to, the villains taking the piss and the losing tossers crying into their free beer!

This particular Friday night's celebration was the first after New Year's day, which that year had fallen on a Friday. The previous week's high AWOL figures in the 'Gents Only' probably accounted for the high turnout that night. Otherwise things were much as normal. Some schools of three card brag, nap and pontoon were in full flow with the stakes easing ever upwards as the sharks gently fleeced their lesser prey. Stories and news, racing tips, tragedies and deals, overlaid by ribald banter and seedy jokes, occupied the rest.

The atmosphere was noisy, relaxed and safe, just as we liked it, when in walks Spider Webb accompanied by the two Hammond brothers, Percy and Eddie. Everyone had a quick gander and an involuntary silence momentarily enveloped the bar but, true to form and their natural skills of self preservation, all present immediately resurrected their activities in an attempt to give the not-so-welcome trio the impression that their entrance had either not been noticed or was regarded as a non event. Nobody was fooled.

The obvious origin of Spider's nick name belied how well it fitted his physical form, his nature and life style. He was a bony, spiky, figure of a man, whose lack of decent flesh on his bones made his movements appear rapid and jerky as he scuttled about here and there spinning webs of deception to catch any snippet of information that might be used to further his own, or his current paymaster's, ends. His current paymaster was Tony Day.

Tony Day was the only ex-small time villain we knew who had actually snatched the elusive pot of gold we all strived for. Tony had made it, financially at least. Probably because he'd made it and we hadn't, none of us were too keen on the bloke. It was interesting though that, nevertheless, most of our crowd liked it to be known that we knew him, in fact more than just knew him. We would proudly announce to the world that he started out with us, he had grown up with us, he had wheeled, dealed and stolen with us. We were mates, he was like family, he would do anything for us and we would do anything for him.

Most of this, of course, was complete bollocks, but it was the impression we liked to project. It was true that he started out with many of us in petty crime but his diversionary legal businesses of dealing in war surplus and scrap metal had proved to be immeasurably more profitable than his dabblings with any of us on the wrong side of the law. We rationalised this by asserting that it was the money he made from his dabbling in crime that enabled him to be successful in his legitimate businesses; not to have done so would have belittled our golden road of hope to a cobbled lane of hopeless despair.

Although we were envious of Tony having made it, buying the motors and women we dreamed of, Tony was in fact more envious of us. He craved our life style, as he imagined it. He envied our active and regular involvement in the mystery, subterfuge and danger of real crime, the high excitement of creeping warehouses and robbing banks wearing balaclavas over blackened faces. The daft bastard had no idea of what it was really like, but what Tony imagined of our lives to be was his elusive pot of gold.

To satisfy his fascination with the criminal world Tony had opened up the Castaways Club, a nightclub near the middle of town which also provided illegal gambling for invited guests in a back room. The Castaways did the trick for Tony. Not only did it make him even more money, it also gave him a regular link with the local villainry and brought in the go-getters of the so-called respectable Brummie business community. Most of us would go up there on a Saturday night, either with our ladies of first choice or looking for the ladies looking for blokes like us, and they were not a few, drawn like moths to the aura of easy spending and a white silk scarf draped loosely over the shoulders of a charcoal grey Crombie overcoat. Tony would often join us for some banter, find out what was going on, and perhaps pass on information about various forms of short term but profitable opportunities that were either in the offing or doing the rounds.

So you see, although Tony did not make his living in the rough and tumble and risk of everyday crime, he didn't exactly walk the straight and narrow. Through his legitimate businesses and contacts he had got to know a fair number of the business and wealthy groups well enough to establish face-value friendships and trust. He had contacts at both ends of the social spectrum and used them. He was a fixer. If one of his legit acquaintances wanted to have a bloke slapped about for messing with his missus or for ducking out on a deal, or if a bit of arson could solve their business problems, Tony would put them in touch with someone who could help them out, at a price. On the other hand, if they let something slip about a particularly valuable consignment of merchandise which was open to cherry-picking, Tony would pass the info onto one of us lot, for a slice of the cake. Through the Castaways Tony became the man to know. He loved it.

He also loved the limelight, to be in the public eye. It was his greatest weakness and, although we didn't know it then, ultimately it would lead to his and our downfall. At the Castaways, he'd be up on stage at the drop of a hat, introducing the acts, publicly welcoming any well-knowns to his club, councillor this or that, the Aston Villa reserve right back, any prick who Joe Public might have heard of. He'd be up there doling out presents for birthday girls, grannies and old farts, and even singing with the band. He was forever in the local papers giving a hundred quid to some poor undernourished kids with no limbs or brains, or making donations to old soldiers still shitting themselves as a result of the war. He was always ready to piss on anyone who was on fire. To the ordinary 'have nothing' folk of Birmingham, Tony was a local lad made good who was now doing what he could for those less fortunate than himself. To those of us who knew the real Tony Day, he was a lucky, self-promoting, self-seeking bastard.

Tony employed Spider as a go-between and to keep his ear to the ground. When there was work or a tip-off involved, it always came through Spider. He also had to let Tony know of everything that was going on and, when contracts had been completed, to collect the percentage due to Tony. The other two who came in with Spider were Percy and Eddie Hammond, two brothers, Tony's two chief minders. Now, when you're talking about really vicious bastards, there are always two brothers somewhere in the plot, it's a simple fact of life. I know films, books, the lot, tend to romanticise things, but I'm telling you straight, in the case of bad brothers they get it right, it really is the way it is, God knows why. Anyway, with them in tow, none of Tony's own business interests paid protection money to anyone, and nobody defaulted on a payment due to Tony and remained mobile. It's not unkind to say, however, that when the big bloke was dishing out the brain cells, the Hammond brothers were not first in line; indeed it's rumoured that they weren't in the line at all, and the few cells they had got had been scraped off the pavement after they stoved in some poor bastard's head with an iron bar. But what they lacked in brain power, they made up for in physical brawn and viciousness.

They were really big blokes, both of them six foot plus and big with it. They always dressed as if they were ready for a fight, which they generally were. They wore studded steel cap boots and sharp heavy metal-buckled belts. The belts were not worn to hold their pants up. They were a weapon, worn and used to beat the shit out of any unwitting fool who crossed them. As back-up, they each carried a cut-throat open razor which, in a show of bravado, they would sometimes spin and twirl like some B movie cowboy with a six-shooter. They sensibly preferred the razor to a knife. A razor will cut and maim but, unless you are stupid enough to slash the neck's main artery, it will not kill. More so, if carried with a shaving brush and a stick of soap, it avoids any charges by the law concerning possession of an offensive weapon. Occasionally the brothers would be charged with criminal offences, usually causing grievous bodily, but they rarely made it into court on account of their victims seldom pressing charges when it came to the crunch and, if any silly bugger did persist, there would be a noticeable lack of witnesses ready or able to testify.

To my knowledge there was only one bloke to have given them both a good working over and walked away unharmed and that was Mick. One night they were giving Mick some threatening ear-ache when he suddenly reached out and banged their heads together, head butted each of them while they were still reeling and, when they hit the deck, he gave them a good kicking too. Although I was there, I didn't have to do anything. I just stood and watched until he finished. When it was all over, he calmly turned to me and said, 'turned out nice again,' which was a popular catch phrase at the time.

They were out of action for three or four weeks and, from then on, they generally steered clear of Mick and, by association, me. Prior to working for Tony, they had made their money by beating up people to order and some small-time protection deals. Unfortunately for them, these two violent psychopaths simply lacked the grey matter to fully go it alone, hence they worked for Tony, who probably paid them more than they would have made on their own anyway.

It was the three of them, the Hammonds and Spider, coming in together that caused the stir in the Bartons that night. Spider had to be there on some sort of business for Tony, and having the brothers with him signalled that it was important business. As he went up to the bar, Spider generally acknowledged those blokes who might expect to be noticed. At the bar he ordered a pint of brown and mild for himself and 'one for each of the lads,' referring to Percy and Eddie. When he gets his drink, Spider leans back on the bar and, trying to appear casual, surveys who's about. He gives the impression that he spots Mick and me, who were sat the other side of the room, incidentally.

'Hey Ronnie. Hey Mick', he calls out and comes over to us. 'How are youse two old mates doing then, long time no see, would youse both have a drink wis me?'

He then looks at us face on and we looks back at him, face-on.

'Ah go on then,' says Mick. 'You've talked me into it, you smooth-talking Irish weasel.'

'What's it to be?' Spider asks. 'Name your poison, have what youse want.'

As Spider was not known for buying drinks willy nilly, we suss that he's under orders from Tony and that Tony will be footing the bill. Mick decides to make hay while the sun is shining.

'I'll have a pint of best then,' he says, adding as an apparent after-thought, 'and seeing as you're paying Spider, a double whisky chaser.'

Before Spider can reply, I chip in. 'Yeah, I'll have the same as Mick, thanks Spider.'

Even though he's not paying for the drinks himself, Spider looks sick, but can do nothing. Ray, having ear-wigged the scene, is already dribbling two double whiskeys from two separate optics. When Spider returns to our table with the drinks he says, 'Cheers then lads. Well, I ask again, how are youse two doing then?'

Almost in unison Mick and me say, 'Win some, lose some, you know how it is Spider.'

This was Spider's opening. His face immediately takes on a sorrowful and anxious turn.

'Ah yes, I do lads, only too well I do.' He shakes his head mournfully and pauses for a while, but then, quite suddenly, he takes on a hopeful, almost inspirational, look. 'But youse know something lads, this could be your lucky night.'

He pulls closer and half whispers, 'Tony has a little proposition that could sort a lot of things out for youse two, and one or two others youse might know, and when I says sort out, I mean sort out in a big way.'

Mick and I feign surprise. It had been clear to us from the moment Spider 'accidentally' clocked us that Tony must have something biggish lined up for us.

'And what might dat be den?' Mick asked in a mock Irish accent.

Spider pulls up even closer and hisses, 'keep it quiet. This is not the place, nor the time.' He glances furtively round the room.

'Tony's having a fews of the old crowd round, the ones youse can trust, you know, for a fews drinks, at his place, Sunday afternoon, round about tree o'clock. Do yers fancy coming on over? It could be well worth yers while, I'm telling yers.' Mick and me look non-committally at each other and nod without showing any hint of our aroused curiosity or interest.

'Yeah, we should be able to make that all right. Tony owes us both one.' Spider looked both pleased and relieved at Mick's eventual confirmation.

'But look now, lads, I don't want youse to make too much of this, but Tony and the lads,' he indicates towards the Hammond brothers, 'would like youse to keep this under yers hat, youse knows what I mean?'

We nod again and before we can say anything Spider is up on his feet and moving on.

'Right on then, that's just fine then lads, I'll be seeing youse then, enjoy your drinks.' He makes off as if heading back to the bar and the Hammonds, but then happens to notice Stan Leach and his side kick Bertie Bates, a right couple of jokers and fly-by-nights, but good blokes nevertheless.

'Hellos there Stan, and youse too Bertie, howse youse two doing then? Hold on let me get youse both a drink.......'

On his short journey back to the bar Spider repeated this little ritual with near enough every group in the 'Gents Only', presumably to cover up exactly who had been invited along to Tony's Sunday Band of Hope meeting. Eventually he gets back to the bar and the Hammonds. They chat for a few minutes, finish their drinks and make for the door, Spider spouting fond farewells as he leaves. As the door closes behind them Mick asks me, 'what do you make of that lot then?'

'I'm not sure,' I reply, 'but for sure it's not a run of the mill do. It's got to be big otherwise Tony wouldn't have sent those two mean bastards to enforce the peace.' This was true; except for perhaps Mick and me, a request from the Hammonds to keep schtum had the power of a Gestapo officer's invitation to join in with the singing of 'Deutschland Uber Alles'.

'Sunday it is then,' says Mick and calls across to Ray. 'Do us another couple of pints Ray, we'll give the chasers a miss this time.' The joke raises a laugh around the room, restores the momentum and soon business is back to normal as though the piranhas had never been in the pool.

2 The Come-On

The following Sunday afternoon sees Mick and me driving out to Tony Day's place near the Lakes at Earlswood which are on the south side of Brum, just past Solihull, a posers' paradise then and now. We go down in Mick's newly acquired 3.6 Jaguar which we decided would have a far racier impact than my staid but more muscular Rover 105.S. Tony's place was a rambling old manor house called Wullford Hall and surrounded by barns and outbuildings and acres of fields and trees. It was real pose. Bobby Dyke, Birmingham's own banana king, went on to own it in the sixties.

In front of the house there is a bloody great gravelled forecourt with, on this particular Sunday, some reasonable motors parked along one side of it. In front of the main entrance, a number of familiar characters are standing around in some very bright unfamiliar winter sunshine. We've got our timing just about right, two minutes before three o'clock.

'Years of practice,' says Mick.

'Bloody jammy, as always,' says I.

Mick parks up conspicuously away from the other motors so that the Jag can be viewed in splendid isolation. We get out slow, and saunter over in a sort of soft shoe shoulder swinging shuffle, revelling in the aura of the Jag, which is the best motor there apart from Tony's ostentatious white Roller. We're also looking good. Naturally, we are wearing the standard outer uniform of any aspiring Brummie bad lad back then, dark trilby hats, Crombie overcoats and white silk scarves. But underneath we had the latest clobber and so, to let the assembled bunch have a good gander at it, we held our top coats open by keeping our hands in our trouser pockets. I was wearing a black jacket with a heavy gold fleck and sporting the very latest Corsican collars (they never caught on!), slim line black trousers without turn-ups, black suede shoes with inch thick crepe soles, and a maroon slim-Jim tie with a fake diamond pin fronting a white cut-away collar shirt. Mick's a near look-alike, except his jacket is grey with a silver fleck. We thought we looked pretty slick and the abusive cat-calls from the lads showed that they thought so too!

Although everyone's more or less in a crowd, we see them in their regular teams of two or three. First there's Stan Leach and Bertie Bates who, as I mentioned earlier, were a couple of knuckle head smash and grab artists. No finesse about these two at all. Everything for them is spur of the moment stuff, they see something they want, crash, bang, wallop, they take it and run. How they got away with it for so long, God only knows. Next there's John Cooper and John Davies, known respectively as JC and JD. Their speciality was lifting bulk wagon loads. JD had extensive connections with the 'legit' wholesale trade and consequently was able to move large amounts of stuff on quickly, safely and very profitably.

Then there's Ernie Roberts and his two lackeys, Terry Isles, otherwise known as Ikey, and Mickey Barnsley, otherwise known as Barney. Ernie was the business brains of this safe busting trio. Ikey and Barney were the safe crackers and blowers. They just did what Ernie told them to religiously and enjoyed the good life the proceeds gave them to the full, which means that they were always skint. These three knew every inch of Birmingham's jewellery quarter. They had probably crept every workshop and factory in there at some time or other, and Ernie was always able to get a good price for the merchandise they acquired with no questions asked. Then there were two other big blokes who neither Mick nor me recognised and, last but not least, Spider and Tony's two minders, the thicko Hammond brothers, Eddie and Percy.

Spider was acting it up as mine host and the brothers looked like a couple of newly recruited bouncers, not quite sure what to do, where to put their hands or where they should stand but desperately trying to look hard. It's clear that Mick and me are the last of those expected to arrive because no sooner had we joined the others than Spider moved to the top of the steps leading up to the studded oak front doors and called out to the assorted mob. 'Come on in nowse lads, we'se kicking off in the Terrace Lounge, Tony'll be down widge youse all soon enough.'

He leads us all up the steps and into the house like a bunch of schoolgirls on a day trip. We go into the 'Terrace Lounge', as Spider called it and it's bloody enormous, genuine pukka English Manor, with wood panelling, oak doors, wopping great crystal chandeliers, the lot. The only thing that wasn't your real original aristocrat was the over-the-top full size Bar, complete with mirrors, coloured lights and optics, taking up the whole width of one end of the room. That was pukka Tony Day! Spider walks on down and goes behind the Bar.

'Now, can me and the boys gets youse all a drink while youse waiting?'

It was clear to all present that Percy and Eddie were not well pleased about either being referred as 'the boys' or the idea of acting as bar slaves to anyone, let alone our mob. Fortunately Spider picked up their over-acted reaction, and with a bit of nimble quick thinking retrieves the situation to everyone's satisfaction.

'No, no. I'll tell youse what, better than that, whyse don't youse all help yerselves? That way you can get exactly what youse all be wanting.'

Before his words had stopped bouncing off the oak panelling, everybody's in behind the Bar scrambling for drinks. The scrummage eventually settles down and soon the best of Tony's exotic spirits and liqueurs are being strained through nicotine stained teeth or bleached porcelain, de-scaling furred tongues en route, and all from his best cut crystals.

Once everybody's stocked up with the liquor of their choice, we all start relaxing, having a Sunday afternoon chat while sizing up, and costing up, this place of Tony's. At the opposite end of the room to the bar there's a small film screen set up and several rows of chairs lined up in front of it. Mick and me wandered over to try to suss out what it's all about.

'Tony's probably got in some Tom and Jerry Cartoons for us all to watch,' Mick says with a knocker's smile.

'Dirty movies, more like,' says I.

We turned to look back up the room to assess more fully who is there and, perhaps as importantly, who's not. First thing we agree is that every bastard there, apart from the two big blokes who neither Mick nor me had clocked before, is a member of the Bartons 'Gents Only' villains club and who also put in fairly frequent guest appearances at the Castaways. The two irregulars stood out like beards in a nunnery. It was the way they held themselves, the way they dressed, just a bit too formal, a bit too straight-laced. I suggested ex-military, but, as Mick pointed out with little finesse, so were all the others there, including us. But these two were different, they sort of held back and surveyed the rest of us rather than getting involved. As for what you might call 'our mob', Tony knew every one of us from way back and we had all got on reasonably well socially for years.

It was when we considered who wasn't there, that it clicked. It was the loose tongue loud mouthers who were missing. All of those there, including Mick and me, were known to be tight-lipped, even more so in times of trouble. There were none of the 'grass on your mother' brigade here. This lot would see their mother murdered before their own eyes, and they'd still maintain to the law they hadn't seen or heard a thing. Mind you, the bastard that did it would be dead or disabled within a fortnight because everyone of them were unmerciful and revengeful crusaders when severely riled. It was also clear from the way they held themselves that the two unknowns would not feature strongly in any local town crier or big fairy contests. The loosest loud-mouther in tow would be Tony himself!

Mick and me are still following these lines of thought when the main man himself breezes in. As always, he's dressed and groomed immaculately, hair Brylcreamed to an oily satin finish, charcoal grey pin-stripe three piece suit with a black slim Jim tie fronting a pristine white shirt with starched collar and cuffs. It's all finished off with a tie pin and a pair of gold cuff links in the shape of a palm tree, the symbol of the Castaways' Club, a massive gold watch and matching bracelet, and so many bloody signet and sovereign rings you wondered how he could wave his hands about so much as he talked. Tony was the ultimate poser, he always had been, but now he was bloody up-front successful, it grated with a lot of the blokes. Success on display tends to get right up the arse of the unsuccessful.

'Hello, hello, hello everybody. Sorry to have kept you all waiting, lads,' he beams, and without breaking step or wind comes straight over to me and Mick. 'Great to see you Ronnie, and you too Mick, I'm glad you could both make it, the grapevine tells me you're doing well....' Blah, blah, blah, he doesn't pause for breath, just off with the spiel like a fucking street market trader, with Mick and me hardly getting a word in edge-ways.

But Tony was only doing the socials, he wasn't telling us anything and he really wasn't interested in anything we might want to tell him.

When he decides he's soft landed us sufficiently he's off like a trap five dog, doing a circuit of all the others, chasing the same tried and tested decoy hares as he did with us. What we had sussed, however, was that we had been first on the circuit again, just as we had been when Spider did the rounds in the Bartons. We know now that whatever Tony's got in mind, he's got ideas of Mick and me being up at the front, which usually means taking most of the fucking flack. We also know that not a few of the others will have noticed the pointers too.

When Tony's finally ironed everyone's sensitivities, Spider, with ace timing, sets up a slide projector in front of the screen and starts to dim the lights.

'Yes, thank you Spider for reminding me, you're right, we must get on, we've got a lot to get through,' Tony says as though Spider had acted independently rather than under strict orders.

'Right lads, let's make a start up this end by the screen. I've got some holiday snaps I want to show you.'

Despite a chorus of abusive but good-humoured responses to this idea, everybody troops up and sits down within no more than thirty seconds. We all wanted to know what this meeting of the Aston Villains was all about.

As we fall silent Tony moves to the front. Always one for the theatricals, Tony was going to enjoy and savour this opportunity. He pulls out a large Winston, unwraps it slowly, clips it like a Jewish doctor and lights up amidst much smoke and rehearsed puffing. He also takes his time pouring himself a large whisky into a glistening cut crystal goblet. He was a pain in the arse but, I have to admit, he could do great theatre.

'Right lads,' he starts, 'Again, I'm glad everybody managed to make it over here today, and I suppose you're wondering what Uncle Tony has in mind for us lot now!'

'Too bleeding right we are,' calls out JC and we all laugh in agreement.

'Well, you'll have sussed that what I've got in mind is a big one, and I mean big, so big it's probably going to blow your fucking minds. And it has got to be big, because counting Spider, Percy, Eddie and myself, there's fifteen of us here today. Now, just for argument's sake, let's say the job I've got in mind brings in five grand. Not bad for a team of two but shared out between us lot, hardly worth getting out of bed for. But I'm not talking about five grand or even fifty grand, I'm talking about money you haven't even dreamt of!'

Tony now had our closest attention, and he knew it.

'Right, because nothing like this has ever been attempted before, except maybe by our old mate Adolf, you'll have to bear with me while I fill you in on some background before I get on to the job itself. Spider.' He nods to Spider who turns on the projector and puts up a slide. It's a picture of Tony's missus, Thelma, a tasty bit of stuff by any standards, and she's on a beach in a swimming costume. There's a chorus of cat calls and wolf whistles. Tony grins widely.

'I thought that might get your attention. I took this picture last year when Thelma and me had ourselves a little holiday on the island of Guernsey. Now, when I wasn't seeing to Thelma's needs,' there's another chorus of jeering, 'I was finding out what makes the place tick.' He nods to Spider again who puts up another picture of Thelma. This time she's standing in front of a jeweller's shop, a real massive place which went right round the two sides of a street corner, with big gold lettering, 'J & S' on all sides. Thelma is stood to one side in the picture so that the shop's windows are in full view. We could see that they were crammed to the eyeballs with what looked like good expensive stuff.

Illuminated like a salesman's spectre in the glare of the projector, Tony begins to explain. 'Guernsey is a bit of tax-haven. They don't pay as much tax as us poor bastards over here, so stuff like jewellery is cheaper, and rich bastards from over here go over there to buy the stuff. So there's bloody jewellers' shops all over the bleeding place.'

Spider whips through slides of Thelma in front of about half a dozen different jewellers' shops. He then puts one up of the 'J & S' place again but this time it's obviously night time and the nine or ten windows shown in the photo are all lit up.

Tony says, 'I took this one well after ten o'clock on a Saturday night, and at a rough guess I reckon that each window had about five thousand pounds worth of glitter on display, so in total you're looking here at about fifty grands worth of stuff. But do you notice anything far more interesting?'

'Too bloody right I do!' Stan Leach, who as you may remember, was a premiership smash and grab artist, calls out incredulously, 'there's no fucking grills!'

'Precisely,' says Tony with a smirk. 'As Stan puts it so elegantly, there are no fucking grills, on this one or on any of the other shops I showed you.'

Spider zooms through slides of the others, again all taken at night and it's the same story. No 'fucking' grills on any of them.

At this Bertie Bates stands up and points disbelievingly at Tony.

'You're expecting all of us lot to go over to bleeding Guernsey to do a few poxy jewellery shops? We can go down New Street, grills or no grills, and do that as part of a good night out. You must think we're as bloody barmy as you are.' Bertie may have been exaggerating a little bit, but the gist of what he said was about right. So there's an audible mumbling of support for Bertie's sentiments and some of the lads started to get to their feet as if to leave.

'Hold on, hold on,' says Tony, moving in front of the screen and waving everybody back into their seats, 'I did tell you you'd have to bear with me for a while. Those pictures were just to give you an idea of what we'll be up against.' The standing lads sat down again but pointedly sat on the edge of the chairs to establish their readiness to leave unless Tony had something better on offer.

'Now, as I was saying, Guernsey is a bit of a tax haven so its main business, apart from tomatoes and bleeding royal potatoes, is money, and where there's money, there's always banks fighting each other to nick a share of it.'

He signals to Spider who puts up some pictures of banks. First up is a Lloyds, a seemingly massive white Roman-style building with a green dome. Next up is a National Provincial with fluted granite Greek columns, then a half-timbered mock Tudor TSB which turns out to be right next door to a Royal Bank of Scotland. Then there's a Midland which is right opposite the J&S jewellers. Then there's a Commercial Bank, followed by a Williams and Glyns, the Old Bank, a Barclays and finally a picture of The Merchant Bank. I can still see that picture of the Merchant Bank. It was a stubby little granite building with two entrances, one of which had two large white marble columns on either side. I remember thinking at the time that it looked more like a court house than a bank, not knowing then that a barbaric form of justice would indeed come to be executed within its walls.

'All of these banks,' Tony goes on, 'are on the one main High Street, with Lloyds at the top, The Merchant and Barclays at the bottom and only one hundred and sixty yards between them.' Spider puts up a slide looking up the High Street. The street itself is cobbled with a narrow pavement on each side. The whole street is barely wide enough for two motors to pass even using the pavements. Despite a slight twist about half way up, we can see its whole length. Lloyds stood out clearly at the top and we were able to locate most of the Banks we had just seen. Ten of them all lined up and, like a row of skittle pins, just waiting to be knocked over!

'Fucking hell,' Stan Leach whispered but bat-eared Tony picks it up.

'Yes, fucking hell again, and they're all loaded, with cash, gold, jewellery, all salted away by mainland banks, companies, rich bastards, criminals, you name it, salted away to avoid tax or the law. Throw in all the brass from growing tomatoes and potatoes and you're talking about big money in every one of these banks.'

Tony paused and looked around again. He now had our undivided attention. 'I showed you the pictures of the jewellers just to give you some idea of their idea of security. They think that because they're an island, as long as they control what goes in and what goes out, they don't need high grade security. For fuck's sake, they've only got a dozen coppers at the most on duty at any one time, and there's fifteen of us here! They think that because it's a little island and everybody knows everybody else's fucking business, they don't have to worry about big time crime..... They've got a shock coming!' He draws on his cigar and scans our practised dead-pan reactions. 'Now for a bit of a history lesson.'

Spider puts up a slide of a bunch of Gerry soldiers smiling their stupid faces off. There's an instantaneous roar of abuse. Tony waits while we calm down.

'Right listen up because here's something you might not know or remember about the war. On the thirtieth of June, nineteen forty, thirty or so Gerries landed at Guernsey airport and took it over without firing a shot. They then drove down to the main town, St Peter Port, and took that over too without any fighting or bother. Less than two hours later the States of Guernsey, the so-called

Government over there, surrendered to them. Now get that. Thirty Germans took just two hours to capture the whole of Guernsey and never fired a single shot.' He paused for effect. 'And that's what we are going to do, we're going to take total fucking control of this poxy little island and strip it clean, the big banks of their fucking millions, the jewellers' shops of their glitter; anything we fancy, we'll take!'

Tony was almost shouting with excitement now, his eyes wild with passion, this was seriously real business.

'We'll be able to take whatever we bloody well want!'

⌘   ⌘   ⌘   ⌘   ⌘   ⌘   ⌘

The Plan

There was silence. We're all a bit stunned by Tony's passion and proposal. Certainly I'm thinking he's finally flipped, gone over the top, and I'm also thinking that most of the others are thinking along similar lines. It was Bertie Bates who pipes up first again.

'And you really think that us lot can take over a whole fucking island without the Wehrmacht and Luftwaffe to back us up? You've gone bloody loony mate!'

Tony doesn't bat an eye-lid. 'Maybe,' he says, 'but before you make your minds up whether you're with me or not, I want you all to take a good look at yourselves and ask why has Tony, Tony the fixer, sorted out us bunch of barmy bastards from the rest? Let me tell you why. First, each and everyone of you is a robbing bastard in some way or other, everyone of you would nick the halfpennies from your dead granny's eyes given half a chance. Second, everyone of you is as hard as a dead bull's bollocks, and you know how to keep your traps totally shut when there's a need.' Mick looks across at me, we'd sussed that bit out all right.

'Third, me and the lads,' Tony gestures towards Spider and the Hammonds, 'have also been doing some quiet checking up on each of you. We know, for instance, that everyone of you went through the war and have experienced front line action when some real shit was hitting the fan. Take Mick and Ronnie, for example,' he says looking our way. 'They'd barely got there boots on before they are caught up in the Dunkirk fiasco. Soon as they're back from there, they're shipped off to North Africa. They go over with the Scilly landings and

30

then back here for D-Day for a repeat evening performance in France.' Mick and me nod to acknowledge he's right.

'And you've all been through the same sort of shit. Do I need to go on? Of course not. None of you is your average Jack, your average thieving little git, who knows nothing and has never done anything and never will. You lot are different, special one-offs, that's why you're here and that's why I know we can pull this off. If we were still in the war and this was a no opt-out operation, you'd say it was a pissing cake walk'.

We fell silent again, most of us feeling a bit cocky after Tony's build up. We also realised that the bit he said about if we were still in the war was right on. It was probably worth hearing what he had in mind.

'This is how we're going to do it. We go in on the fifth of June, a Saturday night, at midnight, I'll tell you why and how later. For now let's stick with taking the place over.' Spider puts up a picture of a two-storey building on a street running down a steep hill. It's a white plastered place on a granite block base. In the middle, there's some steps which lead up to a pair of doors. On either side of this entrance, sprouting from the wall, is a blue Police lamp.

'This is Guernsey's one and only police station. It's about hundred and fifty yards up from the High Street. On any night, even on a Saturday, there's usually only about six coppers in there and six others out and about. There's guns in there, but they're all safely locked up, and the ammunition is locked up in another cupboard. The gist of this is, if they're taken by surprise, it would take them five minutes to get their bleeding guns out. So the first part of the plan is take it over, lock, stock and barrel. That's down to me, Percy and Eddie, Dave and Barry here.' He indicates to the two unknowns who acknowledge his gesture with the slightest synchronised movement of their shoulders.

Whether it was the mention of the Police Station or what, an explanation for their disquieting mannerisms Mick and I had noticed earlier was suddenly clear. The way they held themselves, moved and looked, was classic red cap behaviour. They had got to be ex-military police. 'And Ronnie.' The mention of my name intruded into my musings about 'Dave and Barry', my first reaction being a silently uttered 'shit.'

'And we're armed. We take over the station using whatever force is necessary and lock all the coppers up in their own fucking cells. With all their coppers out of action we can do what we like. Next.'

Spider puts up a slide of a large radio mast, with Thelma stood in front of it. He then puts up another showing an isolated, red-tiled white bungalow with two small white sheds and the same radio mast right next to it.

'This is the island's main radio mast. While my team's sorting out the coppers, Mick, JC and JD will take this place over, there's only a caretaker engineer and his missus to deal with, and blow up the transmitters in this shed,' Tony points to one of the sheds, 'and then drop the mast. Once that's done, we've cut off the island's only radio communications link with the UK mainland and the continent.'

Spider puts up another slide. It's another single-storey whitewashed building but this time there are two radio masts on show, both much smaller than the mast at the radio station, one at each end of the building. Tony continues. 'This is the island's telephone exchange and local radio station. The place is always empty at night apart from two receptionists. At the same time that the main radio station is being sorted, Ernie, Ikey, and Barney will be blowing the switchboards and dropping these two masts. This leaves Spider, Stan, and Bertie.'

Spider puts a map on the screen and Tony starts to use a pointing stick to guide us around the map. 'They'll go to the Airport to do likewise to the Control Tower. Can you believe it, even the bloody Airport is closed down by eight o'clock? The whole island's closed up by eleven o'clock, even on a Saturday night.' He pauses with a look of mock disbelief. 'Anyway, when this lot's been done, it's everybody down to the Police station except, that is, for Spider, Stan, and Bertie who go on to knock out any radio communication's tackle that might be usable in the Harbour Masters office which is at the entrance to port.' Spider puts up a photo. 'As there's usually no big boats in after five o'clock on a Saturday, the office should be empty and shouldn't pose any problems.'

Tony susses we're all a bit stunned and also very impressed. The showman is up front again. He pauses, re-lights his cigar and pours himself another whiskey.

'By my estimation, within twenty minutes of us landing, we'll have got control of the police force, the island will be cut off from the outside world, and every phone on the island will be out of action. As we'll be the only armed and organised mob on the island, it will be ours for the taking. There'll be nobody to oppose us and we'll have at least twelve hours, and probably a lot more, to clean it out, and get clear away.' He stops spieling to take a swig of his whiskey, to suck deep on his cigar, and to survey our reaction.

He did right because the mood in the room had definitely changed. You could almost feel it. We were all thinking about this spiel of Tony's and resentfully having to admit to ourselves that the loony bastard could be on to something. Then the questions start; questions which show most of us are considering biting the hook.

'So how to we open the vaults?'

'We don't, the bank managers will do that for us.'

'And why do you think they're going to do that?'

'If you've seen your wife and kids go off into the night with the likes of Eddie and Percy here, wouldn't you open up if we asked you nicely?' Eddie and Percy grin sheepishly, the daft prats taking this as a compliment.

'And where's the wives and kids to?'

'In the cells with us, down at the police station.'

'And how do we get these bank managers down there?'

'We collect them, in police cars.'

'So we'll spend half the night running a bleeding taxi business?'

'Here's the names and addresses of all of them, they all live within ten minutes of each other.'

'And what about all the other chasing about?'

'From north to south, Guernsey is only just over six miles long, about a fifth of the distance from here to the Castaways.

'What if someone comes in after we've taken over the Blue Lamp?'

'Dave and Harry are ex-military police and, after the war, they did three years with the Met. They know the routines and one of them will be behind the desk, in police uniform, all of the time we're there.'

'What about gongoozelers going up and down the street while we're doing the banks?'

'We close off the High Street at both ends with a police barrier and two of us patrol it as uniformed coppers.'

'With all the communications down, how do we keep in touch with each other?'

'Ex-WD walkie-talkies and short-wave field radios. Ronnie and Mick served with the Signals Corps, they'll handle that side of things.'

The questions go on but one thing seems clear, Tony has got the whole thing sewn up. Then Mick slowly and noticeably gets to his feet. We all shut up.

'Right Tony, I listen to what you say, and I agree, because it's a poxy little island, we could take the place over all right. But it's the fact that it is an island that makes it a headache. Listen a minute. You are talking about emptying the banks, the jewellers and what you will. Now, I've had some of that sort of action in the war and I tell you, money takes up big space.' Mick stops, reaches into the inside of his waistcoat up by the arm-pit and pulls out a wedge of notes.

'See that, there's a monkey there in fivers.' Sounds of admiration echo around the room, even I'm impressed. 'Now imagine we got five grand, ten times as much.' He moves across the room, picks up Tony's over-large cigar box and holds it up.

'You might just about squeeze it in this. Now imagine that it's fifty grand, ten times as much again, possibly a large suit case? Now think of five hundred grand, ten times as much again, and you're talking millions Tony, and we're going to try to get that lot and ourselves off an island without anybody noticing? Talk fucking sense man, it's a great idea but it's fucking dream-world!'

Mick's got a point and we all know it, but again Tony is totally unfazed.

'And that Mick, my lovely, is why it's never been done, because it sounds impossible if not bleeding crazy.' He nods to Spider who puts up another slide.

'Most of you will recognise this couple of old favourites.'

Too bloody right we did. It was a picture of two DUKWs, military amphibious six-wheel drive trucks, affectionately known as 'Ducks'. Capable of up to fifty miles an hour on land and five and half to six knots an hour in water. Pay load up to two and a half tons, or twenty-five fully-equipped men. Mick and me were trained how to use them and knew them inside out. We'd been with the very first batch that went into Sicily and then, after a piggy-back on one of the big transporters, drove one onto Sword beach and then on into

Normandy on D-Day. Mick can see the answer coming so sits down.

'As part of one of my war surplus deals I brought these two tight-arsed bastards a couple of months ago. They are stood out the back in my barn as we speak. I've had them both overhauled from top to bottom, they're in perfect working order, ready to go just as if it was D-Day all over again. And that's why I settled on the weekend of June fifth and sixth. This year is the tenth anniversary of the landings, so to celebrate it a bunch of Yanks and ex-Tommys are going to relive the landings by sailing over to France from Weymouth in anything that will float, but they particularly want the sort of tackle that took part in the original landings to go over with them. So, we're going to be sailing with them.'

Tony paused again but as nobody spoke he continued.

'Ronnie and Mick have solid experience in navigating and handling Ducks so they will be in charge of that side of things. Now as the old Ducks are not the quickest of boats in the water, it will take us ten or eleven hours to get to Guernsey. Our estimated time of arrival on the island is just before midnight on the fifth. In less than three hours and well before day-break we should have cleaned the place out and be heading for the beaches just up from Cartaret on the French coast. It will take us about another three hours to get over there, give or take a minute or two. Once there we drive up to Cherbourg and, before any bastard has got to know what's going on, catch the early morning ferry for Portsmouth and a life of Riley with everything you've ever dreamed of!'

There was no doubt in anybody's mind that Tony had sussed this one out right up to the hilt. It was more than just bloody possible, it was a racing cert!

3 Countdown to D-Day

It was three o'clock when Mick and me had arrived at Tony's that Sunday afternoon and it was well after nine o'clock when we left, a good half-hour after all of the others had gone. We were last because Tony wanted to have a quiet word with us on our own. As soon as there's just the three of us, he told us straight. Without us the plan was a no go. It wasn't just that we were needed to handle and navigate the DUKWs and the communications problem, we were there more than anything to provide back-up for Tony and to keep this bunch of individualistic bastards together as a team, if only for the duration of the operation. Barry and Dave would act as long stops for us if things ever started to get heavy.

Tony, for all his bombast, for all his spiel and showmanship, sensibly recognised that when push came to shove, he might not be able to hold his own with this hard-nosed mob without some substantial back-up. For that, he was depending upon Mick and me, supported by his two new boys, if and when he or we thought things were getting a bit too hairy. It was also an implicit recognition that he knew that the protection he currently enjoyed via the brothers was very much dependent upon how much they'd had to drink the night before or if they had an unexpected offer from a more generous paymaster. Very wisely he had little, if any, faith in their loyalty to him.

As we drove back to the city Mick and me mulled the afternoon over. True enough, we were more than flattered by Tony's unspoken acknowledgement of our prestige and standing in Brum's thriving gangland. We agreed that this was fair enough as any fool should be able to recognise that we were head and shoulders above all of the other dickheads pushing for such dubious recognition. But above all, we had to admit that Tony probably had a bit more upstairs than we had previously given him credit for. For starters, he never actually asked any of us whether we wanted in or out of the job which, given its scale and risks, would have been the natural thing to do.

He'd picked the team so well he knew that there was no need to ask. Mick and me knew the Bartons' crowd and none of those he'd collared could have turned it down, not because of the amount of loot involved, but for the sheer neck of it. Sea landings at night, taking over an island, cherry picking banks, shit, after ten years penned up in civvi street we would have all probably done it just for the chance to have some real butt-clenching, piss-yourself excitement again. And, despite what Bertie Bates had said before he knew the full scene, even if it had been just for 'the poxy jewellers' shops', it's likely that we'd have still gone for it, it was too good a jape to miss! Besides, we were all getting on a bit. Most of us were well into our thirties, so there wouldn't be many chances left for any of us to make big money and have any useful life left to spend it. And there certainly wouldn't be many, if any, more like this one. This was a once-in-a-lifetime opportunity to pull off a big one with a reliable mob. We didn't know much about Dave and Barry, the two ex-MPs, but we reckoned that Tony wouldn't have pulled them in if they weren't up to it.

Despite that, Mick still didn't fully trust them. 'Once a copper, always a copper,' he repeated somewhat monotonously every time I tried to speak up in their favour. He did accept, however, that it was going to be useful having two ex-coppers fronting up the Blue Lamp and the road blocks. The rest of us would probably tell any curious members of the public to 'fuck off' rather than politely ask them to, 'move along there please, Sir, Madam', which is almost second nature to the average condescending rozzer.

Tony had also worked out that going through the plan was going to take some time because, at six o'clock precisely, in comes the lovely Thelma with barrow loads of food and we take a scheduled half-hour tea break! Tony had planned the whole job as if it was a full-scale military operation. He had laid out two giant size maps on his snooker table, one of the whole of Guernsey and one of St Peter Port, the main town. He had marked out all the routes we'd take, with the key points and places circled or displayed. He'd got models of the police station, the radio and telephone centres, the masts, a German pill box positioned on the landing beach, and even the two DUKWs and the other motors we would be using. He had dozens of photographs, floor plans of key buildings, street plans with precise measurements of the distances involved, no detail was too small or overlooked.

Although I knew Mick was sizeably impressed, he kept muttering almost non-stop. 'He thinks he's bloody Montgomery!' For sure Tony did revel in playing the role of overlord but, nevertheless, the level of detail and consideration he had given to all the angles involved boosted the confidence of everyone of us. It was a solid salesman's ploy, and Tony was a solid salesman if nothing else.

As we had anticipated, Mick and me were to be key players. During the war we both served with the Royal Signals Corps based at Blandford Forum, only twenty miles or so from Tony's planned departure point of Weymouth. Consequently, we were fully trained to set up effective radio communications in any situation, including battle conditions. For this job of Tony's one of our tasks was to establish and maintain radio links between each of the teams.

While in the Corps, we also mastered the art of being able to drive any vehicle of any size over almost any terrain the army or war could throw at us. It was no surprise then that, when the Corps had to select men to train in handling the first new-fangled DUKWs from the US, we were plucked out of the hat. Much of the waterborne aspects of this training had been in Weymouth bay itself, so not only did we know Ducks inside out, we also knew how to get them in and out of Weymouth bay with no trouble. It would be like old times.

Tony code-named the job 'D-Day', which was hardly original, but it did fix the date in our minds. There were just twenty weeks to get everything together, and this included one week's holiday in Guernsey for each team to familiarise themselves with the lie of the land and general situation over there. Tony had put together a training programme based on the jobs we had to do both in our small teams and in the whole group. Sessions were to be on Sundays at Tony's place.

Week one was simply a repeat of this first session to iron out any problems or glitch areas anyone had come up with in the interim and to finalise the overall plan. Week two was to renew acquaintances with the two Ducks, give them an airing, and to rehearse launching, sea-going, beaching and loading routines. Week three, weapons and hardware; week four, the radio team; week five, the Blue Lamp take-over team; six, the telephone exchange team; seven, the airport and harbour team; eight, everyone for picking up the bank managers and doing the banks; nine and ten, full run throughs including getting away! The whole cycle to be repeated over the next ten weeks.

It might seem like overkill but, with the exceptions of Stan Leach and Bertie Bates, who were always spontaneous bastards, all of us knew the value of careful planning and preparation, particularly when something totally unexpected runs amok when you're in the middle of no-man's land.

So Sunday afternoons became a regular run out to Tony's. Start time was always at three but finishing time depended upon how long it took to get through the afternoon's rehearsal item. Once we got going, it soon became apparent to even the most Doubting Thomas just how essential all this preparation was. On week two, for example, the Ducks were on the agenda. As Tony had said, they were in perfect nick and fired up first time on the button. Within the minute, me and Mick were racing the bastards round Tony's acreage with the others screaming abuse at us as they were thrown about in the back. Suddenly, however, the bastard I'm driving splutters to a halt. I knew right off that it was out of juice.

DUKWs were notoriously thirsty buggers. Mick and me then discover that these two are still fitted with the standard issue fuel tanks, and there's no way we would ever get across the channel on the amount of gas they could hold. This is the reason why we'd been piggy-backed across on D-Day. By our calculations we would need at least one hundred and sixty gallons to do the trip! So whatever else needed doing, fitting extra large fuel tanks to each of the Ducks and nicking a fully loaded petrol tanker were now high priorities. But it was obvious to all that, if we hadn't done these rehearsals, our grand adventure would have ended with us floating about out in the middle of the channel praying for a gas station to float past.

We then gets into rations, latrine requirements, unloading the necessary equipment, particularly the very heavy oxy-acetylene gear for flame cutting the radio masts, getting down to Weymouth, getting in and out of the water, loading the haul, the list just went on and on. By the time we finished, we were glad that there was at least one other week focused on the Ducks. The two Ducks were nick-named Gert and Daisy. I got Gert and Mick got Daisy.

The weeks passed by and we were becoming a close-knit team. We spent more and more time together as a social group. Friday nights in the Bartons, Saturday night at the club, Sunday training and then to the Bartons. Those of us from the old school became closer mates, although it always seemed to be a bit strained with the brothers. We got to know a bit about Dave and Barry, the two ex-military police blokes, too. After leaving the services, they had joined the London Police Force which not only opened their eyes to the criminal world but also provided them with an advanced crash course in do-it-yourself crime.

Early success in some small jobs done on a moonlighting basis went to their heads and, in no time at all, they were up in the big league of armed robbery, no less. And pretty soon after they were doing five years in Winson Green Prison. While in there, they made mates with a favourite old uncle of Tony's, who was in for handling stolen goods. One day, one of the other birds worked the old uncle over in a bad way for no good reason. Without being asked and on the basis of friendship alone, Dave and Barry beat the shit out of this nark so badly that he'll never be right again. They would have been hammered by the screws if they had been nobbled but the done-over bastard wasn't going to chance another seeing to, and he refused to say who had done the business on him. The other birds, after weighing-up the situation, also judged it to be in their best interests to say nothing.

News of this good deed, however, got to Tony and he was so full of gratitude and admiration that when they were released he offered them a fresh start away from the London fuzz. So they came up to Brum and started to make a tidy living from Tony's connections and tip-offs. They still had the looks and mannerisms of coppers which could put a soul on edge, but they enjoyed a laugh and pretty soon me and the others decide they're OK and eventually, although reluctantly, so does Mick.

As we became closer mates, we also began to fully appreciate what each of us knew or could do too. Take week three: weapons and hardware. Tony had pulled together enough gear to equip Monty's Eighth Army. There were two Bren .303 light machine guns for fixing to the Ducks. There were enough 9mm Sten guns for one each, six Lee Enfield .303 rifles, half a dozen Webley .380 revolvers and four Browning 9mm automatic pistols and enough ammunition and grenades to last for the duration.

This armoury sent Stan and Bertie into spasms of ecstasy. These weapons were like long-lost friends to these two chancers. They could strip and rebuild them blindfolded, and blast a whisker off a gnat's bollock at one hundred yards with a rifle, or ten paces with a pistol. It was very noticeable too, that whenever they peered along the sights of a fully-loaded .303 Lee Enfield, they became cool, calm and controlled, the impetuosity of their smash-and-grab jobs dissolving visibly around them.

We got a similar display with the explosives from Ikey and Barney, Ernie's two foot soldiers. While Ernie might have been the brains of the trio for setting the jobs up and disposing of the stuff acquired during their frequent excursions into the jewellery quarter, when we watched and listened to Ikey and Barney doing their stuff with explosives, we were more than a little impressed. These two could load and wire the gnat's bollock and blow it off without killing the gnat!

After this lot, it was something of an anticlimax when me and Mick got to demonstrating the use of the walkie-talkies and short wave radios. 'Roger, over and out', I can tell you now just doesn't compete with artillery and short fuses! JC and JD had similar problems in whipping up enthusiasm about the logistics of shifting bulk or heavy loads quickly and efficiently. But, sure as not, we were learning top quality stuff from top quality blokes.

Only the Hammonds failed to impress. They didn't appear to have much to offer other than viciousness and open razor twirling. Spider, similarly, lacked any specific skills, but he was proving himself to be one bloody good quartermaster and dogsbody, and we quite definitely needed both if we were to pull this off, and get away with it! As the weeks went on, Mick and me also began to develop a liking for the little squirt.

The 'holiday' trips to the island were equally informative and useful. Tony provided each of us with a daily itinerary of places to visit, routes to take, and features to note. Mick and me went over with our two ladies, Mavis and Marg, twin sisters, for a week. We even took them window shopping so that they could choose the jewellery they wanted! On our last day there, we took advantage of some glorious weather to combine business with pleasure. We bought two bottles of the finest champagne, two fat lobsters, buckets of prawns and fresh French bread and had a picnic on the cliffs over looking Saints Bay.

Guernsey is very much like a triangle, the two short sides more or less facing east and south. Saints Bay is on the south side of the island, less than a mile from St Martin's Point, the start of the east coast. St Peter Port, the island's main town, is further up the east coast. Any vessel approaching Saints Bay from the south or west is totally out of view from the St Peter Port look-outs.

The bay itself has a small, gently sloping, fine and firm shingle beach surrounded by cliffs. Running up through the middle of the cliffs is a steep gully which carries a hard-surfaced roadway up to the island above. Slightly below the skyline of the cliffs, and to the left of the gully when viewed from the sea, is a three- storey cylindrical granite Nazi pill-box which dominates the bay and its approaches. But even this abomination could not undermine the beauty of the place for us on that day.

The sea was deepest blue, shining and shimmering as it stretched out and away across the bay's rocky shorelines and on to the horizon. On the cliffs, the warm sun had brought out clouds of small white and yellow butterflies which fluttered drunkenly around us. Bees hummed in the shoulder-high bracken and wild flowers. All around us, where we sat and lay, were the sweet scents of new life and new growth. We made love with the girls in the long grass. For the briefest of moments we were in paradise, but it was short lived. As we lay back looking up at the sky afterwards, Mavis suddenly sat up and proposed a toast. 'To success and the future!' she chirped.

The future. Mavis's chirpy toast brought to consciousness the dark realisation that the next time we came to Saints Bay it would be at night. We would be armed and we would drive out of the sea, across that beach and away up that road called the 'Route de Saints' to, whatever happened, for better or worse, a new life, be it a paradise or a hell. Whatever we felt now, it was as though we had no choice but to stick with it, it was as inevitable as death. Is this why Tony had picked us all? Once in, too proud to back down, too pig-headed to lose face? I don't know, but in that moment of bliss, I truly questioned the sanity of what were we doing, of what our lives had become, and of the uncertainty that lay ahead. I shed a silent tear that day, for our loss.

4 The Crossing

To present a 'business as usual, nothing untoward happening' picture to the world, the Barton regulars amongst us spent the evening of Friday the fourth of June, as usual, in the 'Gents Only'. We did not, however, stay for our 'as usual' after hours drinking, gambling and yarning. We had a good excuse. On that Wednesday, Lester Piggott, who was then an apprentice lad of only eighteen, had won the Derby on 'Never Say Die'. He'd romped home, a bloody thirty-three to one rank outsider, and everyone of us had put our shirts on the beauty, thanks to an informed tip-off from one of Tony's racing crowd. Mick had picked up over six hundred quid! He jested that with his winnings, there was no need to stick with the job, but then he'd thought to himself, 'if Tony's that good at picking winners, I'm sticking with him!'

Needless to say, we all had similar thoughts and consequently we had a right royal celebration on the Thursday night until the city's own dawn chorus of squeals, rings and roars of trams and double deckers sent us begrudgingly home. So that Friday night, as soon as Ray called time, we headed for home to get some shut-eye before getting over to Tony's for three-thirty, or as Tony liked us to say, '0330 hours.' Prat!

Once at Tony's, we changed into Army battle dress adorned with the requisite accessories of fire-arms, ammo belts and grenades. Just putting on that sort of gear psyches a soul right up. We were battle-ready and ready for battle. Tony, naturally, chose for himself the highest-ranking uniform available, a Major. The Hammonds became Lieutenants, very suitable, the rest of us said, for two thick planks. Dave and Barry, very appropriately, returned to their old role as military police, while Mick and me settled to be Signal Corps sergeants again. JC and JD became corporals, Ernie a lance corporal and the rest, with the exception of Spider, became cannon-fodder privates again. Spider was made padre, much to everyone's primitive amusement, his Irish accent nicely complementing his well-worn dog collar. From that moment on, the order of the day was no names to be used until the job was finished. We would address ourselves only by the ranks shown on our uniforms suffixed by the initial of our Christian name. I became Sergeant R and Mick became Sergeant M.

It was 0400 hours precisely, just before dawn, on Saturday the fifth when, as planned and rehearsed, we set off for Weymouth in the two ducks. The drive down was uneventful with little in the way of traffic to slow us up. Nevertheless it was approaching mid-day before we looked out across Weymouth bay from the top of the Ridgeway road that winds down to the town from the Dorchester side. It was the sort of morning that breathes in the memory. A warm sun was breaking lazily through a typical light Weymouth sea mist. A slight breeze was blowing in from the west and the sea in the bay and beyond lay unruffled and enticing, soothing all fears or thoughts we might be harbouring of turning back. It was a day very different from the last time I had looked at this scene.

That was ten years earlier on D-Day. The invasion fleet had been on hold as high seas and gale force winds battered the south coast from Cornwall to Brighton. After days of waiting, the storm eventually broke on June the fifth and the vast armada finally set sail that evening. So luck was on our side, there was no question of delaying our crossing, and we took it as a good omen. We had been hoping for fine weather but, in all truth, we would have gone in anything but the fiercest of storms. The myths about DUKWs not being particularly seaworthy are just that, myths. The Yanks used to surf-board them onto the beaches out in the Pacific and there's a tale that one Duck in the Philippines rescued the crew of a sinking ship with a sixty knot gale blowing, while the shits in another so-called more 'sea-worthy' craft refused to chance it. Our only worry about rough seas was the knowledge of what twelve hours of being tossed and thrown about would do to us physically rather than any fear of joining Davy down under. The fine weather was, for us, a bonus and one which might even make it a pleasant trip.

During the trip down, the top canvasses had been fitted to both ducks so that, apart from Mick and me who were doing the driving, everyone could grab a bit more shut eye as and when they could. By the time we made the turn onto Weymouth's magnificent Georgian promenade, however, all of the lads were awake and the whole town was in carnival mood. The sea-front hotels were decked with flowers and flags. Bunting and more flags were strung from every lamp post. It was like VE day all over again, and the sight of Gert and Daisy trundling along the front fitted the atmosphere perfectly. The crowds lining the prom and beach waved and cheered us on. We felt like conquering heroes and we hadn't even started! The lads were hanging over the sides waving, blowing kisses and giving V signs, Churchillian style of course, to all and sundry.

We were feeling on top of the world, overwhelmed by the atmosphere of carnival, our mission almost forgotten. But in the blink of an eyelid, our elation was blasted into no-man's land. We had just cruised past the pier and were approaching the brightly painted Victorian cast-iron clock tower, which stands half-way along Weymouth prom, when a copper stepped out in front of us and waved us down.

'Shit, what the hell does he want?' I muttered to Tony, who was stationed alongside me and now looking like death warmed up. I pulled up just short of the copper but, as he walked around to the side of the Duck, I immediately sussed that all was well because he was giving us a broad welcoming smile, very different from the usual condescending copper's scowl me and the lads were accustomed to. He calls up to me.

'Good morning Sir, are you intending to take her across or are you for the display of vehicles?' Pompous prat, I thought.

'We're going across mate,' I shout back down to him trying not to let him have a good look at my Cannock Chase. 'It's the only way to travel.'

'Too true, sir, I only wish I was coming with you!' I can almost feel the whispered obscene ripostes of the others in the back to this idea.

'They say you'll have this fine weather all the way. Anyway, just keep going along the promenade till you get to King George's statue. A few yards past him, there's a ramp on your left which will take you down on to the beach. There's an area marked out, you can't miss it.'

'Thanks a lot,' I shouted back but my reply was drowned out as I wound up Gert's massive six cylinders to full throttle to get her away, with Daisy following right up her back side.

Sure enough, as the copper had said, just past the statue, there's a ramp which takes us down on to the beach. On the beach to our left, there are vessels and craft of all shapes and sizes waiting, I reckoned, for the tide to come in. On our right, further up the beach there are rows of non-amphibious military vehicles, mostly Jeeps, Austin

Champs and British motor bikes, although I did spot a couple of Sherman tanks. Everywhere it's the proverbial organised chaos, just like D-Day but with marshals instead of ex-public school officers running about trying, but failing miserably, to organise anything. Some of them see us and begin exaggerated arm waving and frantically pointing little flags here, there, and fucking everywhere, each trying to outdo the others, whilst each, presumably, intending to show us where we should park up.

While I'm still trying to make sense of this communications mayhem and general chaos, I cannot help but notice that Daisy, with Mick nonchalantly waving to us, has roared past and is heading straight for the sea. This move of Mick's takes the officials up front by surprise, and they scatter in his wake. Before they can regroup, my foot's down hard on the accelerator too and we go haring after Daisy. We both hit the water, contrary to all regulations, at about twenty-five miles an hour, sending great tidal waves along the entire length of the beach.

The watching crowds obviously love it, but we can see the officials are raging, waving their little flags and leaping about like rampant Morris dancers. Within seconds, the rising bow wave and deepening water lifts Gert's wheels from the beach. I engaged the prop drives and, as soon as we were in a sufficient safe depth, disengaged the wheel drives. Mick, in Daisy alongside, had done likewise and both Ducks were in their element once more and we were on our way. Tony, realising that we had become a main event spectacle, climbs onto Gert's foredeck in his full Major regalia and gives an impressive formal salute to all those watching from the beach, prom and pier. The crowds of sightseers cheered and waved us on to the apparent annoyance of the marshals, who were still raging at each other with yet more exaggerated arm waving and pointing of flags.

The Ducks took to the water like, well, ducks to water. Within minutes they were effortlessly cruising at nearly six knots, steaming past the flotilla of other vessels moored in the bay, all patiently waiting for the official 'off' as the saintly and common-or-garden tend to do when real life beckons. As we left them in our wake, we looked back.

The sea mist had burnt off and the whole of Weymouth bay was in sunlit display. To the east, the giant hillside carving of King George mounted on his white horse riding out of Weymouth was clearly visible, and further to the east, in the distance across the bay, lay the Needles and the Isle of Wight. To the west, the stubby white lighthouse at Portland Bill was getting smaller and the wide sweeping view across Lyme Bay was opening up. Above, beyond and around Weymouth town itself, we could see the rolling green fields, wooded hills and white cliffs of the south Dorset coast bathed in bright sunlight. It was a spectacular sight, far removed from the grime, shit and desolation we had left in Brum less than eight hours before. Little wonder that even this bunch of hardened villains were moved by it.

As the bay disappeared from view, however, so did any feeling the others might have had for the wondrous works of the almighty, and they settled down in both Ducks to playing cards. The stakes were bigger than usual with IOUs being accepted as readily as cash. Once we had established all was well with the Ducks and the communication systems, the others took it in turns to take the controls to give Mick and me a chance to catch up with some badly needed shut-eye on the back benches. I fell asleep to the cries of victory and disbelief, as the rest of the lads distracted their anxieties from what lay ahead with the turn of a card.

The sky above was a deep crimson when Tony woke me. The sea was still calm but it was now sunset. On the horizon I could now see the black shape of Guernsey which seemed to be balanced precariously on the edge of this darkened red sea. It was a beautiful, but strangely foreboding, sight. I clambered back up to the driving seat to take over from Ernie who was at the controls, and flicked on the radio transmission switch.

'Hello Daisy, Gert to Daisy, are you receiving me?'

'Hello Gert, yes, you lazy bastard we are receiving you loud and clear,' it was Mick's voice. 'While you've been in the land of nod, I've been taking the Padre and three of the other ranks to the cleaners, half their future earnings are in hock to me.' Obviously Mick had not enjoyed the long comatose sleep that I had, and yet he sounded less the worse for wear than me.

'Thank you, Daisy, I trust that you have checked our position, course and estimated time of arrival, as well as lining your pockets.'

'I have dat, Sergeant, Mick replied now mimicking Spider, 'and to be sure all's well with God and the world.'

'Thank you Daisy, next radio contact in one hour as scheduled, over and out.'

'Over and out 'tis then,' Mick replied still mimicking Spider. He really must have given his bunch a hammering at cards, and without any surreptitious assistance from me or my shifty dealing which, back then, had earned me the proud but dubious title of 'Wheeler Dealer'.

Shortly afterwards we were moving east along the south coast of the island. The sunset had dimmed to a red glow sinking into the far horizon behind us. The rhythmic flashes of the Hanois lighthouse were also behind us and fading, while those of the St Martin's Point light were growing brighter as they guided us to our destination ahead. Guernsey's black silhouette stood stark against the cloudless and star-littered sky and a pale new moon hung low beyond St Martin's Point. It was on a night like this that Mick and me had landed on Sicily. As on that night, we were sailing in total darkness and total silence. We showed no lights, navigational or otherwise. Cigarettes could only be lit up below the gunnels level. All eyes were scouring the black coastline when, from Gert's silvery grey gloom, Bertie Bates' voice whispered excitedly. 'There it is, I can see it, look, there, just after nine o'clock!'

Sure enough there it was, a faint but distinct flashing yellow light half-way up the darkness of what we knew would be Saints Bay. This was the signal, the guiding light, we had been waiting and searching for. I swung Gert a full ninety degrees and steered a direct course for it. White reflective washes of moonlight from Daisy to our right showed that Mick too had made the turn. When the St Martin's light disappeared behind the cliffs of the Pea Stacks and Jerburg point, I flashed Gert's twin headlights twice, slowly and deliberately. All eyes were focused on the yellow light and waiting for a response. It was probably only seconds but, as always in these sort of situations, it seemed like minutes before it eventually changed to green, the signal for all systems go. 'All crew to battle stations!' The lads began putting on gloves and balaclavas and blackening their faces. It was D-Day again, and we steamed on steadily and directly towards the beckoning light.

As we came closer to land, we could see the white crests of waves gently breaking on the beach ahead. Tony called back to the others,

'Get your gear ready!' and I heard the clink of Sten guns against painted steel, the rattle of grenades and ammo belts, and quiet nervous banter. I engaged Gert's full six-wheel drive and opened the throttle. She surged forward and, as her wheels touched terra firma, rose from the water and on to dry land like some great sea monster rising from the deep.

Our coming no longer a secret, I turned on the headlights to pick out the roadway that would take us off the beach and up the Route de Saints, the Road of Saints. Even then, despite the tension, despite the grip of uncertainty, I remember smiling at the incidental irony of the name. Looking back, I could see that Daisy had also landed and was right behind us as we drove up the beach.

The green light that had guided us in safely grew brighter as we climbed upwards away from the sea. It was shining from the second floor of the round German pill box which still stands at the side of the road half way up the cliff. I pulled Gert up at the foot of it and called out into the surrounding darkness. 'All aboard girls!'

Within moments, Mavis, Marg and Thelma appeared, giggling and screaming like three bloody great school girls.

It was little wonder that the girls were so excited. Obviously they knew full well that we were bad lads. At various times in our careers they had had to endure prolonged police interviews, and they had provided alibis for us often enough, but they never knew when or where we were pulling a job. We never told them anything of that side of our business, it kept them and us safe. If they knew nothing, they could say nothing or let anything slip and they probably liked it that way. Now, after years of us keeping schtum, not only do we tell them about a job, we make them an integral and important part of it.

The day before we set out, Marg and Mavis, with Thelma as company, had taken two of my ex-WD three-ton Bedford trucks over to Cherbourg with the documentation necessary to pick up a load of empty metal ammunition boxes. The two sisters had driven large wagons during the war and so it was an easy enough thing for them to do. Thelma, on the other hand, was basically useless, apart from giving fellas the come on. Tony, however, was keen to have her along, probably so that he could keep an eye on her wandering eyes and so that she might see him as the all-conquering hero he longed to be.

Mick and me only agreed to her coming because we felt she'd provide our two girls with somebody else to talk to, and she could be a useful distraction at customs.

After driving down from Cherbourg, they parked up the trucks among the sand dunes to the north of Carteret and hitched a ride to Guernsey on a fishing boat. Just before midnight, they had jemmied their way into the Gerry pillbox on Saints Bay and placed a flashing yellow light in one of the gun-points. This light could only be seen from directly ahead, and so enabled us to sail a straight course to the beach without having any terminal encounters with the jagged rocks lined up either side of the entrance to the bay. When the girls saw Gert's lights flash, if all was well for us to come in, they would shine a green light; if there was anything untoward going on, they were to shine a red light. No light or a red light meant bugger off to God knows where so when the Green showed it came as a bit of a relief. The strategy was simple and effective, and it got us in safely.

'Keep the noise down you silly prats!' Tony shouted at them, obviously oblivious of the decibels created by a six cylinder General Motors engine being held on a steep incline on the clutch! The girls, dressed in Land Army overalls, quickly climbed aboard, helped by too many helping hands keen to help themselves and we continued our way up the gully. Marg clambered up behind me and kissed me on the cheek.

'How's it going then, Tiger?' she asked.

'Same as usual,' I said, 'still pushing on the door marked pull.'

'You always say that,' she laughed and kissed me on the cheek again.

'It's good to see you,' I said with a smile, trying to keep my concentration firmly on the narrow road ahead. 'Everything go OK?

She nodded vigorously in response, and smiled again.

Thelma had climbed up to sit by Tony, but their reunion was somewhat lacking in warmth I thought. Mavis, on the other hand, had charged down to the back of Gert and was crazily waving to Mick in the full glare of Daisy's headlights. Mick flashed the lights on and off to acknowledge their reunion.

We powered up the sharp climb to the top of the gully and drove on together until we reached the junction with La Grande Rue. I turned Gert to the right, the way to St Peter Port and the telephone exchange.

With another flash of the lights, Mick turned Daisy left towards the airport and the radio station which was on the road to Torteval. I spoke to Mick on the radio. 'Gert to Daisy, Gert to Daisy, the time is midnight exactly, zero hour, do you receive me? Over.'

'Daisy to Gert, to be sure, we'se are receiving youse loud and clear all right, and we are now setting our time pieces precisely to the said hour. Over.' It was Mick's voice and he's still mimicking Spider.

'May the Lady be with you, my son,' I said.

'Lady Luck?' he replied. 'Don't youse know that it's unlucky to be superstitious? And besides, luck was on Wednesday when 'Never Say Die' came in. Tonight it's down to us 'cos no other bastard is going to help us. So, never say die, unless it's to the other bastard.'

Marg heard this and looked at me. 'Never say die, Tiger.'

'Never say die, Mick.' I replied into the mike, 'but good luck all the same. Over and out.'

The take-over and looting of Guernsey had begun.

51

5 The Take-Over

After the long steep climb up from Saints Bay it is down hill all the way into St. Peter Port town. Ten hours at sea, even in the most calm conditions, takes its toll on anyone not used to it, and so it did for me. Although Gert was incredibly stable and fairly burbled along now that she was back on terra firma, the road before my eyes swayed and rolled like the calm but restless sea we had just left.

Fortunately, during our reconnaissance holiday, Mick and me had travelled these roads at least twice each day we were there; once on foot, once by car, in daylight and in dark. The result of this disciplined preparation was that I was able to drive the route almost instinctively, giving my senses time to regain their land legs and my mind its criminal poise. But it was strange not having Mick alongside picking out the key landmarks and, even stranger, not having him alongside at the start of a job, particularly a big one. We had always stuck close together in times of risk and danger, working on the age-old principle that two heads are better than one. That while one attacks, the other can defend. That while one rests, the other can keep watch. That being two gives you eyes in the back of your head. We were each other's keeper and each other's security blanket. Together we felt invincible, apart we felt vulnerable. I briefly wondered if Mick was sharing my anxious thoughts, but, despite my feelings of brotherly dependency, I decided that the cool bastard was probably enjoying his moonlit ride with the Valkyries!

Meanwhile, I drove instinctively along our pre-destined route down the Route de Sausmarez before turning left onto Colbourne Road and down to the Telephone Exchange. I switched Gert's engine and lights off and rolled silently and invisibly to a standstill just above the gates of the Exchange. Ernie, Ikey and Barney dropped silently over the side, taking Sten guns, light explosives and a walkie-talkie with them. The heavy oxy equipment was lowered down to them as gently as we could, but each touch of the large steel gas cylinders against Gert's steel shell rang out like a vigilant and deafening alarm bell in the still silence of night. Each time we held our breaths and hearts, listening painfully for any sound which might indicate that our presence had been detected and an alarm raised. Each time there was none, and each time we sighed the sigh of condemned men when echoing footsteps pass their cells and fade into oblivion. When the last of the team's gear was safely unloaded, I released the brake for Gert to continue her silent downhill journey. As we passed the exchange I could see light streaming out of its open doors and I silently wished the lads well. Once out of hearing range of the exchange, I eased Gert into second gear to restart her engine, and we continued on our way towards our unsuspecting and peaceful target, the island's main police station.

Nearing the perimeter of the town, I drove westward so that we would approach the Station from above. We came to a halt at the top of St. James Street. The police station was some two hundred yards further down the hill, opposite a small Hotel whose lights were still burning. The road below us was empty and lifeless. Behind me, in Gert's gloom, I could see the bright-edged profile of Tony's face, illuminated by the glow from a small torch, as he stared anxiously at his watch. It was a scene reminiscent of a Rembrandt painting, an anxious face framed by a circle of light enclosed by dark intriguing shadows etched with emerging pensive souls. The world around us was silent and still, the night air poised expectantly like a crowded stadium before the starter's pistol shot breaks the tension. Our tension was released by Tony's hoarsely whispered, 'Let's go!' The time was zero-ten minutes precisely.

The hill was steep enough to take Gert down to the Station without using the engine. I released the handbrake slowly and Gert inched steadily forward, gaining momentum with each second and each yard. Just above the station I eased the brakes back on and Gert slowed to a near silent crawl. As we passed the alleyway leading to the station's side entrance, Dave and Barry dropped catlike over the side and disappeared towards the side entrance doors which we could see were wide open.

I pulled Gert to an abrupt halt at the main entrance. Before she had come to a complete stop, Percy and Eddie, both armed with Sten guns, and with Tony in close pursuit, leapt off and ran towards the steps leading up to the main doors. After heaving on the handbrake, I was off too, chasing after them like the devil's own. It might have been the slight squeal of our brakes that alerted the rozzers inside to our presence or perhaps just bad timing but as Percy and Eddie neared the top of the steps, the station door opened and I saw a uniformed body framed momentarily against the lighted doorway. It brought back a terrible memory.

When we were fighting our way up Italy with the 56th Division during the war, Mick, me and a third bloke, a good mate called Billy Chin, took cover in the ruins of a heavily shelled house in Castelforte, which is over to the east of Monte Cassino. The Gerries had literally just pulled out of the place after giving us a right hard time of it. Anyway, this mate Billy Chin was a real laugh, always telling jokes, always ready with a quick answer and always ready to nick anything that wasn't nailed down before anyone else could nick it.

This time, however, he was too quick for his own good. While Mick and me were rolling up a ciggie, feeling good at being safe and being able to relax for the first time in a few weeks, he was nosing round to see if anything worth nicking has been left in the house. The last words we heard him say were, 'Just look what we've got here! That's mine.' We both instinctively shouted 'Leave it Billy!' but it was too late.

Mick and me never even saw or found what it was that had excited Billy's acquisitiveness. We heard the explosion and felt its blast as, along with bits of Billy, it bowled us over. Our illusions of safety and respite, along with a good mate, were blown away in an instant. It all seemed so bloody inevitable and yet there was nothing we could do but to curse our helplessness and nurse our grief. In the silence that followed this sudden and unexpected conspiracy of time and fate, our hopes melted into despair and our dreams dissolved back into reality, and, without our hopes and our dreams, we lost our trust in faith and the future.

As I looked up at the figure opening the station door, I saw Billy again and felt the same sense of dread. I instinctively called out, 'Leave it Billy!' Again it was too late. We had agreed that there would to be no killings unless absolutely necessary, that no-one was to be hurt unduly. The plan, the discipline, had been practised and perfected and everything was going according to plan. I was keyed up and confident. Unfortunately, as at that time in Italy, I had momentarily forgotten that it is in such moments that the demons of time and fate conspire to destroy your plans, your dreams, your very being. I heard the familiar brief stutter of a Sten gun and the dull thump of bullets bedding deep into human flesh. The silhouetted figure in the doorway appeared to be held motionless for a moment by string like shadows of spurting blood before, as they faded, the figure fell backwards like a marionette into the lighted hallway, its twitching legs and feet trapping the Station's doors open.

I saw Percy go in over the body crouched like a first World War veteran going over the top at the Somme in the terrifying illumination of an enemy flare. I heard a shout from inside which was silenced almost instantaneously by another rapid burst from a Sten, which I knew would also be Percy's. By the time I reached the doors, Tony and Eddie were already lugging the bloodied and lifeless body of a police sergeant back into the station. I joined their heaving in a blur of disbelief and the need to act. His twisted feet finally slipped off the doors which swung shut noisily before shielding this death scene from the prying eyes of any self-righteous do-gooders in the world outside.

As the doors closed, we heard the sound of boots running along a corridor which lead off to the right of the reception counter. Percy spun round and aimed his Sten for another unnecessary killing. As the boots turned the corner and came into view, we saw it was Dave. Percy was poised but didn't shoot. I blinked with relief, firstly because it was Dave and not some other poor bastard, and secondly that Percy hadn't pepper-potted him with twenty rounds from his Sten at close distance.

'What the fucking hell?' Dave screamed wildly in both fear and anger, eyes transfixed on Percy's still smoking Sten which was pointed directly at him. He then saw the two shot coppers on the floor. 'What the fucking hell? I thought we all agreed no fucking shooting unless we fucking had to!'

Percy stared back at him impassively. 'Shut it!' he said coldly. 'Just shut it unless you want some of the fucking same.'

'Jesus fucking Christ, Percy!' It was Tony now, in a right spin. Although he must have realised that this sort of incident could happen, I think that he had never really believed deep down that it could. 'What the fuck has got into you Percy? Dave is right, we agreed nobody to get hurt unless it was absolutely fucking necessary, and the first fucking thing you do is to gun down two fucking coppers and nearly do for Dave as well!'

Percy, now supported by Eddie, turned fiercely to face Tony directly. He braced his Sten ready to fire. 'Do you want some? You can have some as well if you fucking well like!'

I knew that this was no idle threat or bout of bravado on Percy's part. He had flipped and his eyes were strafing an imaginary battlefield for a possible enemy attack which he would repulse, single-handedly if needs be. I'd seen that haunted look many times during the war. After months of waiting the action finally starts. At this point, for some blokes, their control snaps. All that they want to do is to get the job done and to get out and to get home again. Nothing else matters to them, it's a sort of retaliatory fear, get the bastards before they get you. So they shoot to kill, and anything or anyone that gets in their way is the enemy and will be eliminated without hesitation, thought or compassion. At least Percy had retained enough control not to gun down Dave, but the irretrievable flip-over point is finely balanced, and as I've seen mates kill mates, it's as much luck as judgement which way they fall. I moved in fast.

'This isn't the time or the place, you can sort it out when we're all back home and smiling,' I said, adding with deliberately emphasised sarcasm, 'If it still bothers you then, which I doubt it will.'
With perfect timing one of the shot coppers groaned.

'Look,' I says, 'this one isn't a goner yet and there's a good chance the other one has still got some life in him too.'

I knew for sure the other one, a Sergeant, was dead, but putting up the idea that he could still be alive I thought might provide a temporary distraction inspired by hope.

My intervention had the desired effect and there was a brief silence. In that brief silence we heard slight metallic rattling noises coming from the floor above.

'The gun cupboard!' Tony whispered, as if it were the Grim Reaper himself scraping away at our tombstone up above us.

Instinctively I took off up the stairs, two at a time, calling back to the others as I went,

'I'll sort it!'

Once at the top I waved them back with my Sten gun. I took the two

56

paces to get to the door leading into the gun room. Tony's training programme was paying off again and had given me familiarity with the battle terrain. The army had done its training well too. In my reactions I was back in Italy, tight as an undersize G-string, in the shit and ready for house-to-house sniper clearance, my Sten primed and braced ready for action. I kicked the door open and saw two coppers fumbling frantically to open a grey metal gun cupboard. They corkscrewed around, startled to see a primed Sten aimed directly at them. In stark fear, they dropped to floor. I squeezed the trigger of the Sten. The burst ripped across the ceiling bringing down lumps plaster and curling plumes of dust. In a small room the noise, smoke and mayhem of rapid gun-fire is devastatingly disabling, particularly to those who have never experienced it. My display of controlled fire power blew the coppers' brains. They curled their bodies into tight balls, covering their heads and pleading with me not to shoot. Coppers! Cobblers! I've shit 'em.

'Get up, you whinging pair of bastards,' I said scornfully. 'Just get up and put your fucking hands on your heads and move.' The meek bastards complied instantly and shuffled out taking great care not to look me directly in the eye. Most prisoners, hostages and victims, have this stupid belief that if they don't look their captors in the eye, they will be spared. Silly bastards, the decision to kill deliberately in cold blood involves more than a fearful meeting of eyes.

They led the way down to the reception area which is now like New Street station on a Bank Holiday Monday! Barry had arrived too, with three more coppers he and Dave had taken prisoner when they came in through the side entrance. The whole bloody lot were crammed together almost shoulder to shoulder and, worst of all, our lads were standing about in amongst them as if they didn't know what to do next, except that is for Percy whose eyes were still strafing and looking for the next kill. It was only the recognition and fear of Percy's volatile instability and readiness to kill that was retaining the semblance of stability and peace in the melee before me. Again I decide I'd best take over and quickly.

I stopped on the third stair which gave me a commanding position and view. Following up from where I had left off earlier, I nodded towards the motionless copper on the floor and asked, 'Has anybody bothered to check if that one is dead?'

My authoritative and elevated platform on the stairs gave me the desired edge and everyone turned their attention to me.

'Dead as a door nail,..... Jesus Christ, Percy, what the....' It was Tony.

Percy turned and pointed his Sten menacingly at Tony who immediately fell silent, fear zigzagging in lightening flashes across his face. Percy snarled venomously, 'I thought we said no fucking names and you're at it a-fucking-gain.'

Tony backed away, one arm outstretched as if hoping it would protect him from the wrath of Percy's Sten.

I sussed that he had good cause to be afraid and swung my Sten very pointedly to Percy but spoke to Tony, 'We don't have time for this, Major.' I then spoke to Percy, 'Lieutenant, let it ride.' Percy eased off. I lowered my Sten and left it at that. I turned to address the whole group. 'Now look, what's done is done. You all know what you've got to do, so just do it, you can argue the toss to your bloody heart's content later.'

I pointed to the two coppers I had brought down from the gun room. 'You two, get your dead mate into that office over there.'

Without hesitation, the two coppers began to drag their dead sergeant by the arms across the reception area, his trailing feet smearing a ragged twin-track of congealing blood on the scuffed cream linoleum.

'What state is that one in?' I asked pointing at the copper who was still breathing.

It was Barry who answered. 'Actually he's not as bad as he looks, took a couple in the arm and one in the shoulder and must have passed out. He should live.'

I turned to two of the coppers Barry brought in. 'You two, take him down to the kitchen and patch him up, then the lot of you put yourselves into the far end cell, and no fucking talking or whispering to each other, remember with one dead, we've got fuck all to lose now.'

The coppers were totally shell-shocked and totally compliant. I hadn't wanted the blood and thunder stuff but it had certainly subdued the coppers, they were doing everything we wanted without trouble or question. The chosen two carried the wounded one down to the kitchen to patch him up whilst the third copper trotted off to the cells like a chastened dog to its kennel.

Scanning the room from my vantage point, I spoke to our lot again. 'Right, you know what to do, so get to it and do it.'

Barry and Dave went off to the wardroom to sort out police outfits that fitted them. Eddie and Percy did a systematic search of the station and eventually found another cheeky bastard of a copper hiding upstairs in the ladies' toilets! Tony, meanwhile, was standing around looking lost and as if it's all got beyond him; a perfect impersonation of a real-life Army Major under battle conditions, in charge but absolutely bloody useless!

I opened the front door and went out into the street. Nothing appeared untoward. Gert was parked there as though it was the most natural thing in the world for a war-time DUKW to be sat outside Guernsey's main Police Station in the middle of the night. The small Hotel a hundred or so yards up the hill was closing up and a car was pulling out of the drive, a rather nice Riley 1.5 as I remember it. As it went past, those inside eyeballed Gert and then me. I smiled and waved and the dozy prats waved back before disappearing off down the road. If they had heard anything of the shooting, they had obviously discounted it. Once they were gone, the street became as quiet as an empty grave yard at the witching hour again.

I went down the steps to Gert and gave a quiet whistle. Marg and Mavis popped their heads over the top.

'Pass me down the radio and stuff.'

'What was all the shooting about?'

'Never bloody mind about that, just pass me down the bloody radio stuff.'

'All right, keep your bloody hair on, we haven't done anything!' It was Mavis.

'That's what I'm moaning about, come on, give me the sodding stuff!'

Complaining quietly to each other, the girls heaved it over and lowered it down on to my shoulders. I struggled off up the steps to the station with it. They stood in the Duck watching me!

'Come on,' I hissed at them impatiently, 'move your bloody arses!'

The girls, including Thelma, lowered themselves down and followed me up the steps. As I got to the door, I heard the phone ringing. When I pushed the door open, there's Dave looking like a pukka copper answering the phone as if all is well with the world and his uncle.

'Good evening, Guernsey Police, relief Constable Wilson speaking, how can I help you?' He listened for a while and then says, 'Yes, I'm sorry about that Sir. We've got some Army chaps from the mainland in town, got lost going over for the D-Day celebrations in France,....yes, they've had a drop too, perhaps a drop too much. Anyway that was them firing off some blanks, for a laugh they said ....Yes that's the trouble, when it's as quiet as it is at this time of night, it sounds as if there's a full scale invasion going on again.'

He pauses to listen again, and then laughs. 'I should think you did Sir, anyway, I'm sorry it woke you up but everything's calmed down now and you shouldn't be disturbed again tonight.........Thank you Sir and Goodnight to you too.'

He put the phone down and I gave him a thumbs up to indicate that I'm right impressed. He comes from behind the desk and gives me a hand to lug the radio gear into a small office to the left of the reception desk.

As the three girls followed me in, they saw the blood trails left by the dead copper as he was dragged across the floor. They also clocked the splatters of blood and flesh on the walls and reception desk. There was no doubting that the blood and bits had been only recently separated from some poor soul. When Thelma realises this, before you could spit, she's got her hand over her mouth and running for the ladies' room. Marg and Mavis look at me wide-eyed.

'Don't bother to ask, I'll tell you later, just see if you can get this place cleaned up a bit in case some Nosey Parker waltzes in.' Without further ado or questions, the girls get some cleaning gear from the kitchen and set about cleaning the mess up. I was right proud of them.

Things were calming down. The phone rings again and Dave handles it true to form again. Barry had been busy hooking up my fifteen foot radio aerial on the roof and running a cable down the stair wells to plug into the transmitter. Before I switch it on, I do a quick check of our situation. The girls have more or less cleaned up the reception. Dave is behind the front desk looking and acting for all the world as though he's pissing P.C. 49, handling the phone calls with practised panache until, as expected, the phone suddenly goes dead on him. Barry and Tony were working their way through the station collecting all the stuff we needed, police uniforms for some of the others, car keys, handcuffs and road signs. Percy and Eddie had locked all the coppers into the end cell and were sitting, mute and sullen, in the passage leading to the cells. By the time I had finished the check, the girls were making everybody a cup of tea in the Station common room. What shit there had been had largely missed the fan, and what had hit was now nicely cleaned up. We were on course again. It was zero-twenty minutes, and we were dead on time!

I switched on the transmitter and spoke into the microphone.

'D-Day to all units, D-Day to all units, do you hear me? Over.' I switched to receive and waited. The speaker hissed and crackled, and then a faint but distinctive voice came through.

'To be sure we do Sir, unit one is receiving yers loud and clear.'

It was Mick, and he's still with the Spider impersonations, but I was more than glad to have contact with him again. The way things were shaping up, I could foresee that he might be the only bastard I could fully depend on if or when things should turn arse upwards.

He carries on, still doing his Spider impression. 'The radio Doctor has successfully completed the operation and is now on his way to the Theatre, picking up some friends on the way, over.'

'Thank you unit one, units two and three, do you hear me?'

'Unit two responding, we'se have youse loud and clear, and I'm very pleased to report to yers that it will be some time before the bells are ringing again for me or me's fucking gal, over.' It was Ernie who was feeling so pleased with himself that he decided that he'd have a go at the Spider impersonations too. Despite the hissing and crackling, I could hear Barney and Ikey laughing in the background.

'Unit three, are you receiving me?'

'Unit three here, all's well and we have youse loud and clear, the airways have been cleared and we'se off to give the Harbour lights a bloody dowsing anytime now, over.' It was Spider and while it was good to get at least one straight answer, he did not sound amused. His displeasure cannot have been helped by Stan and Bertie joining Barney and Ikey's uncontrolled giggling in response to Ernie's and his radio announcements.

Despite the mixed moods out in the field, however, everything was in place for the next move in the game and it was down to me to start the play. But I was having manic hysteria problems. The sounds of laughter and giggling pouring from the radio was infectious and I was struggling to keep a straight face and level voice. It felt and sounded prattish but I gave the code exactly as Tony had ordered. 'The harvest has been safely gathered in, I repeat, the harvest has been safely gathered in. Let the festivities begin.'

It was prattish, and yet more uncontrolled laughter poured from the radio. I lost control and began laughing irrationally too. At least some of the lads were enjoying themselves out there, their laughter probably born from relief that for them, all had gone according to plan with no-one hurt getting hurt. For me, it was a human moment of irrepressible respite. I switched off the radio and regained my composure. I remember thinking, let them enjoy their moment, they would be brought back to reality soon enough when they joined us in the Police Station.

6 Cutting the Links

As planned, while Tony, me and the others in the main group were taking over the police station, the others, operating in groups of three, were taking out the radio station, the telephone exchange, the air-port and the Harbour Master's office.

⌘   ⌘   ⌘   ⌘   ⌘   ⌘   ⌘

The Radio Station

It was Mick's job, aided by JC and JD, to take out the radio station. On reaching the top of the Route des Saints, Mick pulled Daisy to a halt to drop off Spider, Stan and Bertie, whose job was to disable any communication systems at the airport and Harbour Master's office. They went fully armed with our standard kit; sten guns, pistols, a pack of grenades and an active walkie-talkie. They crossed La Grande Rue to St. Martin's Church where the girls had left the car they had used to get out to Saints Bay. Mick waited until he saw the car start and head off towards the airport. He then drove Daisy to Pleinmont Point where the Radio station is located, stopping just below the crest of the hill so that they could not be seen from the Station itself.

While he busied himself tuning in the short-wave radio, JC and JD went on foot to check that all appeared normal at the Station. All was peaceful and, apart from the circling red flashes from the warning light perched on the top of the mast, all was in darkness. When they returned to the Duck Mick was sat alongside the slightly hissing radio, feet up on the dash and smoking a roll-up ciggie, looking for all the world as though he was holding three threes in a school of three card brag and waiting for some silly bastard to raise him. JC and JD climbed in and, appreciating what they saw, did likewise.

'Everything OK?' Mick asked when they had settled themselves down without showing any inclination to give him any feedback from their reconnaissance trip.

'Yeah, all quiet on the Western Front,' JD replied after taking his time to light a workhouse roll up, more paper than tobacco.

'Mind you,' JC added somewhat casually, 'there's a bloody great warning sign on the gates saying 'Beware of the Dogs'! We couldn't see any sign of them though.'

'Well it was nice of you to let me know!' Mick snaps back, more than a little irritated. 'I suppose I'd have cottoned on when I found one of them hanging off my bleeding arse!'

'Always ready to help out when we can,' JC answered, his reflected red eyed wink reaching JD across the darkness in a timely flash of the mast warning light.

Mick returned to his cigarette and his thoughts. After consulting his watch, at ten minutes past midnight, exactly as planned, he slid smoothly into action. A thumb and finger flick, perfected over years of practice, sent the remainder of his lighted ciggie arcing across the night sky and he restarted Gert's engine. He engaged full six-wheel drive and, with an air of fatalistic optimism, he smilingly announced to JC and JD, 'When it's time to go, you've got to go!'

He let out the clutch and built up speed quickly, using the gears and pedals with expert synchronisation. After clearing the top of the hill, he used the final slight downhill stretch leading to the radio station's steel security gates to build up whatever speed was left in Daisy's willing power base. She hit the gates at over fifty miles an hour. The gates burst open in a screeching, stretching, and twisting scream of tortured steel and a spectacular display of showering sparks. Mick pulled Daisy up in between the radio shacks and the caretaker's house as though he had just parked up for another Friday night's drinking session at the Bartons!

He snapped to JC and JD. 'Right, you two sort out the mast and I'll deal with everything else,' and casually dropped over the side. As he touched the ground he saw the two huge Doberman Pinchers that presumably had been guarding the interior of the compound bounding towards him, barking, snarling and apparently passionately intent to kill anyone wearing a British army uniform and Mick in particular. Without pausing to check if the dogs did indeed have him lined up as their next meal or were merely pleased to see him, Mick hit them with two short bursts from his Sten. Both dogs jolted to an abrupt halt in mid-air and crashed to earth, their aggressive snarling abruptly silenced, their once polished silken coats ripped apart by gapping jagged flesh wounds and spraying blood. Mick sauntered over to where they fell. One was motionless but the other lay whimpering and quivering, pitifully trying to raise its head and painfully biting at the night air. Mick stared down impassively into its rolling white framed helpless eyes and put two bullets directly into its brain, blasting its skull apart and eliminating all sound and movement instantly.

He turned and strode briskly towards the house where lights were being switched on. He waited by the door, knowing that despite the smashing of the security gates, the sound of gunfire, the abrupt silencing of the dogs and other noises shattering the silence and peace of the night, the caretaker would quite illogically, and stupidly, open the door to find out what was going on! He did and, as he did, he was smacked hard full in the face by the side of Mick's Sten for his trouble. He fell backwards into the room to the accompaniment of his wife's instantaneous panic-stricken screaming. Mick used the same old trick as I had with the coppers in the gun room; he fired a short burst from his Sten into the ceiling and shouted to them, 'Shut up and you won't get hurt!' ...... They shut up. 'Just stay there, don't move, don't say a thing, don't do fucking anything, just stay where you are. I'll be back.'

Outside JC and JD had unloaded the gas cutting equipment and were burning through the first of the radio mast's legs. Mick crossed to the radio shack and smashed the door open. He switched on the lights and surveyed the array of equipment. It was standard stuff in a basically standard layout. From his ammunition pouch, he took three hand-grenades and wedged them equidistant between the control panels, pulling the pins as he did so. He left quickly but unhurriedly, closing the door behind him and pressed himself firmly against one of the side outer walls. Three seconds later, three muffled explosions announced the destruction of the radio equipment. He looked towards the radio mast and saw it was beginning to lean and sway unpredictably as JC and JD burnt through the last of its four legs. The mast was about to topple.

'Thar she blows!' JC cried out triumphantly as he and JD did a triumphant runner to escape the slowly falling and twisting tower which, in a final burst of speed, crashed to earth missing the caretaker's house by a cat's whisker. While JC and JD connected up a dummy flashing red light on the house to cover for the one that had been at the top of the mask, Mick returned to the house. The caretaker and his wife were huddled on the floor trying to comfort each other, the caretaker's face bruised and bleeding from around his mouth and nose. Mick reassured them of their well-being provided that they continued to co-operate. They were too terrified not to. He hand-cuffed them together back to back on two chairs, gagged them with two lengths of WD puttee tape and, after turning off the lights and shutting the door, left.

He climbed back up into Daisy where JC and JD were now waiting and, after rolling and lighting up another cigarette, he took up his former relaxed feet up position alongside the radio. After the brief whirlwind of violence and noise, the night had regained its former peace and tranquillity, the only sound now being the quiet umbilical hiss of the radio and the distant sound of the sea. As Mick flicked another cigarette into the void, the sounds from the radio changed to a crackle and my disembodied electronic voice floated into the night.

'D-Day to all units, D-Day to all units, do you hear me, over?'

Without moving from his relaxed position, Mick casually picked up the microphone and, still mimicking Spider's accent as he had done ever since skinning Spider at cards during the crossing, answered. The three of them listened closely as the other two units checked in and finally heard me give the all clear code for all units to assemble at the police station. Mick restarted Daisy and drove out through the radio station's shattered gates towards St. Peter Port town, stopping at the telephone exchange on the way to pick up Ernie, Ikey and Barney.

⌘　⌘　⌘　⌘　⌘　⌘　⌘

The Telephone Exchange

When Mick picked them up, Ernie's team had effectively closed down the entire telephone network of the island for some considerable time. Their action had started, as had everyone's, at ten minutes past midnight precisely. Walking towards the exchange, they saw that its two doors were wide open and they could hear women's voices coming from the inside. It was a warm summer's night and they reasoned the doors were open to gain some cooling effect from the slight breeze. Without hesitation or breaking step, Ernie and Ikey sailed in authoritatively. Barney followed close behind, closing the doors as he entered. Inside were two plump middle-aged round-faced women receptionists sitting in front of a line of eight switchboards.

'Evening girls,' Ernie chirps brightly.

The two women swivelled round in their seats to face the intruders.

'What's going on here then? You've no right to come in here!'

'Who do you think you are, bursting in here at this time of night?' said the other. Although our lads were blacked up and wearing balaclavas so that only their eyes could be seen, the two girls spoke indignantly rather than fearfully. They were probably reassured by the sight of the Tommy uniforms and had no doubt got used to this sort of intrusion during the Gerry occupation.

'Have to tell you that later my lovely,' says Ernie as he and Ikey casually but quickly reached past the women to pull out the plug-in lines that were connected. 'We're a bit busy at the moment, do you mind if we have these too?' and removed the two headsets the receptionists were wearing. The two old girls were too taken aback by Ernie's ordinariness and his non-threatening polite behaviour to do anything, and screaming wasn't even an option for these two, they were well past teenage hysterics! Ernie fills them in with a bit of cock-and-bull about what's going on.

'Sorry about this girls,' he says, 'but I'm afraid that your work's over for tonight, you see we've got our orders to close this place down. Now don't ask me why, you'll have to ask the powers that be, but our CO says we're on a fizzer for life if we don't disable all the equipment in here so that it can't be used for a few days. He says nobody is to get hurt, but we've got to make sure that nobody, and that includes you two, raises a fuss or does anything silly, at least until tomorrow morning. Now 'cos we've got other things to do, we can't sit here all night looking after yer, nice as that might be, so how are we going to do that then?' He sits sideways on a switchboard, and looks at them for an answer.

The two women look quizzically at each other before one says, 'Well I suppose you could lock us in the toilets, Lance Corporal, that's where the Germans used to lock us up when there was a search or a scare on during the occupation. Once the door's locked there's no way out, there's only one little window and that's too high up for us.'

'And it's barred,' the other one says.

'That'll do nicely then,' says Ernie. 'Come on, you two lead the way.'

'Hold on,' says the rounder one of the two, 'I'll just get our bags with our knitting and stuff in.' She reached under the switchboards, pulled out a couple of large patchwork bags and, after handing one to her mate, leads the way into the ladies' toilets where they both make themselves comfortable in a couple of chairs which must have been genuine relics from the German occupation.

'Rightio girls,' says Ernie, 'that's lovely then. Now you'll hear a few bangs and things but just you just stay in there and I promise that nobody will come to any harm, OK?'

'OK, Luv. Are you sure that somebody will come to let us out in the morning? I've got my old man to sort out, you know.'

'He'll bleeding sort you out if you don't!' the other chortled.

'In that case, I'll make double sure they do,' says Ernie. He winks broadly at them, moves out and locks the door.

Ikey and Barney are beside themselves trying not to laugh out loud. Ernie is not amused.

'Come on you silly pair of buggers,' he whispers, pointing towards the switchboards, 'get cracking on that lot.'

Ikey and Barney immediately rigged up a string of small explosives, fixing one to each of the eight terminals. Because of its proximity to some local housing, this had to be a much quieter job than Mick and Co. could do up at the more isolated radio station. They lit the fuse and all three made a rapid exit. They counted down as they heard the rapid mini explosions from inside the exchange. There were eight.

'Now the masts!'

The two small masts were made of much lighter steel than the large mast at the radio centre and were soon brought down with no trouble and not a lot of noise either. With their work there completed, Ernie goes back to the exchange and calls up to the illuminated small window of the ladies' toilet.

'We're off now then, girls, there'll be somebody up here to let you out in the morning. Watch what you're doing now won't you, don't drop too many! Bye.'

'Ohhh, you cheeky devil. Bye then, Luv, thanks a lot,' the two women chorus back and Ikey and Barney double up again. These two jokers are still giggling when I'm radioing the teams for the all clear. Hearing Mick's take off of Spider sets them off laughing even more and when Ernie does likewise, they collapse onto the telephone exchange's lawn rolling about, smacking the ground and shaking with uncontrollable girlie giggling.

A few minutes later all three are picked up by Mick on his way into the town. When Ikey and Barney meet up with Stan and Bertie, within seconds the lot of them are on the bottom of the duck helpless with laughing. Attempting to comply with Mick's chastisements, to 'keep it down', only served to make them giggle all the more. They were still giggling when they jumped down from the Duck at the Police Station.

⌘ ⌘ ⌘ ⌘ ⌘ ⌘ ⌘

The Airport

The job of taking out the communication systems at the airport and Harbour Master's office had been allocated to Spider, Stan Leach and Bertie Bates. When Tony had reconnoitred the job in Guernsey, the only place he hadn't been able to get a good gander at was inside the airport control tower. He had tried, but no amount of ingenious bullshit could get him a guided tour. So it remained a bit of an unknown quantity. What he thought, however, and we were all behind him on this, was that we couldn't afford the risk of some bastard being able to radio some passing aircraft which might then transmit an alarm on to the mainland. The safest thing to do was to disable the equipment.

The same logic applied to the Harbour Master's but at least Tony had managed to give that a good eyeballing so the team wouldn't be going in there entirely blind. The obvious choices for a team to deal with an unknown situation were Stan and Bertie who, as I have already said, were two spontaneous bastards who thrived on jobs where they had to think and act on the run. Their problem was that once they had things on a roll, they tended to go over the top and wind up the pace until things often got a little out of hand. So Tony had decided, quite rightly, to put Spider in with them to act as a minder, not to protect them from outsiders but rather from their own exuberant excesses if things started going too well for them!

They drove to the airport using the car the girls had used to get to Saints Bay. The airport was a shambolic affair with one single story

69

building acting as the terminal and a mass of other smaller buildings and sheds seemingly scattered randomly around it. The control tower, a two-story prefab, stood isolated a hundred yards or so to the west. There was a six foot wire perimeter fence surrounding the whole airport.

When the lads cruised past the main buildings they were a bit non-plussed to see one of the larger out-buildings lit up like a Christmas tree, windows wide open and music blaring out. Spider dropped Bertie off to have a butcher's at what was going on while he and Stan did a tour of the whole place to make sure that nothing else was amiss. They picked Bertie up on the return trip.

'There's a fucking D-Day party going on in there,' Bertie reports as he gets in, 'and they look as if they'll be there all fucking night!'

'Fucking hell,' replies Stan, 'Tony said the place would be deserted!'

'For Christ's sake man,' Spider says, his expression of despair fully in line with his padre's outfit, 'he wasn't to know something like this would crop up, so's stop yers whinging and figure out what we'se going to do.'

'We could toss in a couple of grenades to make the party go with a bang,' Bertie replied dryly. Stan chortled but Spider was on edge and thought that he might just be serious.

'No fucking way, are youse two fucking barmy or something? Tony says nobody's to get hurt unless it's absolutely fucking necessary.'
Stan and Bertie slap each other with delight at Spider's hasty taking of the bait.

'Well perhaps it's necessary,' said Stan as seriously as he could muster. Spider drives on not entirely sure if they were winding him up or not.

'Drop us off up there, just past the tower and give us ten minutes,' Stan said.

Spider pulled over and Bertie and Stan, taking two loaded backpacks, are out fast and disappear into the dark towards the perimeter fence. Spider watched them go in his rear mirror and then drove on.

Once at the fence, the lads cut their way through and do another quick runner to the control tower which is in total darkness. They jemmy their way in, check the ground floor and go up the stairs to the top of the tower. Three sides of the tower are crammed with radio and electrical gear.

'What do you think?' says Bertie, 'We could pop in a couple of grenades.' They slap each other with delight again.

'No chance,' Stan replied with true disappointment, 'much as I'd like to, too much thunder and lightning with that party going on over there.' They could see the lights of the party clearly from where they stood. 'We'll do an electric chair job!'

They found the tower's main electricity supply and fuse boxes which were on the ground floor. Working by torch light, Bertie turned off the mains supply and wrapped thick wire tightly across each pair of main fuses so that every one was effectively bridged. At the same time Stan was wiring anything that could be wired to anything else on the three equipment banks upstairs. As soon as he's done, Stan calls down to Bertie doing a James Cagney sound-take, 'OK Sir Bertram, the dirty rat is strapped in the chair, let him have it, let the dirty rat fry!'

Bertie throws the main switch on and immediately hears Stan calling down to him frantically, 'For fuck's sake Bertie, get up here and see this lot quick, it's like fucking Bonfire Night.'

Bertie raced up in time to see the finale. In the darkness, the two banks of equipment were ablaze with an electrical fireworks display. Components were showering sparks, glass valves were glowing and fading like red hot pokers and other bits and bobs were just flaring up in small but spectacular silent volcanic eruptions.

'We'll have to try that again,' says Stan and they shook hands with some pride and satisfaction at their destructive creativity. 'Come on, we'd better get going.'

They wedged the door in a closed position and sprinted back to the fence. They scrambled their way though the perimeter wire and joined Spider who was waiting for them in the car as arranged. Without even asking the lads how it had gone, as soon as they are in, Spider puts his foot down for their next target, the Harbour Master's. As they passed the main airport buildings they could see that party was still going strong, obviously oblivious to the devastation wreaked in the nearby control tower. The windows were still wide open and, what was then, the newest sound of Bill Haley and the Comets' 'Rock Around the Clock' was blasting out loud enough to be heard in the car. The record still hadn't been released in England, but Stan and Bertie knew it from the Yankee parties they were always gate-crashing. They start to sing and jive about wildly on the back seat to the complete bewilderment of Spider who had never heard it before.

'Keep it down, youse noisy pair of barmy bastards, does yers want to wake up the whole bloody island?'

Between laughs, Bertie and Stan keep on singing but in more whispered tones. 'One, two. three o'clock, four o'clock rock, five, six......................'

⌘　⌘　⌘　⌘　⌘　⌘　⌘

The Harbour Master's.

The St. Peter Port Harbour Master's office is stuck right out at the end of what's known as the White Rock. The rock itself is about two hundred and fifty yards long and is joined to the mainland by a five hundred yard long stone pier, St. Julian's Pier. The rock juts out from the pier at near enough ninety degrees to form one side of the entrance to the main harbour. Right next to the Harbour Master's office is a small lighthouse which, with its companion on the Castle Cornet pier opposite, marks the entrance to the harbour. Flashing in regular patterns they guide all shipping in and out during the hours of darkness. The office is situated so that everything that goes in or out of the harbour has to pass directly in front of it.

The town of St. Peter Port rises steeply on a hill-side so that the whole of the harbour, including the White Rock, is in full view from much of the town. The harbour in those days was always pretty well full of fishing boats and private vessels which entered and left with the tides. It was important to our success, therefore, to knock out any radio communication equipment in the Harbour Master's to prevent news of our raid spreading via any sea-going craft. Given its position in full view of the town and the surrounding boats, taking it out could not involve any explosions or bright lights. This had to be an A1 low-level job.

Spider parks the car at the end of the pier and Stan and Bertie, fully armed, equipped and buoyed up with confidence after the way the airport shut-down had gone, stroll off towards the office like it's a Sunday morning reviver. Apart from a few lights on some of the boats, there's no sign of active life. Locked doors presented no problems to these two merchants so they were soon in the office. There was no need to turn any lights on as the flashes of the lighthouse illuminated the whole room every few seconds. Within the spans of light, Stan and Bertie could see the office was exactly as Tony had described, just one main transmitter receiver unit with a range of minor stuff scattered about. Their job was to disable the equipment by cutting as many wires and smashing as many valves as they could see but without making too much noise.

They had barely set about their work when Bertie says impatiently, 'this is bleeding ridiculous, we'll be here all bloody night farting about like this.'

'What are you thinking then?' Stan asked.

Bertie didn't answer but simply directed his eyes to the four large sliding windows which looked out to sea and took up most of the wall on that side of the office. The office had been built as an integral part of the stone pier to the seaward side and Bertie had sussed that they could use this to their advantage.

Stan instantly latched onto what Bertie had in mind. His eyes lit up. 'Let's do it!'

They pushed back the two central windows to make one large opening and peered down to see the sea breaking rhythmically and noisily directly below them. After wrenching and cutting the main unit free from its wiring, they carried it over to the wide open window. It was a heavy bastard but between them they managed to hoist it up and to balance it on the window ledge.

They swayed together to get into the joint rhythms of the breakers and the lighthouse beam, before, with perfect timing, pushing the unit over the edge so that, not only was the sound of it hitting the water absorbed by crash of a large breaker against the pier, any white water was washed away by the dense darkness that followed the lighthouse's circling bright light. The unit made an impressive splash, the plume of water rising up beyond the office, making the lads leap back from the open window to avoid a right soaking.

With great delight, they slapped and congratulated each other. Picking up one of the smaller transmitters Bertie heaved that out the window solo using an exaggerated shot putter's twirl and thrust. It sailed out into the night and, although much smaller than the main unit, it still hit the sea with what they rated as a commendable splash.

Not to be out done, Stan loaded another onto his shoulder and does likewise, grinning triumphantly when a distant rising flash of white water indicates that his throw has out flown Bertie's. In quick response, Bertie ripped out the telephone and flings that out even further. Stan picks up a typewriter which he decides is too heavy to throw, so he just drops it out of the window, not even attempting to out do Stan's phone throw.

They were now both fully fired up. They began tossing and skimming anything and everything that could be tossed, skimmed or simply dropped into the sea; paper baskets, plates, a kettle, trays, chairs, everything until the room was cleared. Thinking they were all done they leant back against the wall panting like a pair of knackered steeplechase greyhounds and, between pants, laughing at each other as the room brightened and darkened with the monotonous silent rotation of the light.

As the light made one of its journeys across the room, it seemed to pause, momentarily, as it passed the office clock which was hanging nervously above the doorway. Bertie takes it down. It was round, not much bigger than a discus, and so cupping it in his hand, Bertie does a first rate impression of a discus thrower, twirling himself around several times before hurling it into the night like a flying saucer. Thin, spreading, circular reflections of white water way out in the dark sea signalled when it finally hit the surface. It paused for a moment, and then sank slowly to the depths. When waters of the Atlantic washed over it, it was showing the time of twenty four minutes past midnight.

With their work done and near enough on time, they headed back to the car, closing the office door quietly behind them?'

'How's it go then?' Spider asked as they got in.

'With a splash,' said Bertie and they both began laughing and slapping each other again.

'I'll never understand youse two barmy bastards, 'Spider said, which only caused Stan and Bertie to laugh even more and to begin singing again, 'One, two, three o'clock, four o'clock rock.'

Three minutes later with a verse still to sing, they were in the Blue Lamp with the rest of us.

7 Harvest Festival

The three girls, Barry, Tony and me were sitting around the police common-room table drinking tea when Mick, followed by the others, minus Spider, Stan and Bertie who were still off doing the Harbourmaster's, breezed in. Mick laughed out loud at the sight and groaned in mock admonishment.

'Well I'll shag my granny, just look at you lazy bastards, what do you think this is, workers' bloody playtime?'

We all laugh and Mavis is up in an instant, flinging herself on him wholesale before anyone has a chance to answer.

'Hello Bab,' he says, 'Are you all right?'

Mavis gives him a big smile and nods.

'Make us a cup of tea then, I'm bleeding parched.'

Without any more ado, Mavis bounces off to make him a cup of tea with Marg right on her heels. Thelma, sour-faced, stays put. Mick and the others joined us around the table.

'Well, how's it going then?' Mick asked.

'You might well ask,' Tony responds immediately, 'Percy's killed a copper and nigh on killed another one. Just shot them for no good reason. He then made to have a go at me, he'd have shot me too if Ronnie hadn't have stopped him. He's gone crazy.'

Mick appeared to be completely unfazed by Tony's anxiously dramatic outburst.

'Any other problems?' he asks, turning from Tony to looking directly at me. As was often the case with Mick, I'm right impressed by his reaction, or lack of it, but before I can say anything Tony chimes in again.

'This is fucking serious Mick, he's put the hangman's noose around all our necks.'

Remembering what happened to Chris Craig and Derek Bentley, who had killed a copper during a robbery only the year before, Tony was probably right. When they were cornered by the law, Craig, a sixteen year old kid, shot and killed a copper. It was Craig who pulled the trigger but it was Bentley who got topped for it; just for being there. That's the British establishment's idea of justice and retribution.

But for us there and then I was with Mick's pragmatic view. What was done, was done and there was no point dwelling on it, so taking up Mick's gambit, I also ignored Tony's legitimate and frenzied scare.

'No, apart from that everything went according to plan.'

'Well, if you will play soldiers, somebody's likely to get hurt. Where are the bros now?'

'Out the back keeping an eye on the coppers in the cells and guarding the side door. How did your caper go?'

'Straight down the line, I'll tell you later.'

The girls arrived back and started handing cups of tea around. Mick gets his first.

'Soon as we've had this then, we'd better get started hadn't we?' he says sipping his tea.

Thelma suddenly stands up, grabs the tea pot and two cups, bangs them down noisily on a tray and announces, 'I'll take a cup to Percy and Eddie.'

'Watch out that crazy bastard doesn't shoot you,' Tony muttered sarcastically.

'Why don't you grow up?' Thelma retorted sourly, pouring out two cups of tea as she spoke. 'As Mick just said, people get hurt when they play soldiers, Percy was just doing what had to be done, at least he'd got the bottle to do it.' With that and a swivel of her well-shaped hips, she turns and leaves, carrying the tray and two cups of tea.

I remember thinking to myself at the time, this was a very different Thelma to the one who had been puking up at the sight of a few drops of blood only ten minutes ago. The atmosphere in our tea party was now less than jolly. Nobody knows what to say or do. Eyebrows conspicuously raised, we all look round at each other in a silent 'What the hell was all that about?' ritual.

Before anyone took the chance to offer some inane, perhaps insane, comment, Mick, the soothsayer, speaks. 'Right, we can't sit around here all night numbing our arses, where's these coppers' uniforms?'

As Tony, Mick and me were to remain in army gear, this was clearly a move by Mick to get everything going again, and it worked. There's nothing like a burst of activity to divert the brain cells from dwelling on matters they're not too keen on.

Barry and Tony had laid out a dozen or so police uniforms and helmets on the cupboards running around the sides of the room and the lads who were to act as coppers started to try them on. They were in an in-between state of dress when Thelma came back into the room in a minor state of panic.

'Percy and Eddie told me to tell you there's a police car just pulled up the side with a couple of coppers in it, and what do you want them to do about it?'

Mick looks at me and answers flatly, 'Ronnie and me will handle it.'

We each picked up an Enfield rifle on our way out to the side door. For what we had in mind, an Enfield with its heavy wooden stock was a much better tool than a lightweight Sten. We step smartly down the passage and, just as we get to the door, the two coppers come through it rabbiting away to each other about the two Ducks parked outside. They see us and, though surprised by our sudden appearance, one manages to ask, 'What's with all this then?'

He received a quick and unexpected answer. Mick slammed the butt of his Enfield into his guts and, as he doubled up with the pain, Mick smacked him hard on the side of the head with it. Blood splattered out. The other copper goes into paralysis, probably from the sight and feel of his mate's blood, it often has that effect with people who are not used to it. Before he had time to shake himself out of it I gave him the same treatment and they both end up on the floor moaning and writhing about in slow motion. The door leading to the cells opened and we were joined by Eddie and Percy.

'We could have handled these two,' says Percy.

'We know you could,' Mick replied. 'Ronnie and me thought we'd save you the trouble that's all, but you can them take down the cells if you like.'

Eddie kicked one viciously. 'Right, on your feet you pair of bastards and into the fucking cells before you get a lot more than what you've bargained for.' Even at the time this seemed to be a prattish thing to say as it implied that they had somehow 'bargained' for what Mick and me had just dealt them. But that was Eddie's way.

The coppers struggled to their feet and stumbled towards the cells, hurried on by the jabbing barrels of the brothers' Sten guns.

'Now gently, gently,' Mick says knowingly to the brothers. 'We don't want anybody else getting hurt do we? Otherwise you never know where it might end up.' The brothers knew Big Mick well enough and they knew what he meant well enough. They would have been fools not to.

We returned to the rest room to find Spider, Stan and Bertie safely back and also enjoying a welcome-to-base cup of tea. Stan and Bertie were drinking theirs as they changed into police uniforms. Dave comes in from the front desk holding a large black folder and announces for all to hear,

'I've checked the duty roster and there's no other rozzers out and about, so we've got the lot that's on duty tonight, all nicely locked up out the back.' A small cheer went round the room. It was half time and, despite a couple of mishaps, we're in the lead with everything to play for!

⌘ ⌘ ⌘ ⌘ ⌘ ⌘ ⌘

It was apparent that the slightly unexpected turn of events had blown Tony off course and, although it was his show, it was obvious that he was not going to be able to manage things from the front for the time being. In his fantasies Tony had dreamed about being part of a big real life caper, he had craved for it, but now he was in it, all he wanted was out, to turn the clock back, but he was having to face up to the fact that there was no out and that time never moves back. For him now, it was like being on a small boat in a big storm on a big ocean, he was shit scared but there was nothing he could do but clench his buttocks and ride it out.

I moved my eyes from Tony to Mick and cocked my eyebrows. Mick nodded. I didn't need to say anything. Mick had also sussed the score and agreed with me that if things were to keep going according to plan, someone would need to take over Tony's leading role, and that it would be best for all concerned if that somebody was us!

I called down the passage for Eddie and Percy to join us. As soon as they came in, I started spieling as if it were all part of the plan.

'Right, it's two minutes past-half twelve. We're near enough on time and right on target so let's get to it. First, the car and van pick-up teams. Dave has the keys and handcuffs for you, take your weapons but don't, don't, use them unless you really have too, we're in enough shit as it is without adding any more to the pile. Stick to the schedule and radio in to Dave when you have made your pick-up or if there's any problem we need to know about down here. First stops are Lloyds and the Provincial, so Tony and the rest of us will have the Ducks down there well before you arrive back with the first pick-ups. The girls will stay here to look after what women and kids come in, and Dave will be manning the front desk and radio at all times. Barry and Tony will look after the road blocks. Everything from now on is as we planned. So don't worry about what's going on this end or shit yourselves if a copper flags you down, 'cos if one does, it'll be one of us.' I smiled, looked around and paused for a breather.

'Right, any questions? Any problems? Speak now or forever hold your piece.' Nobody spoke. I sensed the mood was right; everyone was ready to go, it was pay off time at last, this is what we had signed up for. ' OK, let's go to it, good luck and ....never say die.'
Mick and some of the others murmured in reply, 'Never say die.'

⌘　⌘　⌘　⌘　⌘　⌘　⌘

As we stepped out of the station the enormity of what we had achieved in the thirty minutes or so since we had landed on this honey-pot island hit me. We now had effective control over the whole of Guernsey. We were an armed, trained, organised and determined outfit. The police had represented the only possibility of any effective opposition to our take-over and we had cut their bollocks off quicker than a vet can neuter a sedated tomcat. Right now, half of the force were compliant prisoners of ours in their own cells and the other half were billeted around the island in blissful ignorance of our presence or unlawful intent. The force's only useful and available weaponry was in our hands. All of the island's means of internal communication by telephone or radio had been destroyed, so that we were now the only group capable of communicating with each other over distance. All possible links to the outside world had been destroyed, so there could be no last minute rescue by the US cavalry in this do. It was a classic textbook coup d'etat. The island was ours for the taking, and we were about to take it!

8 Pay Off Time

Bringing in the bank managers was the job of two teams of three. Percy, Stan and Bertie made up one team and Eddie, Barney and Ikey the other. The two teams were to use two of Guernsey's own police cars to bring the managers into the station. As and when we were ready, each of the managers would to be taken from the station to open up their respective banks to be, shall I say, asset stripped. With Percy and Eddie acting like a couple of loose cannons ready to fire off at anytime, Mick and me were not too happy about them being sent out to bring anybody in who might offer some resistance.

There was, however, not a lot we could do. It was far too risky to start making any major changes to our plans or to rejig the composition of the teams at such a late stage in the play. To have done so would have rendered the months of training and preparation we had done irrelevant and consequently increase, rather than decrease, the possibility of generating further casualties and shit-yourself situations. We could only hope that the saner lads would, through self-preservation if nothing else, curb any further excesses on the part of the brothers.

Mick and me managed to hold hurried, secretive con-flabs with Stan and Barney. Firstly, we alerted them to the minor changes we had made to the overall plan. Secondly, we put it down hard that it was up to them to make sure that the brothers didn't step out of line again and, if they did, to put them out of the running permanently, without trial, inquest or hesitation. In practice, if you stick rigidly to the last of these, it avoids all the soul searching pain of the first two. Just do it without thinking. It's often excused as acting under orders by the powers that be. Basically it's an edict for conscience-free atrocities and the right to blame others who will never be called to account.

The plan now was that the saner lads were to get the managers out of their homes while the brothers remained in the cars, engines running. Putting them in charge of the motors, we reckoned, would give them a feeling of importance and avoid them feeling any loss of face. The change, however, was intended solely to keep them cocooned in the cars whilst the other lads blagged the managers to go with them peacefully using cock and bull stories about serious threats against their banks, them and their families. Not so cock and bull in reality, but the idea was simply to get the managers and, where relevant, their wives and families down to the station as quickly as possible and without any unnecessary violence or fuss. Once at the station, the managers were to be put in the small interview room with the very dead bloody copper. Being locked in a small room with a bullet riddled body at their feet, knowing they could be next should they displease us, would, we reasoned, convince them, far more than any threatening words we could come up with, that they really were in Deep Shit Street. In addition, the knowledge that we had their loved ones God knows where, we also reckoned, would inevitably ease their way into doing whatever we wanted them to do without any feelings of guilt or stupid heroics on their part. They could always say to themselves and others that they did it for their families.

The two collection teams were supported by a third team of two, Spider and Ernie. Using Guernsey's one and only Black Maria, they were to follow up behind the police cars to bring the manager's wives and families back to the police station. Once there, the hostages, for that's what they were, would be confined to the station's common room. Spider was to stay in his padre's outfit as we felt that this might help to keep the silly bastards calm should anything untoward spook them. The van could hold a dozen comfortably and so it was to remain out in the field until full and then deliver them, a full load at a time, down to the Lamp. It was far safer to have the wives and whoever under one roof and under our control rather than to leave them at home, frightened and in a state of panic, not knowing what was happening to their men-folk. The procedure was in line with our plan's main guiding principle: Safety First.

Finally there was the group who were to control the police station. This comprised Dave and the three girls. Dave was to stay on duty at the desk to deal with anything that might come through the door, to man the radio, and to provide any muscle should it be needed. The girls were to look after the womenfolk and children when they came in, keep them happy, cosseted and ignorant. Tony and Barry had the job of sealing off the High Street and to keep it clear of Nosy Parkers while the rest of us opened up the banks, did some eye-ball valuations and then loaded everything worth taking into the Ducks ready for our get-away.

Those of us making up this last group stood at the entrance to the station and watched silently as the two police cars followed by the Maria disappeared up the hill. We loaded the stuff for setting up the road blocks into the Ducks and, without starting the motors, rolled them down the hill to the top of the High Street. I stopped Gert alongside Lloyds Bank while Mick rolled on past to park Daisy outside the National Westminster. JC and JD hooked metal slide chutes, specially made for the purpose, to the Bank side of each of the Ducks. These chutes ran at an angle of about sixty degrees from the Duck gunnels down to the Bank doors. The chutes were designed specifically to move steel ammo boxes. The boxes would be slid down the chutes empty and hauled back up once fully loaded with bunce from the banks. Maximum speed, maximum ease, minimal effort. Brainchild, courtesy of JC and JD.

While JC and JD were rigging the chutes up, Barry and Tony set up regulation police road blocks at both ends of the High Street to close the area off. Once done, Barry and Tony patrolled the barriers as additional protection. Tony had more-or-less regained his composure now and was enjoying strutting about playing an Army Major again, while Barry was looking every bit a regular copper. To any unsuspecting Nosy Parker, the scene would suggest a joint army and police operation involving the Banks rather than a bunch of thieving bastards stripping their island clean! All was ready for us to extend a warm greeting to our first bank manager.

Mick and me strolled up to the top of Smith Street where, from the corner, we could see both the Police Station and Lloyds Bank. The first of the cars returned to the station and we watched as four figures, Percy, Stan, Bertie and one other, go in through the main doors. We returned to Lloyds and told the others to make ready. Minutes later, we saw the same four we had watched go into the Station come out and start walking down the steep slope of Smith Street towards us.

When they reached us Stan, for reasons only known to himself, decided to play the formal military bit and stamped to attention. He saluted and in regulation army-speak barked at me, 'May I introduce you to Mr. Gomerseal and pass him over to your safe-keeping

Sergeant?' A pathetic figure of a man dressed in a blue towel dressing gown, vivid striped pyjamas and fawn tartan slippers stood before us. He looked a broken soul, his shoulders hunched and head sunk deep into his chest. He looked like anything but the typically haughty god almighty Bank Fuhrer that most Bank Managers considered themselves to be in those days, and that some of the bastards still think they are now.

Stan continued. 'Mr. Gomerseal is the manger of this Bank and he has kindly agreed to open it up for us so that we can make our substantial withdrawals without any further delay.' He poked Gomerseal in the ribs with the barrel of his Sten gun. 'It's a sort of 'thank you' to us for keeping his wife and two kids safe from danger, that's right isn't it Mr. Gomerseal?' Gomerseal nodded his head without looking up.

Picking up on Stan's army speak, I replied tersely.

'Thank you Corporal, I'll take over from here. You and the other men carry on with your duties.'

Stan, grinning ear to ear, salutes again, does an exaggerated regulation about turn and, followed by Bertie and Percy, marched off back up the hill.

'After you, Mr. Gomerseal, Sir,' I said, guiding him with the barrel of my Sten gun to the pair of solid oak doors just inside the Bank's Romanesque entrance porch.

Rummaging about in the large loose pockets of his dressing gown Gomerseal shuffled forward, pulled out a bunch of large keys, selected one, slid it into the lock, turned it and pushed the doors open. As they opened I shoved him forward into a large reception area. It had a marble tiled floor which exaggerated the clatter of our hob-nailed boots. Stan and Bertie followed us in and turned on any light switches they could find. Prompting Gomerseal with my Sten again, I said, 'Now turn the alarms off and do it quickly, we don't want them going off now, do we?' He shuffled into an office, unlocked a steel cabinet and turned off a series of alarm switches with another key.

'Well done, you see, you work with us and you and your lovely family will be all safe and sound. Now the vault and the personal security boxes if you please.'

We followed Gomerseal to the door of the main vault. He stopped and stood motionless before the vault in what we took to be a symbolic, if only momentary, acknowledgement of his duty to resist.

'I hear that your wife and kids are tucked in safely up the road, Mr. Gomerseal, is that right?' Mick asked quietly. Gomerseal turned his eyes to see Mick conspicuously examining his Sten gun as if looking for a defect. Gomerseal nodded sorrowfully when Mick eventually looked at him for an answer.

'Well then, it's best if things stay that way isn't it, we don't want any more nasty accidents tonight do we?'

Gomerseal shook his head; the poor sod was to terrified to speak. Mick continued as if he were talking to a child. 'No, we don't, do we? So you know what you've got to do, just feed in the right numbers, open the door and we can all get back to our beds, all safe and sound.'

Gomerseal reached his hand out towards the combination dial on the vault door, his fingers trembling like the legs of a skinny greyhound on heat. Grasping the dial tightly reduced his tremors somewhat and he turned it left and right several times before spinning the large steel lock wheel in the centre of the door to finally open the vault. Still holding on to the wheel, he leaned backward so that his body weight swung the heavy door open with a minimum of physical effort. It was done as a priest conducts a solemn ritual, a silent rite of proscribed procedure which proclaimed the repetitive pattern of Gomerseal's daily life-draining enslavement.

'There, I knew you could do it, well done!' Mick said and both him and me stepped into the vault. We felt like a couple of war-raised kids walking into a sweet shop when sweets came off ration. We were surrounded by money, wads of it, trays of it, boxes of it, money everywhere we looked, and it was all ours for the taking. I picked up a loose wad of five pound notes from a tray and tossed it high in the air so that the individual notes floated down like giant snow-flakes.

'We've bloody well done it, we've bloody well done it!' I whispered to Mick as if to dispel my own feelings of disbelief.

'Don't count your chickens, we're still far from being home and dry,' Mick replied although even he couldn't totally mask the excitement on his face as the large white tissue paper five pound notes wafted down around him. He caught one as it floated past him. After scrutinising it closely, he folded it twice lengthways. He took out his cigarette lighter and lit the end of the folded fiver. He pulled a cigarette from behind his ear and lit it with the burning five pound note, gave a massive grin and says, 'But we can start counting the fucking eggs, can't we?'

I called out of the vault to the others.

'Hey, Privates C and D, come and get yourselves an eyeful of what we've got in here, and bring some boxes with you too!'

JC and JD, as requested, came in bringing four ammo boxes with them. Soon as they step into the vault, they're kicking through the tissue fivers which are lying all over the floor. Now these two are not generally your excitable schoolgirls. A show of emotion for them was more like the distant rumble of thunder that you'd miss if you weren't tuned into it, rather than the eruption of a volcano in your front living room. They came to a standstill amongst the carpet of fivers and looked warily around the vault. I was just thinking I could hear the distant rumble when the bloody volcano erupts. They suddenly exploded into paroxysms of ecstatic disbelief, jumping up and down, yelling and whooping! You've got it, just like a bloody great pair of school-girls! They were still jumping when they shouted at Mick and me, 'Well, let's start doing the business we came for then, what are we standing about here for?'

With that, we all started tightly packing wad after wad of bank notes into the ammo boxes. In our excitement we almost forgot about Gomerseal who was standing at the entrance to the vault watching us impassively.

'Come on, you idle bastard,' Mick says to him, 'don't just stand there like a bleeding zombie, give us a bloody hand.'

Reluctantly, Gomerseal joined us and began to neatly and orderly stash wads of money into the boxes. Although he didn't display our sense of urgency in his work, I'm bloody sure that he was packing more into the boxes than us and probably at a faster rate; experience and efficiency, as always, triumphing over exuberance and greed.

When five or six boxes were full, JC and JD dragged them out. JD climbed up into Gert and JC pushed a loaded box up the steel chute. When it got within his reach JD hauls it up and stacked it inside. Within minutes we'd got the whole thing working like the production line at the Longbridge factory, with empty boxes going in and the same boxes going back a few minutes later heavy and laden with cash.

We estimated that each box held somewhere between fifteen and thirty thousand nicker, depending upon the denomination of the notes. JD was stacking them neatly into Gert at a rate of around two a minute. He worked for fourteen minutes and in that time every last promissory note of whatever denomination or origin in the Lloyd's vault was cleared out.

Next, with noticeably less quivering and shaking, Gomerseal began systematically to open the personal security boxes. The lads followed him along, throwing anything that looked worth the effort, which basically meant money and jewellery, into more ammo boxes. Everything else, which included a surprisingly large number of handguns, was tossed to the floor as rubbish. Leaving the lads to finish off the bits and pieces, I radioed to Dave to send down the manager of the Provincial which was next on our withdrawals agenda. In no time at all Stan and Bertie arrived with the new bloke and we swopped him for Gomerseal who they then escorted back to the station.

This new bloke, as I recall, was called Dobinson and, just like poor old Gomerseal, was a bag of nerves and gave us no trouble. The net result was that we did a carbon copy job of emptying the Provincial just as we had Lloyds. When Bertie and Stan had pulled in all of their allocated Bank managers, they joined us to help out with the clearing operations. With them helping, we were able to clean out the next bank, the TSB, and load everything into Daisy in less than ten minutes flat.

The routine was now set. Mick and me leap-frogged the Ducks down the line of Banks, received the respective managers and had the vaults open, ready and waiting for the clearing team to move in as soon as they had emptied out the previous place. When the last of the Bank managers had been picked up and were safely tucked in at the station, Ikey and Barney joined us and the clearance time became even better. We were knocking them off like nine pins; Lloyds, Provincial, TSB, Royal bank of Scotland, the Midland, the Commercial, Williams and Glyn, and the Old Bank. Never in the history of banking had so much been withdrawn so quickly by so few!

9 Making a Killing

With things going that well, it was inevitable that something had to crop up to disrupt the smooth flow of the operation. The first hint of possible trouble came while the lads were clearing the Old Bank. Mick and me had moved on to get the next bank, The Merchant Bank, to prepare it for clearance. Gert was in position and I radioed to Dave for Percy and Eddie to bring the manager down. I was feeling as confident as if I was asking the milkman to leave an extra pinta, so Dave's response came as a bit of a shock.

'You'll have to watch this one,' Dave said, his voice sounding a cautionary warning.

'There's something dickey about this bastard, he's different from the rest for sure. His name is Adrian Mordant and he's got a right bob on himself. No wife or family so the lads had to rough him up quite a bit even to get him down here. Percy and Eddie are looking after him now and he seems to be behaving himself. It was pretty obvious we weren't going to get much out of him so I pulled Gomerseal out for a chat to see what I could find out from him about what makes this Mordant bloke tick. Once I let Gomerseal know that he was in the clear now he'd done his bit, he became quite chatty. We're almost best mates! '

What did Mick say about Dave and Barry? 'Once a copper, always a copper,' and god bless them for that I say. The rest of us probably wouldn't have let this bloke's resistance bother us, but the copper in Dave instinctively knew the old rule; if someone ain't behaving normal, the chances are something ain't normal. So he checks it out.

'And what did you find out?'

'Well it's a funny do all round. Gomerseal reckons this Mordant geezer was Guernsey born and bred till his folks buggered off to Austria when he was just a kid. Nobody knows much what happened next until he turns up back here again within a year of the war ending. He was all skin and bone when he returned, probably only weighing about seven or eight stone. Gomerseal thinks Mordant must have had it rough as he has never talked about what happened to him over there, or what happened to his folks except he once said that they'd been killed by the Nazis. He reckons he must have spent some time in a Gerry concentration camp or something like that. Anyway, soon after Mordant gets back, this Merchant Bank, I'll tell you about that in a bit, advertises for a new manager and, against all the odds, Mordant gets the job.'

'A set-up?'

'Well that's what Gomerseal thinks. But the Bank's a funny do, too. Gomerseal reckons that during the occupation the Gerries took it over all legal like, paid for it and everything, and then ran it as a normal bank. It was used mostly by the Gerry soldiers and people in their pay. Then, as far as he knows, just as soon as the war ends, some Swiss Bank took it over from the Gerries and sent some of their own blokes over to run it. Next thing you know, they make Mordant the manager and most of the Swiss bugger off back home. Gomerseal thinks they used Mordant to pacify the locals, him being Guernsey born and bred and all that, but he never really seemed to fit in.'

'And what else does he say?'

'Well not a lot, he says Mordant keeps himself to himself. He's always at the Bank and regularly works way into the small hours. He's a case of all work and no play. Gomerseal says most of the Bank's business seems to be in international finance, it sends stuff all over the world, although it has built up quite a bit of local business now, mainly through agreeing loans which most of the other Banks refuse to handle.'

'And what was his mother's maiden name?' I asked, teasing his thoroughness.

'I never got.... you bastard.' He laughed, accepting that he'd been caught on the hop.

'Well done Dave, but what do you reckon?'

'Well, he's a strange one for sure, and a tough nut with it. He's nowhere near as compliant as the others have been. You'll have to let him know that you mean business right from the start. It might be a good idea to keep the brothers with you, he seems pretty wary of them. I'd have a good sniff around that bank, there's something about it that just don't ring true. Gomerseal says as much but he can't put a finger on it. Anyway I thought I'd best to fill you in and warn you he's not the same as the others. I'm sending the brothers down with him now.'

'Thanks for the advice Dave, we'll bear it in mind. Over and out.'

I switched the walkie-talkie to hold and turned to Mick who had been alongside listening.

'What do you reckon to this lot then? This will be the awkward bastard Ikey and Barney mentioned.' Ikey and Barney had told us that they'd had a bit of bother with one of the managers but they hadn't really given us any details.

There was a long pause before Mick replied.

'The bloke's got to be more than a bit dodgy for the lads to hand him over to Percy and Eddie to sort out.'

Looking up the High Street, he dragged hard on his cigarette, dropped it to the floor and killed its brightened glow with a slow twisting action of his boot.

'Anyway, we'll find out soon enough, here they come.'

We watched as Percy and Eddie marched down towards us with a third bloke, presumably Mordant, in between them. It was noticeable that despite being in pyjamas, dressing gown and slippers, just like all the rest, Mordant was actually marching too and, although it looked bloody ridiculous given the way he was dressed, it was undoubtedly the march of a trained soldier. He was not shuffling along or cowed as all the others had been. He marched in precise military fashion; back straight, head held erect, with his eyes fixed directly ahead. And when the group reached us, while Percy and Eddie simply came to a halt, he snapped to attention and looked me directly in the eye. I scanned his face. There was blood oozing randomly around his lips and nose and there was a swiping gash on the left side of his head. One of his eyes was all but closed from heavy bruising. It was obvious that he had taken a heavy beating before he had agreed to comply. I spoke to him in typically formal but intrinsically sarcastic British army fashion, completely ignoring his appearance.

'Thank you for joining us, Mr. Mordant, now if you would kindly open up for us please,' and pointed to the Bank's entrance .

Without replying he moved forward, removed a bunch of keys from his pocket, selected one and opened the door with it. We went in and he turned on the lights.

'And now the alarms and then the vault if you would be so kind.'

· He nearly managed a smile as he led us through a door to a vestibule area housing the alarm system controls and the entrance to the vault. After switching off the alarms, he crossed to the vault, entered the combination, spun the lock wheel and swung the door open. Then without saying a word, he turned around, walked back across the room and sat down defiantly on a chair in the middle of the room. Apart from this show of bravado, his ready compliance to this point didn't sit easily alongside with what Dave had told us over the radio. No hassle, no bother, he just opened up the vault as requested. Mick and me had a look inside. It was much like the others we'd seen, racks and shelves crammed with trays and boxes of money. By then, however, we had seen so much money it no longer impressed or excited us. It was Mordant's behaviour that was more intriguing.

While Dave the Copper might look for evidence and facts, I tend to work on gut reaction, instinct, twitchy nose and the like. Why had he opened up so easily? Even Gomerseal had tried to put on a bit of a show. And now here was this Mordant guy, sitting there with a faintly arrogant smirk on his face almost as if he'd pulled one over on us. There was something decidedly funny about him and about this situation. I remembered that Dave had advised us to have a good sniff around this bank and so, twitchy noses poised, Mick and me prowled around the place, going from room to room, not really knowing what we were looking for, or if we'd recognise it if we saw it.

Having found nothing untoward, we went back to Mordant who was still sitting bolt upright looking straight ahead. I leant on a wall and looked at him, vainly hoping for inspiration. Mick casually rolled a cigarette, lit it and strolled across to Mordant. He bent down to put his eyes a few inches from Mordent's and stared at him, occasionally clouding both of them in cigarette smoke. Mordant just sat there, almost expressionless, yet looking arrogantly back into Mick's eyes. Suddenly Mick steps back and, still staring at Mordant, announces. 'Whatever it is, it's in here.'

Mordant's eyes flinched momentarily, which told us that Mick had hit on something. This was confirmed for us as Mordant stubbornly fixed his eyes straight ahead. Mick walked slowly round the room and then to the door. He looked around the entrance hall and, turning back to me, says, 'It's too small, this place is too small.'

He pointed to one side of the room which was lined with

bookshelves. 'It's that wall, either that wall shouldn't be there or it should have a door.'

Once Mick had said it, it was obvious. The room was short by at least a couple of yards and it was the wall with the bookshelves that was all wrong. There were four sets of shelves, each stacked with box files. We looked them up and down several times but could see nothing amiss. Mick dropped his cigarette to the floor to kill it with one of his customary over-emphasised slow twists of his boot. As our eyes moved from the shelves to Mick's writhing boot, we simultaneously spotted small scrape and scratch marks on the floor. They were right in front of a bank of shelves and precisely prescribed the path of an arc. They could have only been made by this section of the shelves being moved on a pretty regular basis. We each took hold of a side of this set of shelves and pulled. With surprising ease, they swung outwards to reveal a large vault door set in the wall. We had found the thimble!

Mordant immediately became agitated, less composed, less arrogant and I could hardly conceal my feeling of feral triumph when I turned to him.

'Would you now please open this vault for us, Mr. Mordant.'

Mordant pursed his lips in thought before answering.

'I have opened the main vault for you. That is all you need. This vault holds nothing of interest for you. It is rarely used and holds only old deeds and legal documents.' This was the first time he had spoken. He spoke tersely with clipped consonants, and his eyes looked away from me. Except when he was opening the first vault, he had always looked me directly in the eye whenever I had addressed to him. Until then I had found his resistance and superior manner a little unsettling but this attempt to avoid eye contact suggested that he was not as cock-sure of himself as he tried to make out.

'All the same,' I persisted, 'We would appreciate it if we could check that for ourselves.'

'If I could open it for you I would, but I cannot. I do not know the combination. I have opened the vault which holds all the bank's deposits and financial reserves. This one is used only for legal material which will be of no interest or use to you.' After his earlier compliance I was taken aback a bit by this unexpected defiance but before I could come up with a reply, Percy, who had witnessed the latter part of this scene together with Eddie, butts in.

'If you don't know the fucking number, who the fucking hell does?'

It was a good question.

Mordant turned and looked at Percy as if he were a fool, not a wise thing to do, and answered very disdainfully.

'The Bank's legal adviser. I repeat, the vault contains only old legal documents, therefore only he needs to go in there, and therefore only he needs to know the combination.'

'You fucking lying bastard.' Eddie takes up the case and shouts directly into Mordant's face before turning to me.

'He's fucking lying Sergeant, if anything happened to this fucking legal adviser bloke, who could open the vault then, eh? Someone else has to know it and it's likely to be this bastard. And another thing, if there's only legal junk in it, why is it hidden away? It's fucking amazing that you and Mick even found it.'

Percy chips in. 'He's right Sergeant, let me and the Lieutenant make the bastard open it up, or we'll open him up. It's up to him.'

What Mordant made of the peculiarity of two Lieutenants asking a Sergeant for permission to take action God only knows, but I had to concede the brothers had a point, particularly the bit about why was this vault so well hidden if it only contained worthless legal stuff? On top of all that, I reasoned that whatever was in there, it had got to be important otherwise why was he refusing to open it up? I decided it had to be opened, and opened quickly. He'd already had a taste of Eddie and Percy's interrogation etiquette, whereas Mick and me were unknown to him, and so I nodded to Eddie for him and Percy to take charge. Mick and me moved away from centre stage to leave the brothers to it.

It was a hasty decision taken, I tell myself now it was because we were running to a tight schedule and couldn't afford the time to be messed about by this prat. Mind you, I've spent a lot of time thinking about the consequences of this decision ever since. Mick used to console me with, 'Time and fate. Fate and time. You just happened to be there.'

Placed in charge, Percy puts his face right into Mordant's. 'Now, I'm not asking you, I'm telling you, open that fucking vault, now!'

'I have told you, I cannot. I do not know the combination. If I knew it I would open it. You must believe me.'

'Give me your left hand,' Percy said to Mordant. Mordant was clearly terrified by these two but he shook his head resolutely in refusal.

Eddie moved behind Mordant who was now holding onto the chair with both of his hands as if his life depended on it. Eddie hit him at the back of the head with the butt of his heavy Webley revolver. 'Give him your fucking left hand!'

Mordant's head jolted forward and his face twisted with renewed pain. He reached his left hand out hesitantly to Percy, still clinging to the chair with his right. Percy grasped Mordant's outstretched hand across the palm so that Mordant's fingers were facing upwards and fully exposed. As he did so, Eddie locks his right arm around Mordant's neck and clamps his left hand over firmly over Mordant's mouth. Simultaneously, Percy clinically snaps Mordant's finger's downwards, breaking them noisily like dead twigs. Mordant squirmed in agony, the whites of his eyes pushing deep into his forehead as he struggled to scream through Eddie's coarse fingers clamped solidly over his mouth. Eddie tightened his hold on Mordant and Percy kept his grip on his hand. Mick and I stood motionless as Percy continued the interrogation.

'Now, open the fucking vault,' he shouted. Mordant shook his head, tensing his body and tightening his one handed grip on the chair. Unsure of the terror I had unleashed, I shouted at Percy.

'Come on, Percy, for fuck's sake leave it, perhaps he is telling the truth, and besides, we've got the main vault open.'

'Fuck it,' Percy screams back at me. 'He's fucking lying! I know his sort, there's something in there that he's fucking desperate to hang on to!'

With that he pulls out his razor and flashes the blade in front of Mordant's eyes, ' I'm telling you to open that fucking door.'

Mordant shook his head again and Eddie eased his grip to let him speak.

'I've told you, I cannot. I do not know the combination. If I did I would open it. Believe me, please believe me. If I knew, I would tell you. I would open it.'

Percy glanced at Eddie who repositioned himself to strengthen his hold on Mordant. Before we had time to blink Percy's razor was flashing around Mordant's hand catching the light like a Catherine wheel. Blood starts gushing everywhere. Eddie was having a job to hold Mordant who was going berserk in the chair. Percy stepped back triumphantly holding a severed finger while a second fell to the floor where it slowly and silently began clenching itself as if it were experiencing some ultimate agony. Eddie released his grip over Mordant's mouth. Mordant was screaming and writhing as Percy tried to force the severed finger he held into Mordant's mouth.

'Open the fucking vault.' Percy shouted at him, 'Or I'll shove everyone of your fucking fingers down your fucking throat until they come out of your fucking arse!'

Mick and me had seen a lot of people who had been physically tortured in the war but, even so, the sudden barbaric nature of this mutilation stunned even us. Before we had chance to react or stop it, however, Mordant was screaming dementedly, 'Stop! Please stop! Please stop! I will open it, I will open it!'

Percy looked across at us very smugly and, sounding well pleased with himself, said, 'I told you he was lying.'

Grasping his mutilated left hand in a vain attempt to staunch the flowing blood, Mordant staggered to the unopened vault door. Pushing the hand deep into his stomach and doubling over bodily to lock in the spurting blood, and perhaps to find some respite from the agonising pain, Mordant fed in the lock's combination with his uninjured right hand. Once done, he scuttled like a crab back to his chair, his face contorted with pain and fear. We turned the lock wheel, swung the door open and went in.

The scene which greeted us knocked us speechless. The interior of this hidden vault was like a Nazi shrine. One wall was plastered with Nazi posters and paraphernalia. On another, above a small desk, there was a Nazi flag draped above a framed photograph around which hung a heavy gold chain necklace and Nazi medallion. Still speechless we tried to take in and make sense of what we saw.

It was Percy who broke the silence.

'Well, look at this lot here then, no fucking wonder he didn't want to open up!' Percy was pointing at the photograph. The picture showed a group of young SS officers clustered and smiling around Hitler, the bastard Fuhrer himself. One of the officers was shaking hands with Hitler and holding the same gold necklace and medallion which was hanging from the picture. Although this SS officer was younger, it was unmistakably Mordant. A little more hair on top and greased down flat, the facial features more angular and skeletal, but it was Mordant all right.

Mick reached out and lifted the gold necklace from the picture and turned the medallion over. On the back there was an inscription in German which he read aloud, 'SS Grupenfuhrer Adrian Mordaunt, Fur Dienste an den Fuhrer. Adrian Mordaunt, for service to the fucking Fuhrer!'

Answers to Gomerseal's questions began to fall into place. This was why Mordant, or Mordaunt as he was probably known in Germany, never spoke about what happened to him in the years after he left Guernsey. This is why he had got the banking job against the odds. It all fitted. It all made sense. Standing besides me, both Percy and Eddie visibly tightened up.

'The fucking bastard, it's him, it's that fucking bastard out there, he's nothing but a fucking SS bastard!' Eddie spat out the words with searing hatred.

The brothers swung around and burst out of the vault, moving in on Mordant like two predatory lions in a final death lunge for their prey. Mordant looked up, his face and body frozen with fear. He saw Percy's razor spiral downwards before it slashed deep into the left side of his neck, slicing through the main carotid artery. Blood sprayed out like water from a severed hose-pipe. Mordant clamped his right hand over the wound. As he did so, Percy's razor arced through the air again, this time slicing through his neck on its now exposed and raised right side, completely severing the brain's other main artery. In co-ordinated milliseconds, Eddie pulled Mordant's head upwards by the chin and dragged his razor savagely across his throat, the razor jolting inwards as it passed through the resistant gristle and the void of his windpipe. Mordant's head was now only attached to his body by a thin layer of flesh at the back of his neck and his spine which, for a split second, blinked a silvery white within the spraying crimson blood.

Mordant clamped his hands around his neck in a desperate but hopeless attempt to support his severed head and staunch the spurting blood. As Eddie released him, Mordant's mutilated body crumpled to the floor, his eyes bulging and rolling, his mouth biting at the air as his body writhed and slithered in his own warm blood on the polished linoleum. We looked on in silence, the only sounds being Mordant's hoarse hollow gasps for air which whispered around the room like the breath of phantoms seeking refuge from their inevitable destiny of eternal silence. It seemed like minutes before Mordant's convulsing body found its own eternal rest and peace.

At the time, the vicious behaviour of the brothers seemed both inexplicable and inexcusable. Some years later, however, I discovered that there had once been a third Hammond brother called Hank. This brother had been captured while on a special duties mission during the war and had died after weeks of interrogation and torture by the SS and Gestapo. To add to this, the brothers themselves had been with the twenty-first Army which liberated the Belsen concentration camp. On their arrival, and without any warning or preparation, they were ordered to bury the massive piles of maggot infested skeletal corpses with bulldozers. For days on end, they pushed and shovelled mountains of decomposing human bodies into cavernous lime-filled mass graves before neatly levelling the death sites so that the sensitivities of others could remain undisturbed by these inescapable reminders of the fragility of our so-called civilisation. Little wonder, then, that they had become dehumanised, stripped of emotion or empathy for the feelings and pain of others. Little wonder, too, that they killed Mordant, the former SS officer, so readily and so unmercifully. Denied, as they had been, of any chance of revenge or retribution for their own suffering and for the suffering they had witnessed, what they did is at least understandable and, for me, to some extent forgivable.

At the time, however, Mick and me were not best pleased with this Hammond's horror show.

'What the fuck do you think you two are fucking playing at? You fucking barmy pair of fucking bastards, haven't you fucking got us all into enough shit for one fucking night? Fucking hell, fucking hell, what a.....' It was Mick, he was mad and stamping about like a wild man. I'm sure that if he'd have had his Sten with him he would have mown the brothers down there and then without hesitation or regret.

'He was a fucking Nazi, he deserved to die.' Although Eddie spat the words out, he said them quietly and deliberately. 'The only pity is that he didn't die more slowly.' The quiet authoritative nature of Eddie's unapologetic response contrasted with Mick's rage and seemed to calm it.

'Anyway, what's done is done,' I intervened. 'We'd best get this lot tidied up before Tony or any of the others come in, if Tony sees this mess, it will blow his bleeding brain again.'

To my surprise the brothers nodded in agreement and dragged Mordant's blood-drained body away. They returned with some towels and began mopping the pools of blood up off the floor. These two uncompromisingly proud, vicious bastards were on their hands and knees, cleaning up like old Mother Riley or Mrs. Mopp, and they didn't seem to mind. I like to think that they too had been affected by what had just happened.

While the brothers cleaned up, Mick and me went back into the Nazi vault. Once we were able to ignore the Nazi crap, we could see that we had hit upon an unexpected jackpot. The place was stuffed with money, most of it in foreign currencies, tied up into neat bundles with thin pink cotton tape. The biggest stash was in Argentinean pesos, there were also Chilean and Portuguese escudos, Swiss francs, American and Canadian dollars, even Irish pounds. If we could launder Guernsey's own Mickey Mouse Money, we would certainly be able to launder this lot! And there was a lot!

In the corner, at the far side of the vault, alongside a small wooden desk, was a stack of wooden ammo boxes.

'What's that lot doing in here?' I asked looking at Mick.

'There's only one way to find out,' says Mick moving towards them, 'and that's to take a look.'

The lid of the top box was loose. Mick pushed it away and it clattered noisily to the floor.

'My giddy fucking aunt, what do we have here then?'

The question was entirely rhetorical. We both knew what it was the moment that unmistakable iridescent glow illuminated the vault. It was gold, pure fucking gold. For the first and only time in our lives, we had literally struck gold. We had reached the end of our personal rainbow; we had found the mythical pot of gold! Mick knocked the lid off another box using a gold ingot he took from the first as a hammer. That box too was packed with solid gold ingots. There were eleven boxes in all and they were ours for the taking!

Mick picked up a bar, lifted it up and down, pursed his lips and judged it to weigh in somewhere around four pounds. Legal gold was selling for around twelve pounds a troy ounce, so we reckoned that each bar was probably worth well over six hundred nicker, and a brand new Ford motor car was under four hundred! We estimated that there were eighty or so bars in each box. This made each box worth not far off thirty grand, and there were twenty-three boxes. Today that would probably be well over thirty million nicker or more! It was all too much and too sudden for me to take in. Nutter psychologists would probably say I was in denial, but whatever it was I couldn't stay focused. I began looking around for confirmation, for something, anything, that said this was real, that this was really happening, here, now, to me.

Mick meanwhile silently grinned as he stroked the gold bars in a state of mesmerised semi-shock while I, being a more inquisitive bastard, took to eyeballing what else was inside this vault. I turned to the small desk which was alongside the bullion boxes. It had a large ledger lying open on it. I sat down and ran my eyes over the open pages. I flicked through the rest of it, quickly scanning each diligently completed page. The ledger provided the confirmation I was unknowingly seeking. It showed monetary transactions in close detail, with money and gold coming in from all over Europe, particularly Switzerland, and then going out to countries all over the world, notably Argentina and Chile. The dates, the amounts of cash, the currencies used, where and how payments were to be made, and the names of the recipients were all meticulously recorded. Even I was able to recognise some of the bastards listed. There was Martin Borman, who had been Hitler's Deputy, Alois Brunner, Klaus Barbie, Anton Gecas, Konrads Kaljs, dozens more, all top-ranking Nazi war criminals still on the run. What this ledger showed was that we had stumbled across a Nazi money laundering set-up which was financing Nazi war criminals on the run right across the world. The brothers were ultimately right, Mordant, or Mordaunt, whatever his fucking name was, deserved to die.

There were more records and ledgers in the desk drawers. I pulled a few out at random and skimmed them quickly. In some ways I found some of these more shocking. They contained details of the Gerry occupation of Guernsey, spelling out the names of those few local big-Whigs who had collaborated with the Gerries. The daily records showed that these traitorous bastards had helped the Nazis identify and track down any Jews living on the island, condemning them to the horrors of the concentration camp. They had confiscated Jewish properties and land and legally sold it on to themselves for the price of a packet of fags. They had selected other islanders for deportation, had profited from the use of slave labour, and had aggressively enforced German laws to suppress any opposition to the occupation by islanders.

One bastard, who was the Island's bailiff, had even gone over to Germany to do propaganda broadcasts. There was nothing these traitors hadn't stooped to. Whilst, at dreadful personal risk, the rest of the islanders had done what they could to resist and hamper the Gerries, these bastards had been lining their pockets on the suffering and deaths of their friends and neighbours. The records also showed that enormous sums of money were being transferred to mainland England too, much of it to aristocratic bastards who were only one shag removed from the so-called Royal House of Windsor, formerly the German Houses of Saxe-Coburg-Gotha. If Mordant had deserved to die, so too did many of these bastards.

⌘　⌘　⌘　⌘　⌘　⌘　⌘

Percy and Eddie had done a first-rate job of clearing up by the time the others arrived. Bertie Bates was the first to breeze in. 'Bloody Nora,' he says, a meaningless but favourite expression of his. 'What have you lot been doing down here?'

Fortunately, we didn't have chance to answer before he carried on. 'You've been down here twenty minutes or more and you haven't even made a fucking start yet! We've all been working our bollocks off while you lazy bastards have been holding a mothers' meeting!'

Without replying I beckoned him to follow me into the second vault.

'Bloody Nora,' he says again, this time with real astonishment, as he encounters the Nazi paraphernalia. He then sees the money and then the gold.

'Bloody Noraaaaa.....' He pours over the gold bullion boxes for a second or two and then snaps out of his yellow-brick trance. 'We'd better get to it, it'll take some time to shift this lot.'

'Too bloody right,' I said to him. 'You and the others clean out the other vault while Mick, me and the brothers make a start on this one.'

At this, he dashes off calling to his side-kick as he goes, 'Stan, wait till you see this fucking lot in here.'

I turned to the others. 'Right, Percy, Eddie, you two get the gold boxes up into the Ducks. Even them out between the two. They're heavy bastards so tell the 'Js' to stow them as low as they can, and balance them out, so that we don't get stability problems out at sea.'

The brothers set to work without a word. They were both two big strong blokes but even working together they had difficulty in moving the boxes out one at a time, let alone pushing them up the slides into the Ducks. While they were moving the first of the gold boxes, Mick and me started ramming the foreign currency notes into the ammo boxes. When the brothers were out of the vault and out sight, I told Mick what I'd sussed in the ledgers and records.

'What do you reckon then?' he asked. 'Take them with us?'

'Take them if you're not sure. What they going to take up? Two boxes at most, if we decide they're no use, we can always dump them.'

'OK, we take them, but keep it to ourselves, the others might not be too pleased about us taking up time and space pratting about with they'll see as waste paper.'

So while the brothers were carting out the boxes and Mick was stashing away funny money, I filled a couple of boxes with any paperwork that looked interesting or possibly 'useful.' I scratched a cross on each side of the boxes and then just moved them out with the others. Nobody noticed. As soon as we'd done the rest of the cash, we joined the bros in moving the bullion. To this day I don't know why I thought those ledgers might be useful to us, it's more than likely that I really am just a nosy bastard and wanted time to have a better look.

10 The Getaway

In a severe bout of what's known as displacement activity, the physical work of clearing out the Nazi vault had temporarily absorbed my mind to blot out all thoughts of Mordant's gruesome and bloody death. But, with the clearance work done and with Percy standing before me at the entrance to the vault illuminated by the bitterly bright lights of the vestibule area, such thoughts irresistibly prised their way back into my consciousness. He stood before me like some sort of latter day Frankenstein monster. The police uniform he wore was so stiff and blackened with Mordant's dried blood that it creaked like starched canvas when he moved. On his face and hands small scabby crusts of yet more dried blood were flaking off him as if he were a maturing leper.

'Jesus Christ, Percy,' I said to him despairingly. 'What do you look like? Go and get yourself cleaned up and into a decent set of clobber before any of the others realise the state you are in. God in heaven!.. Jesus fucking wept!... Try to think what you're fucking doing to the rest of us.... What do you look like? At the rate you're going, you're not only putting the noose around our necks, you're pulling the fucking drop lever too! Shit a brick, Percy, just look at yourself man!'

I was beginning to rant. The strain had got to me too and I was beginning to lose it. Within seconds Eddie came in to see what I was shouting about and positioned himself protectively alongside Percy.

Mick, with his innate sixth sense for diffusing such situations, stepped in. 'Remember what I said about the dead copper, what's done, is done and can't be undone.' He spoke as if we were involved in a minor set to back at the Bartons. 'In for a penny, in for a pound, after the first one is dead, it don't really matter a lot, one, two or a dozen, they can only top you once, so the best thing we can do now is to make sure the bastards don't catch us, and the best way to do that,' he paused and looked at each of us in turn, 'is to keep our heads, keep calm, do what has to be done, make no more mistakes and let things drop when they need to be dropped.....' He paused and looked at us, head held slightly down at an angle, eyes looking upwards, eyebrows raised, top lip enveloping his bottom lip and with his chin thrust outwards so that his cheeks pouted.

'Agreed?' He says, his upraised eyes flitting between us. The brothers nodded in agreement while I, feeling chastised, mumbled almost inaudibly, 'Agreed.'

'Right,' says Mick. 'Percy, you go and get yourself cleaned up and sorted out at the station, and tell the others there that we'll be up in a minute to let them know what's going on.' Percy nods again and heads off without comment or further ado. Mick then turns to me.

'Ronnie,' he says, 'I want to have a bit of a confidential con-flab with Eddie here, it will only take a minute or two. Tell you what, while we're doing that, you get all the lads who are down here into the front reception, I think we ought to have a bit of a pow-wow to see where we go from here.'

I knew that whatever he had in mind, Mick would be backing me up rather than knifing me in the back and would be acting in the best interests of all of us; it's called 'faith in a mate' and there doesn't seem to be much of that about nowadays. Anyway, I made to leave without question or comment but, as I was leaving, I couldn't stop myself from looking back. Mick had his face thrust right into Eddie's, his finger prodding and poking Eddie's chest as he spoke fiercely but quietly.

I never really got to the bottom of what Mick actually said to him but I knew then and I still know now that for sure it was something along the lines of any more misbehaviour by the brothers, either of them, and they, both of them, would not have the chance to misbehave again. And I know this much too, the brothers knew Mick to be a man who wasn't profligate with his advice, so much so that when it was given, it was advisable to listen very carefully and take full heed of what he had said. I also know that very wisely the brothers did not put a step out of line from that moment on until we were back in Blighty. Thereafter, mind, it's true to say that they made up for lost time, and made up for it with aggravated interest!

While Mick was having his fatherly chat with Eddie, I got the others Villains into the reception area. Barry remained at the door to keep an eye on the road blocks and guard the Barclay's manager who was already down with us ready to open up. This poor sod was having to wait because we were running late now, due mainly to the time spent dealing with Mordant and getting the Nazi loot out.

No sooner were we assembled than Eddie came in from the back room to join us looking as though he's found a pound and lost a fiver. He was closely followed by Mick. Without any deference or reference to Tony, Mick took centre stage. He handrolled a ciggie and lit up while we all looked on. I noted to myself that he'd learnt a lot from Tony, but he needed to understand that a roll-up ciggie is no contest for a bloody great Winston.

'Right, we haven't got time to prat about, so I'll get straight to it. First the bad news. Most of you know by now that we've got at least one dead copper on our hands and that there's another who is still tossing up whether to live or die, so whichever way you look at it, we're in deep shit if we get nobbled.' As most of the lads were in blissful ignorance of Mordant's death, Mick choose neither to broadcast it nor hark on about it. He continued.

'Now the good news. You probably all also know by now that we really have struck fucking gold, eleven big boxes crammed with the stuff, and that's on top of the foreign cash and all the loot from the other Banks.' He drags hard and long on his roll-up while we remain silent. He looks quizzically at the roll up, and gradually begins to emit ripples of smoke from what seemed like numerous unknown orifices in his head until he is shrouded in an aura of swirling and drifting smoke. From within this haze of smoke, he eventually says, 'So what we have to decide now is, should we cut and run right away while the going's good?.... Just get out as fast as we can, which, given the delays we've had, is still cutting things a bit fine.... Or should we stick with it, empty the Barclay's, which is the last on our list, and then head for home?'

He returned his immediate attention to his roll-up, which fizzed like a fuse wire with each of his exaggerated inhalations, his cheeks drawn in until they appeared to touch. He held it before him, peering at it intensely as though it was some unknown curiosity rather than he concede to scrutinise our reactions.

We stood around him as a group, each waiting hopefully for someone else to speak up. I had sussed Mick wouldn't want it to be me, so I kept schtum. When he looked towards us again, perhaps not surprisingly, it was Bertie Bates who was first to speak.

'Well, the way I see it is, why don't we do both? While you and

Ronnie sort out the Lamp and get everybody from up there down here and ready to go, the rest of us will clear out as much as we can from Barclay's, and as soon as you're back down here and ready to go, we go.' He looked mightily chuffed with himself and grinned around at all of us. 'Might as well make a clean sweep of it while we're at it, and now that we're all out of bed anyway.'

Bertie's suggestion made eminent sense and was tacitly agreed by a nodding of heads and a ripple of mumbling with no further discussion.

'Everybody OK for that then?' asks Mick. When nobody says anything, Mick continued.

'Right, let's get to it then, but remember we can't hang about wiping down when we're done, so wipe as you go.' With that, he strides out of the bank at such a pace I had to break into a canter to keep up with him. As we pass Dave and the bewildered Barclay's manager standing by the main door, he shouts back, 'And don't forget to lock this daft bastard up somewhere safe when he's opened up!' The bank manager looked bemused at being referred to as a 'daft bastard' for no rhyme nor reason.

I thought the steep climb back up the hill to the station might slow Mick down a bit, but no way, he had the bit between his teeth and he just wanted to be away off this island fast. When we get to the station, I'm puffing and panting like a knackered greyhound but he bounds up the steps and through the doors like a Derby winner. Solid Dave is still stood behind the front counter.

'What's up then?' Dave asks, obviously deducing from Mick's sudden entrance that there's something going on.

'No problem!' Mick replies. 'It's Dunkirk time, we're getting out, we're ready to go. Where are the others?'

'Your two girls are down the back just keeping a general eye on things. Percy is having a shower upstairs and Thelma's taken some fresh gear up for him to change into. How the hell did he get in that state?'

'Have to fill you in on that little episode later, my son,' Mick answers somewhat condescendingly. 'It's nothing that can't wait. Ronnie, you get the girls and make sure that the place is left clean down here, Dave you give them a hand too, I'll get Percy and Thelma and we'll wipe down up there.' And with that, he makes off up the stairs two at a time.

I find the girls and tell them it's time to go. We all put on rubber gloves, get some damp cloths and start wiping anything that might have any of our finger-prints on, working our way systematically from the cells at the back to the front counter. When we meet up with Dave, who has been cleaning back from the front counter back, we know there's no prints in the bottom half of the station at least. Back in reception, we find Mick working his way down the stairs cleaning the handrails. A few seconds later Percy and Thelma, looking strangely sheepish, appeared on the landing at the top of the stairs.

'About bleeding time,' Mick snaps. 'Have you wiped everything you might have touched on the way out?'

'What do you think?' says Percy and they each hold out a towel as if in evidence.

'Well make sure that you don't touch anything else as you go.'   He turns to me.

'Is that it?' He sounded agitated.

'Reckon it is,' I answer.

'Come on then,' he says abruptly, 'let's get the fuck out of here!'

When we were all outside Mick locked the station doors and threw the keys into a cluster of dense bushes edging some gardens opposite. 'Might as well make everything as difficult as we can for the bastards,' he says and sets off at the double back down the hill to the High Street. We chase after him like a bunch of hungry reporters following some minor celebrity. I knew Mick was more than up tight over something, something that had happened after he'd gone looking for Percy and Thelma, just what I didn't know for sure although I did make a bloody good guess.

We were on the beaches at Cartaret when I finally got the full story out of Mick. When he'd gone upstairs looking for Percy and Thelma, he went straight along to the shower room and walked right in. What greeted him was the sight of Percy's white arse humping Thelma on a table. She'd got her legs wrapped up around his shoulders with her land army overalls hanging loose from one of her ankles and jerking about like an empty scarecrow in a gale. There was so much moaning and groaning going on they didn't hear Mick go in and, in their breathless state of ecstasy, carried on with the business in hand.

Mick remained by the open door patiently waiting and watching until their finish was heralded by a spasmodic collapse and much puffing and blowing. Mick sniffed loudly and disapprovingly to indicate his presence. As might be expected, the effect was dramatic. Percy jumps off backwards, slips on the wet tiled floor and falls over, goes completely arse over tip, bare skin and flesh flashing everywhere. He must have hurt himself bad but he's scrabbling about on all fours interested only in finding a towel to cover his nakedness. Thelma, red-faced, swings down off the table and tries frantically to pull the dangling overalls up to cover her nakedness but with little success. It was as if they thought that if they covered up quickly enough, Mick wouldn't notice what they had been up to! Mick told me that he had a job not to laugh.

'Turned out nice again,' Mick says. 'And now that you've got that lot out of your fucking system, perhaps you wouldn't mind getting yourselves dressed and help to get this top floor wiped down, we're out of here as soon as we're done.' With that, he picked up a wet towel and walked out closing the door behind him. He then turned to wiping anything that might have any of our prints on it with the towel. He was finishing off the staircase hand rails as we, having finished cleaning the main floor, returned to the lobby.

But that whole Thelma and Percy scene was not funny, it was bad news. In the Navy, it used to be considered as bad luck to have any woman on board a fighting ship. To most villains, the same rule applies to taking a woman on a job, and we'd got three of the jinxes riding along with us for good measure! Be that as it may, but something that serious going on between Thelma and Percy had got to end in big trouble. For some time Mick and me tried to reason that it might have been just a one-off horny session for Thelma, maybe brought on by excitement or fear, or perhaps seeing Percy naked in the shower, something like that, anything like that, mainly because we just couldn't imagine any woman in her right mind being attracted to that vicious bastard. It's strange what you can bring yourself to believe when you're in deep shit.

After leaving the station, still chasing on Mick's heels, we turned onto the High Street and saw that the lads were still busy loading stuff from

Barclay's into Gert. Daisy was parked outside the Old Bank, slightly up from the J&S Jewellers, and as we reached her, Mick barked out to me, 'Right, tell them to move their arses, and no arguing, I want to be out of here, now, no messing!' With that he climbed up into Daisy and started her engine.

I moved on quickly and, doing the best drill sergeant-major impression I could muster, I bellowed through the open doors to the Barclay's clearing team, 'come on now, my lucky lads, the demob train leaves in ten seconds, just leave everything and get out, the clock starts now, ten........ Nine......' I climbed up into Gert still shouting the count, 'five......four....' and started the engine on the count of three. The lads come out through the bank entrance like the front row punters in a new year sale, desperate to snatch the best bargains. With legs and arms flying, they scaled up best they could up into the ducks. 'Two ....one!'

As I called 'one', I released the clutch and Gert lurched forward. An instantaneous screech of rigid steel plate being dragged across the cobbled street together with the reflections of showering sparks in shop windows indicated that all was not well. In Mick's slightly unnecessarily frantic rush to get away, we had forgotten to unhitch the loading chutes. Working on auto pilot, I slammed the brakes on hard, which brought most of those still in the process of settling into the back crashing forwards into the front bulkhead. It was pure bloody luck that nobody got hurt badly.

'It's the chutes, you haven't unhitched the fucking chutes!' I called out in primitive frustration.

Bertie and Stan were the first on their feet. They levered the chute free of Gert's hull and let it drop to the ground where it decided, after some noisy gyrations, to come to rest in front of Gert's back wheels. I tried to drive over it, wrenching through forward and reverse gears, but no way was it going to happen. Bertie and Stan saw the problem and leapt over the side to drag the chute clear. Seeing that those in Daisy were having problems unhitching their chute, they ran back to lend a hand. Daisy's chute was eventually freed and they pulled it clear. I watched in the mirror waiting for Stan and Bertie to return. I can still see them now, two mischievous goblins spotlighted by the limelight spilling out from the unprotected jewellery-laden windows of J&S.

Two of life's great chancers with only a few panes of fragile glass keeping them from barrow loads of their wildest dreams. I remember instinctively thinking, 'Oh shit!'

Taking an end of the chute each, they swung it back and forth before tossing it lengthways in the general direction of the shop. It took out the three main windows fronting on to the High Street in one shattering blow. It was as if the place had exploded. Almost instantaneously Bertie and Stan were bodily inside the windows, laughing and tossing everything they could get their hands on, trays of rings, necklaces, watches, you name it, up and over into Daisy's hold. With trays of jewellery flying and falling around them, it was mentally impossible for Ikey and Barney to restrain themselves from joining in the 'fun'. Taking two Enfields with them, they jumped over the side and used them to do all the windows that run along the side of J&S into what's known on the island as the Commercial Arcade. This is Guernsey's own jewellery quarter and there must be a dozen or more high-class jewellers' shops within fifty yards or less. Like the Banks, they're one after the other.

In the rear view mirror, I can see that our four stooges are having themselves a party, and are now having to run backwards and forwards to the Ducks to toss in the plundered gear. This means they are moving up into the Arcade proper and I know that once they do that, there will be no stopping them. Someone had got to put an end to their party! Shoving Gert into gear, I wound up the throttle and began to move off towards the harbour, albeit somewhat slowly. Seeing me do this, Mick did the same. Seeing their only means of escape from the island trundling away from them produced the desired response. All four came charging after us as if chasing to catch the last bus home, which for them it was. They just about managed to clamber back on board but not without some considerable difficulty, due mainly to some judicious work with the brake and throttle by Mick and myself, and much, much, cursing from the four lads.

We drove the two Ducks down the remaining few yards of the High Street and turned left onto the Quay. As we passed the squat granite town church, which was off to our right, its clock chimed three. Despite everything, we were only half an hour behind schedule. The chiming of the clock started Bertie and Stan singing again, 'One, two, three o'clock, four o'clock rock.' Spider starts cursing them again as 'barmy bastards' while I concentrated on driving. I steered Gert under the imperious glare of Guernsey's statue of Prince Albert, who was clearly not amused by this nocturnal intrusion of his domain. His statue stands on a small traffic island at the entrance to a pier which is named after him. The pier has a slipway almost immediately at its head which slopes gently down to the water, ending with a level stretch about twelve feet long. It's ideal for launching small boats, but is barely wide enough for a normal motor car to go down, let alone a wide-arsed Duck.

When we turned on to it, the top of the slip was ten foot or more above the water in the harbour. We had calculated, quite wrongly as it turned out, that the tide would have been much higher at the time of our departure. This was a real cock-up in our planning. Anyway, now, with the water so far below us, to have dropped a wheel over the edge could have spelt disaster with a capital D, so I edged Gert down the slip with her steel hull scraping along the side of granite pier. I've been told that the gouges and scrapes we made into the blocks that night can still be seen to this day. In the silence of the early morning, the sound of the engines and the screech of steel dragged brutally along hard rock must have been loud enough to waken the dead, let alone those asleep nearby in the town.

But I had other worries on my mind. Quite illogically, the Albert Pier slipway does not slope away gently into open water. It dead-ends very abruptly at the face of a massive abutment to the pier which spans its entire width. We had known this all along, of course, but as I have already said, we had calculated that the tide would be far enough up the slip for us to be afloat with plenty of room to make the necessary turn before we ploughed into this solid wall of granite. With all the weight we had on board now, there was no way we would be afloat before hitting the wall, the tide was barely two feet above the bottom flat section of the slip. There simply wasn't a sufficient depth of water for us to float off. Furthermore, as usual, Daisy had got her nose right up Gert's back-side, there was no hope of backing up. I immediately sussed that we were in deep shit when we should be in deep water!

One of the few beauties of being in a situation where there is only one way out is that you don't have to prat about deciding which way to turn or go, it's simply a case of eyes closed, fingers crossed, buttocks clenched and go for it. Slamming the throttle to the floor, my cautious descent of the slipway became a headlong charge towards the very solid dead end wall which remained firmly and unflinching before us.

We ploughed into what little depth of water was there, the flat face of Gert's bow throwing up a huge bow wave in front of us. I pulled hard on the wheel to turn out into the harbour, hoping that our speed and weight would carry us off the slipway. As I've said before, I'm no religious freak, but there are times when I think I could have become a believer, and this was one of them. As we hit the water the huge bow wave that we had created smashed against the flat face of the wall at the end of the slip. Almost instantaneously it came crashing back towards us with the lifting force of a tidal wave. The wave went under Gert's sloping bow as I was making the turn and, amidst much crashing and splashing, we were lifted upwards and off the slip to plunge into the reassuring deep water of the harbour!

Mick, in Daisy, however was not so fortunate. Following so close behind us, Mick was largely unaware that there was a major problem until he saw Gert suddenly charge off down the slip in front of him. By the time he had assessed the situation, there was no time to build up the sort of speed we had achieved. Moreover, when Daisy finally hit the water, our displacement and departure had drawn most of the water on the slip away with us. The net result was that when he turned to crash Daisy off the slip, her front wheels just dropped over the edge and she belly flopped, grounding like a beached whale across the bottom of the slip, bow down in the water and rear end still hanging up on the slip. Mick thrashed through the gears repeatedly, forward, reverse, forward, reverse. The wheels turned, the fronts flailing uselessly in deep water, the rears sending up clouds of smoke and steam from the slip, but there was no discernible movement. He was well and truly grounded!

The tide was on the rise and so we could just have sat there until the tide came in enough to float Daisy off, but this really wasn't an option. Running late, as we were, any more delay would kill off any chance we had of making the Cherbourg ferry on time. There was also the outside chance that some 'sheriff's posse' was even now in hot pursuit.

Hardly likely as we had shut everything down but, nevertheless, in the circumstances prevailing at the time, a real worry. We either had to abandon Daisy or face capture and a life behind bars.

In desperation, I reversed Gert slowly and steadily until our stern was pressed against Daisy's bow. Using what ropes we had, we strapped the two ducks tightly together. With a thumbs up sign to Mick, I put Gert's prop on full drive and drove a flood of water under Daisy's hull. The effect was like a rising tide which lifted her momentarily from her grounded position on the slip. Mick gave Daisy's wheel and prop drives all she'd got and, riding on the backwash of our floodwater as it rebounded from the side of the pier, she waddled off the slip into deep water like a real live duck. Both Ducks were now fully afloat and the two crews cheered. The hitching ropes were untied and the Ducks separated. I swung Gert around and, with Mick following up with Daisy, we began our escape. It all took less than five minutes. It felt like hours.

Our exit from the harbour was signposted by the dark silhouettes of the massive pier and walls of Castle Cornet, a thirteenth century job, which towered menacingly above us on our starboard side, its gun batteries, placed to deny invaders from the sea entrance to the town, thankfully now no more than historical curiosities. The castle's pier extends beyond the castle itself and ends with a lighthouse more-or-less directly opposite the one adjacent to the harbour master's office Bertie and Stan had rubbished earlier. The two lighthouses mark the frontier between the enclosed safe waters of the harbour and the inherent dangers of the open sea. They came into view as the Albert Pier slipped past on our port side and we were now heading for the open sea at full throttle!

Although there was still a long way to go to get home and to get away with the job, a tangible feeling of jubilation swept through all those of us sailing in Gert, with perhaps the exception of Tony and Spider. Stan and Bertie were noticeably ecstatic and had switched from belting out 'Rock Around the Clock' to Big Joe Turner's original and ruder version of 'Shake, Rattle and Roll', with Marg and Mavis enthusiastically da-da-da-ing the accompaniments.

At the appropriate verse, they sang directly to Thelma.

'Well I believe to my soul you're a devil in nylon hose. Da de da da.

Da de da da. The harder I work the faster my money goes.'

Thelma loved it. Failing to appreciate the irony of their words, she joined in with the singing and dancing! I watched Stan and Bertie's impromptu performance in Gert's rear view mirror. It exemplified and symbolised their sheer love of life and excitement. They optimistically believed that this life is the best that's on offer, so enjoy it how and when you can. Neither the past nor the future held any fears for these two sons of adversity. For them life was here and now, each moment to be enjoyed and savoured before it speeds irretrievably into the past to be lost for ever. Not for them my memory's cinematic repeats of two coppers being unnecessarily gunned down, or the hoarse whispers of Mordant's dying convulsions. They had witnessed none of these things. For them, their memories of the night were only of daring do-or-die from which they had emerged triumphant. As if to confirm these silent thoughts of mine, still singing, they each picked up an Enfield rifle and aimed at the lighthouses standing at the harbour entrance.

'Shake, rattle and roll,.... I'll take the right,.... and you can take the left,' sang Bertie. 'Da, da, da da,' sang the girls. Stan joins in with singing and two shots rang out in synchronisation with the final 'shake, rattle and roll.' The lights on the two harbour entrance lighthouses went out. With a triumphant yell, they threw the Enfields over board and jived with each as best they could in Gert's now very limited available space for dancing.

'Youse barmy pair of bastards!' Spider shouted at them in anger. 'What the hell did youse have to do that for?'

'Those two flashy bastards have irritated me on and off all night,' says Stan still jiving. Bertie laughed and began to dance a 'What the fuck's up with you?' dance right in Spider's face. Spider responded with a despairing look and sad shake of his head.

Leaving the imprisoning harbour walls and the towering darkness of Castle Cornet in our settling wake, we made the turn for the Carteret beaches. The sky was beginning to lighten on the distant horizon, as if signalling that the night was nearing its close, and only a bright future beckoned us from ahead. Carteret lay in an easterly direction, beyond the rock strewn passage between the small islands of Alderney and Sark. The St Martin's lighthouse soon faded away behind us and we headed towards the imminent sunrise which was filling the sky with ever brightening light. It was the start of another fine summer's day.

The early morning sea air was crisp and clean. The two Ducks fairly burbled along, leaving long lanes of quietly swirling white waters in their wake as we rode with a tide drawn southwards to refill the vast basin of Mont St-Michel's Bay which it had drained only hours before. An occasional gull circled and swooped above us, fleeting shadows against the growing red sky of morning. The beauty and agelessness of the dawn of a new day absorbed my senses and washed away any lingering fearful memories of the night. Marg moved up and sat beside me. She buried her head and arms into my chest for warmth and comfort and instantly fell asleep.

I looked back and saw that, of all of those on board, I was the only one not sleeping. Though tired too, I did not envy them in their sleep. For them, the Elysian peace and tranquillity of this ephemeral sea and sky was exchanged for uncertain dreams. I looked across to Daisy and raised an arm. Mick lifted an arm in reply. We were united. We were two Viking chiefs bringing our longboats and warriors home to safety, our sojourn and victories acknowledged and proclaimed by the gods in this celestial and earthly display of their majesty and power. Few men can have experienced such a consummate elation of the human spirit as I did that summer morn. The memory of its ecstasy haunts me still.

11 Getting Home

Three hours after leaving the harbour at St. Peter Port, the lighthouse at Cap de Carteret shone bright on the horizon, guiding us to our landing point on the French coast. The sun had risen higher and was now paused momentarily on the mountainous range of sand dunes that spring from the wide flat beaches which sweep down to Carteret from the north. The low sunlight cast long black shadows from the dunes across the wide deserted yellow beaches whilst bathing the crests of the dunes in burnished gold. As we neared land I whispered quietly to Marg. 'Come on love, it's time to get going again.'

She stirred and blinked around, trying to establish where she was. She didn't speak.

'Wake the others up, it'll be touch-down time any minute now.'

She lifted herself from my chest and climbed unsteadily back to the others, shaking and waking each one in turn as she went. As they woke, each one shook themselves like newly wet dogs and gazed silently at the lines of white breakers rolling across the vast approaching beach. Feeling the wheels touch the beach below, I engaged wheel drive again. The wheels grabbed at the firm land beneath and drove us steadily through the breakers up and out onto the beach. Marg pointed to where there was a small break in the dunes some two hundred yards to the north, and I drove towards it.

As we passed through this short sandy canyon we could see the two Bedfords parked where the girls had left them less than twenty fours hours before. Twenty four hours, a single day. It was only a little more since we had set out from the garden city of the midlands in the two Ducks for Weymouth. Tennyson once asked, 'a day less or more, at sea or ashore, we die, does it matter when?' If any life has the chance of even one such day, the answer is 'Yes indeed it does!'

With such thoughts I parked Daisy close alongside the first Bedford and Mick pulled Daisy up close alongside the other. The engines of the two Ducks growled to a relieved halt and we were surrounded by the silence and beauty of the morning. The calm seemed almost sacrosanct and everyone set to the task of transferring our night's earnings to the two trucks in almost total silence. The canvas side-sheets were raised and tied. The load of empty ammunition boxes the girls had collected to avoid problems with documentation on re-entry at Portsmouth were unloaded quickly. A small prefabricated cage of steel mesh, which had been stowed flat during the girls' journey over, was erected in the centre of each wagon directly behind the solid rear of the cab. These cages would be the hiding place for all but the girls during our journey back home.

The gold bullion boxes were the first to be loaded onto the wagons. They were stacked two-high inside the cages to act as seats for those of us who would be travelling home hidden inside them. Two small twelve volt battery bulbs were hooked to each roof grill to provide some light. Two one gallon water carriers, filled with drinking water, and a Jerry can, for toileting purposes, urine only, were placed inside.

Next, using the money filled ammo boxes as building blocks, walls were built around the cages leaving only a small doorway to each to enable the intended occupants to crawl through and into the cages. More boxes were laid on the top grills to make a roof and we now had two liveable priest holes hidden deep within a well ordered stash of ammo boxes. Once all the money filled boxes had been stacked all around the cages, the empty boxes were used to build protective outer layers until the trucks were heaving at the canvas straps. As the lads got on with this business, Mick and me turned to disposing of the Ducks.

We drove the two Ducks back onto the beach, stopping well above the incoming tide, and set about our business. All DUKWs have six large brass drain plugs, three on each side on the bottom of the hull, to enable the water, inevitably shipped during any amphibious action, to be drained away once back on dry land. To avoid the inevitable disastrous consequences of going to sea with any one of these plugs not screwed tightly in place, a rigid routine is drilled into all DUKW commanders. Firstly, whenever a plug is removed it is immediately stowed in its own specially designated place in one of two racks either side of the driver's seat. Secondly, before launching into water, the commander must ensure that all six plugs are correctly fitted and the hull fully watertight.

During our training these two aspects had been drummed into us until they became second nature. Now, here we were doing the exact opposite, and it didn't feel right. The Ducks were going to sea and we had both removed a plug from each side of the two hulls.

Once we had climbed back on board, we gave an OK thumbs up to each other, engaged wheel and prop drives and set the two Ducks moving alongside each other towards the sea. Ten yards or so before hitting the water, we both jumped down to the beach, leaving the two Ducks to trundle on without us towards to their fate. We watched and waited for a short while to check that Gert and Daisy, these two faithful brothers-in-arms who had carried us through all of this and had never let us down, were indeed heading out for the open sea on this, their final mission. When all seemed well, we made our way slowly back up the beach to the trucks. On reaching the breach in the dunes we turned and stood together to watch them again.

They were now well out to sea and settling deeper into the water. They had moved together and were travelling and sinking in close unison. Quite suddenly, Gert's bow rose briefly above the water line, as if giving us a final salute before she disappeared beneath the waves, leaving only a short-lived whirlpool to mark her passing. Daisy did likewise seconds later. Stupid as it sounds, for me it was like witnessing the death of two close friends.

'I knew that we shouldn't have named them,' I said.

'Come on, you sloppy bugger, don't go all maudlin on me now,' Mick replied, as if mocking me. I looked across at him. He held up one of the drain plugs he had removed from Daisy and slipped it into his pocket with a smile. In reply, I held up one I had removed from Gert and we both laughed. He was strange bastard, Mick, hard as nails ninety-nine per cent of the time, and yet he could be as sentimental as me over things which others would find of little consequence or meaning.

When we got back to the trucks, one was ready to go. The cage was completely hidden with its payload of blokes inside, sheets tied down, all ship-shape and engine running. After giving our girls a quick peck and grope, we crawled through the small tunnel through the boxes into our cage, where Tony, Percy, Eddie, JC and JD were already installed. Through necessity, the cages had to be small, no more than seven feet long, five wide and five high, so naturally, space was tight before Mick and me squeezed our way in. Once we were in, to use one of Mick's favourite expressions, we were 'crammed in tighter than a fat lady's G string.' It was not going to be a pleasant trip home.

The girls filled in the entrance tunnel with more empty boxes, dropped and tied down the back canvases, and set off for Cherbourg. It was just after seven in the morning. Despite all, we were in good time to catch the morning ferry bound for Portsmouth. Marg was driving our truck. As she pulled off the dunes onto firm tarmac, she gave three short and one long toot on the horn, the Morse code for V, V for victory. In our dimly lit steel walled cave, even those miserable bastards Mick and me had been lumbered with for the long journey home couldn't help shouting, 'Yes!'

We quickly agreed a programme of one-hour watches so that everyone could get some much needed sleep. Because Mick and me had had no sleep during the crossing from Guernsey, we were allocated the last two watches so that we could get some shut eye straightaway. It was essential that at least one of our group was awake at all times in case of an emergency and to silence any bastard with noisy sleeping habits which, with us all sleeping shoulder to shoulder in a tight upright position, was highly likely! Seconds later I fell asleep.

⌘　⌘　⌘　⌘　⌘　⌘　⌘

It was some hours later when I was drawn back to life again by the incessant drone of the ferry. I had obviously slept through our boarding and departure at Cherburg. My eyes painfully refocused. In the sparse light seeping from our makeshift electrics, I could see that four of the others were awake too, playing a silent game of three card brag, signalling bets and play to each other like trainee bookies. I peered at my watch. It was thirty-five minutes past mid-day. In just over an hour, we should be berthing in Portsmouth. JD signalled me into the game by handing me a fistful of fivers from an ammo box over-flowing with bank notes.

I soon realised that this game was simply to kill time, no more, no less. Nobody was counting or bothering about money, about winning or losing. As soon as anybody ran out of notes, they took another wedge from the box, JD even put a wad from his 'winnings' back into the box! The whole purpose of the game was destroyed. Brag is about betting, bluffing, bravado, winning, losing. Without the threat of loss or chance of triumph, it becomes meaningless. The only bonus was that this was one game of brag which shouldn't end up in a mean-minded fight or resentful argument. It also struck me, however, that if we got home safely with the takings, things would be very different than they had been before we set out. The fistful of fivers JD had given to me as if he was handing round a bag of broken crisps must have been a few ton in itself. None of us had ever seen that much in a pot, even for a game with a big betting school, let alone a single player holding it as a stake. So, no more games down the Bartons with ten bob as the maximum bid allowed open, five bob blind, and an end to the game if the pot gets to twenty nicker!

Tony was in the game and so was Eddie but brother Percy was still soundly asleep chasing fairies. The brothers were on Tony's pay-roll but now, with a million quid or so in their back pockets, I couldn't see them taking orders from him any more. In fact, if anyone was going to lose out in the prestige and power stakes, it was going to be Tony. Sure enough it had been agreed, because it had been his show and his investment, that his cut would be twenty per cent of the total haul, but who the hell was going to kow-tow to Tony now with the size of cut due to each of us? His performance during the raid had hardly been up to Victoria Cross standards, and so the poor bastard had even lost what tiny shred of credibility he might have had in that department too. And on top of all that, Percy was shagging his missus; and how the hell was that lot going to end up?

And what about the rest of us? Ernie would certainly be losing Ikey and Barney as his two foot soldiers, but would he need them now? Even Stan and Bertie were going to have their work cut out spending their share. And there was another problem. With this sort of loot in our pockets, how were we going to be able to spend even a small part of it without arousing suspicion? OK, we might be able to bull shit our way out of a sudden unexplained windfall of a few thousand nicker, but not out of this lot. Why the fuck had none of us thought of this before we kicked off?

I threw my hand in and tossed what was left of my stake of fivers back into the ammo box. I needed to do some thinking away from the game. I leaned back and closed my eyes to give the impression that I was getting some more shut eye, but my thoughts were in turmoil, circling round and round the question of what the fuck do we do with this lot, if and when we got it back? With so much money swilling about, it was going to be hard to get any of the lads to hold back on spending. Siphoning a ton off at a time from, let's say, the occasional two grand job was par for the course, quite acceptable, no problem, all gone in a few months, but a million was a totally different situation. A quick calculation told me that it would take two hundred years to see off a million if we spent a ton a week! And remember, twenty quid a week was a bloody good wage for anybody in those days. Buying a Tony style mansion, complete with swimming pool and a brand new Roller to park out front would give have probably given plenty of change out of fifty grand, leaving each of us with only another nine hundred and seventy-five grand to spend. Then there was the problem of turning the gold into readies. Ernie had good contacts right enough to off-load perhaps a few pounds every so often, but in our truck alone we'd probably got half a ton in weight of the stuff literally sitting right under our arses at that moment. Then there was all that foreign cash! Again there was just too much of it to handle. Basically we were in the farcical situation of having nicked too much of everything and in the back of my mind I could hear old blue eyes singing, 'There may be trouble ahead!.......Let's face the music and dance!'

⌘　　⌘　　⌘　　⌘　　⌘　　⌘　　⌘

The thunderous rumbling of giant propellers straining to bring ten thousand tons of floating steel to a halt, and the deafening sounds of crashing water and clanging steel announced our arrival in Portsmouth. JD turned the cage lights off and we heard Marg and Thelma get back into the cab. The truck rocked slightly as they climbed aboard.

'Fat pair of bastards,' Mick whispered in the darkness and we all laughed quietly.

The engine started and we bounced our way out of the boat and on to the dock. Next stop customs, our final hurdle. The truck came to a stop and we heard the girls get out.

'Hello Boys, how are you two cheeky monkeys today then?' It was Marg.

'I hope you haven't been up to anything we wouldn't do while we've been away.' That was Thelma.

'That gives us a lot of scope,' says a bloke, and we heard him, another bloke and our girls laugh. These must have been the same Customs blokes Marg had told me they had chatted up and flirted with when they came through Portsmouth on the way over.

'Well, you got what you went for then,' says the first banging on the empty ammo boxes lining the sides of the truck with a stick or something.

'Yeah, we got what we went for but not what we might have come for, if you know what I mean,' says Thelma, her voice oozing sexual innuendo. I could hear Marg giving an approving and knowing giggle. The second bloke picks it up and replies, just as knowingly.

'Well, you'll just have to come again, so that we can arrange to make sure that you come when you get it next time. Is this going to be a regular run for you girls?'

'We've got a few more runs to do, but it seems a shame you know for us to go all the way over there, on our own, with nothing to do at night except twiddle our thumbs and look at knitting patterns. Now if we had some company, some one to treat us nice and look after us properly, to meet our every need, if you know what I mean, I'm sure that we'd manage to come,' says Thelma oozing again.

'I think we know just the right couple of handsome blokes that could manage that for you, isn't that right Jonah?'

'I reckon we do, Frank,' says Jonah, 'if we puts our minds to it, and you can give us a bit of notice to fix things up at this end.'

'Well let's go and put your mind to it, Frank,' coos Thelma, 'I may need to take down some of your particulars, if we are going to fix things up.' They all laugh and we hear Frank and Thelma come around to the other side of the truck. There's a sound of scuffling, pushing and panting from the pair of them as they pressed up against the sides of the ammo boxes which acted like amplifiers.

'Steady on, Frank, no, not here, someone will see...no don't undo them, ooh no Frank, no, not here, it's broad daylight, wait till we're down next time and come over with us for the night.'

'I'll come over you all right,' he replied, 'repeatedly, all night,' and there's more scuffling.

120

'No, no, stop, you'll ladder me nylons or something, now pack it in, just look at the state you've got me in, now calm down, you'll just have to be patient. Look, write down how I can get in touch with you when we come down next. I expect we'll be down again next week, and if not then, the week after.'

'Here's the phone number for here,' he says. 'It's probably best if you ring me here. I'm usually off Tuesdays and Wednesdays but, apart from then, I'm usually here. Mind, I'll need at least two or three days' notice to sort things out.'

'I'll let you know as soon as we know,' says Thelma. 'Now we'd better get off, we've got to get back to Liverpool tonight.'

We heard her trot along the side of the truck and climb back into the cab.

'Liverpool!' says Frank, sounding totally mystified, 'but I thought you were from....'

'Oh, and you'll have to get someone for Shirley back there in the other truck too.'

'Just leave it to me,' the prat drools as Thelma calls out to Marg.

'Come on Sylvi, we'd better get going, you can have more of him next time.'

God knows what Marg had been up to with Jonah, I try not to think about it, but she was soon back in the cab. She starts the motor and pulls away with both her and Thelma blowing mating calls to the two Customs prats. We could hear Mavis keeping right behind us in the other truck. A swift lurch to the left and a change to top gear told us that we were out on the open road. We were out of the port, through customs, home and dry, safe and sound, back in Blighty and heading for Brum!

JD turned the lights back on and we started shouting jubilantly at each other, shaking hands, patting each other on the back as best we could in cramped space, all that is except Percy who is now wide awake and wide eyed.

'How can you put up with her behaving like that?' he growled at Tony.

'What the fuck are you on about now?' Tony snaps back, more in surprise than anger.

'The way she was carrying on with that Customs bloke, fucking slut.'

121

'You mean Thelma?' Tony looks bewildered. 'I don't believe you, you must be going soft in the head. Anyway, it's fuck all to do with you, is it? What she does, or what she fucking don't do, has nothing to do with you, and don't call her a fucking slut, what she did was get us through customs with no hassles, and it's fuck all to do with you!'

'Well, I'd give her a fucking good slapping if she was mine, carrying on like that.'

'Well, she is not yours, is she? So fucking shut it.'

Before Percy had time to rise to this, I poked in. 'Will you both fucking shut it, you're like a couple of fucking school kids, the girls got us through without any bother, that's all that matters, now for Christ's sake just forget it, let it drop.'

'Well, your fucking Marg.....' A prod from Eddie prompts Percy to reluctantly let it drop.

A sullen silence descended, when we should have been popping champagne. Considering what was going on between him and Thelma, this outburst of Percy's worried me a lot. If Thelma was playing games with him, she should know that Percy was well beyond the 'let's play games stage,' and worse still, whatever game he's in, Percy is a very bad loser.

Pretty soon we were hearing Marg pedalling the revs up and down as she does a brilliant job double de-clutching through the gears on the Bedford's heavy crash gear box to coax our over-loaded truck up the steep road that snakes out of Portsmouth on the way to Winchester. When the sound of the engine and gears settled into an easy whine, we knew we had topped the hill. It felt as though it was downhill all the way now and JC uncharacteristically cottons on to our revived jubilant mood.

'Yahoooo, let's hear it for Marg!' he shouted and the rest of us joined in, shouting and cheering in a mixture of relief and release from tension and hours of silent confinement.

A few minutes later, the truck slowed down, made a turn, bumped down an uneven track and came to stop. The cab doors opened and slammed and the girls were shouting to us.

'Out you come then boys, time to stretch your legs.'

We heard empty ammo boxes clanging away as they were thrown off the truck. And soon we were staring at Marg's smiling deuce and ace through the cage door way. We were out of that cage like a load of rabbits with a ferret down the hole. Out into the day-light, blinking, gulping at fresh cool air, stretching arms and legs, and laughing uncontrollably. We had done it! Or so we thought.

⌘

Lloyd's Bank, The High Street St Peter Port

12 Home to Roost

We were parked up in the middle a cluster of trees which hid us from the main road on the way to Winchester. Mavis had pulled the other truck up behind ours and the lads were piling out of that one too. You would have thought that we hadn't seen each other for years, it was like a bloody regimental reunion! Slapping each other on the back, handing fags round. Then the girls start handing round bottles of champagne! As a surprise for us, the beautiful darlings had bought half a dozen bottles when they were over in France for us to open just at this moment.

'You know you could have got the lot of us arrested for smuggling that lot in!' It was Barney, smiling his head off while posing to be serious.

'You barmy bastard!' says Spider and we all cheered and began opening the bottles.

As each cork flew skywards we cheered. All our problems and fears for the future were for the moment forgotten. It was VE day over-again!

Percy, however, was standing to one side and still brooding about Thelma's performance with the customs men. Thelma, seeing that he was standing apart, took an opened bottle over to him.

'C'mon Percy, cheer up, have a drink, c'mon join the party, we've done it, we're home and dry, we're safe.'

Percy glowered at her.

'Fucking slut.'

'You what?'

'You heard.'

'Yes, I bloody well did hear. What the hell are you on about? What the bleeding hell has got into you now?

Thelma's raised voice silenced the party-making.

'Carrying on with that Customs bloke.'

'You what?'

'Carrying on with that Customs bloke. We all heard you, you fucking slut.'

Tony went over to Thelma before she had chance to react to this verbal onslaught.

'I thought I told you in the truck to drop it. Its got fuck all to do with you what she does and what she don't. So just drop it you stupid prat.' If Tony had hoped to calm Percy down, his intervention had just the opposite effect. If anything, it pulled the pin from the grenade.

'Prat? Who are you calling a prat? I've just about had you up to here. We'll see who's the prat,' and with that Percy flips out his razor. Tony starts to back up and Percy starts to circle him. 'Who's the prat now then? Eh, Who's the stupid prat now? When I've finished with you, you'll see who the prat is every time you look in a mirror.' There was no doubt that Percy had every intention of opening up new dimensions on Tony's face.

Mick nodded across to me and we made to move.

'Keep out of it, this is between Percy and Tony, nobody else.' It was Eddie. He was standing right next us and he had a Sten. And it was primed and it was aimed directly at us. And Mick and me knew he would use it if we made a bad move. These barmy pair of bastards were right on track to cock up everything we had achieved. Nevertheless we sussed it was politic to hold back. It was then we saw Dave and Barry move.

They were standing slightly behind Eddie so they weren't in his sights. Dave, still wearing heavy standard issue army boots, kicked Eddie viciously behind the knees. Eddie's legs collapsed. As he went down, Dave gave him a boot to the arm holding the sten and simply took it off him as if it was a baby's dummy. When Eddie hit the ground Dave finally kicked him in the head, hard, very hard. Percy turned just in time to see Barry's perfectly targeted head butt as it smashed into his face, his nose and cheek bones exploding with blood. As Percy staggered back, Barry kicked him hard in the groin and, as Percy doubled up, put a boot right into his face. Percy went down. The two assaults were clinical and unhurried, displaying the skills and poise of two ex-Military Police, practised and perfected in breaking up countless squaddie brawls in barrack rooms and bars all over war-time Europe.

The brothers were lying on the ground helpless and groaning. Each time they went to move, Dave or Barry kicked them in the body or to the head, whichever was most convenient as they slowly circled the defenceless duo. Each kick jolted the brothers' bodies as if they had been jabbed by a thousand volts. Move, kick, jolt, groan. Move, kick, jolt, groan. On it went but the barmy bastards kept insisting on moving, so another kick, jolt, groan. It was fascinating to watch, particularly how Barry and Dave were operating. They were doing a job and the job was to teach the brothers a lesson they would not forget in a hurry. And they were doing it without any sign of rage or passion. This was probably what they had done to the poor nark who had had a go at Tony's old uncle in Winson Green, and they'd disabled him for life.

Now they were doing the same job for Tony. He'd not forgotten what they'd done for his uncle, and now they were showing that they had not forgotten what he'd done for them. They were a funny pair of bleeders. It was as if the army had got right into their system, all the loyalty bit, sticking to together; sticking to orders even when the officers are a load of dickheads; standing by your mates in times of trouble and knocking the nasty bastards on the head. They were probably the only people who had never let Tony down, who never despised him in some way or other, and who, at the end of the day, regarded him as an OK bloke.

But they had to be stopped, otherwise there would have been two more destined for the undertaker's slab, and more tightening of the hangman's noose for the rest of us. So despite our tacit approval of their devotion to their task, Mick and me called them off.

'Leave it off lads, you've made your point. We don't want any more dead meat on our hands, they've had enough.'

'If you say so, Mick, but these two bastards have been asking for it. They don't know when to let go, always pushing for trouble. We should have thrown them over board when we were at sea.'

'Too late for that now,' Mick replied. 'You should have thought of that when we had the chance.'

Too bloody right, I thought to myself. How bloody stupid can you get? If we had tossed the brothers overboard in the middle of the channel we'd have saved ourselves a lot of bother. Not only that, there would have been more than a chance that the bodies would have been washed up on some beach somewhere or other. Assuming that the law would have had a modicum of sense, they would have linked the bodies to the raid, some of the witnesses would have identified them, and the chances are that the law would have concluded that the DUKWs had gone down at sea taking the loot and the rest of any gang with them; case closed; everybody happy ever after. At the time, my mind worked through this detailed fantasy in a matter of seconds but I have replayed it nearly every day since and cursed myself for not coming up with it 'when we had the chance.' One thing for sure, however, was that the celebration party had been killed stone dead!

Barry and Dave moved back and Mick, me and some of the others dragged the brothers to an upright position. They were unable to stand let alone walk and so we shouldered them over to one of the wagons. Some of the lads jumped aboard and chucked out some ammo boxes to make space for them to lie flat out. Once they were bedded in, the rest of us had a get together to sort out our next move.

It was decided that Mick and me would drive the truck with the brothers in the back and that our two girls, backed up by JC and JD, would travel with them to soothe their wounds, nurse their pride and generally keep them in order. Barry and Dave would drive the other truck and Tony, Thelma and the remaining lads would travel in the back. By the time we had downed what was left of the Champagne, our spirits were revived, led by Barney and Ikey enthusiastically re-enacting Barry and Dave's doing over of the brothers.

'And did you see the look on Percy's face when Dave nutted him?'

They both laugh.

'Splatt. And when he got the boot in his bollocks? Ooogh.' Ikey mimics extreme genital pain and there's more laughing.

'And Eddie, the way he fell over when Dave kicks his legs in.' Even more laughing as Barney imitates Eddie's fall from grace. They slap each other on the back. They find it impossible to complete a sentence without laughing, continually resorting to exaggerated re-enactments of the beatings. Their antics and laughing, as always, infected us all and before long we were all laughing as if we had just witnessed a Tom and Gerry cartoon, where extreme violence never results in anyone being hurt badly, rather than the real thing. I've really missed those two daft buggers over the years and, whenever I think about them, I can't help smiling. Not quite true, because at the same time, knowing why and how they were eventually killed, fuelled a passionate hatred in me for those responsible for their deaths, and a suppressed life-long yearning for revenge.

Soon after we were back on the road heading for Winchester, then on to Newbury, Oxford and finally up towards Brum through Chipping Norton and Stratford. A left turn at Hockley Heath and we were trundling down the leafy lanes to Tony's place at Earlswood. Tony had left the high doors to the barn open when we left on Friday and so we were able to drive the trucks straight in. As we pulled up, two of the lads jumped off the rear truck and closed the doors. We turned off the truck engines and they clattered to a halt almost simultaneously.

The barn was silent and the smoke from the truck engines swirled across the streams of sunlight spraying through the weathered planking and lightening the gloom of the barn. The lads and girls emerged painfully from the trucks, stretching and bending like newly woken dogs to relieve cramped joints and release the pent-up tensions built up over the course of the raid. You get a strange feeling when you've pulled off a successful job. There are always feelings of relief mixed with exhilaration but these are overlain with a feeling of uncertainty, of 'so what do we do now?' and a gnawing at the back of the brain which tells you that you can never, never, be quite sure that you've actually got away with it. That's what keeps the real villains of this world going, this bitter-sweet cocktail of incredibly strong and competing emotions; few things in life can compete with it, it's like a drug, it's addictive.

We sort of stood around at first, not knowing quite what to say or do. The best thing to do, once all the stretching and bending was over and done with, was to have a smoke. Rolling and smoking a cigarette means that you are doing something, and if you're doing something, you can't legitimately be expected to have to say anything. We all knew this and accepted it, all, that is, except Tony. After rummaging about in a bench drawer, Tony pulls out a pack of his giant Winstons. He offers them round but most stick with their roll ups or cheap Woodbines. Tony lights one up for himself and, after a couple of puffs, he's himself again and ready to spiel.

'Well, I told you we could do it, was I right or was I wrong? It's got to be the biggest job in history, and we pulled it off, us load of bastards and we pulled it off!'

He was jubilant, but the ever-dour Mick (he should have been a Scot) puts a damper on it. 'Up to now, but we are far from in the clear yet.'

'Bloody Captain Cheerful, we're here aren't we, we've got the loot, the law's got nothing to go on, we're in the clear.'

'Yeh, I suppose so, nothing but our Brummie accents, a couple of names, multiple descriptions, eye witnesses and those two bastards in the back of the truck guaranteed to do something daft as soon as they're fit enough again.' Like me, Mick had obviously been mulling things over and coming up with the same not too-welcome conclusions.

'Mick is fucking right,' Ernie says gloomily, 'We might as well have left our names and addresses.'

'Fuck this,' Barney bawls out. 'Let me have my share and I'm off!'

'Don't be a prat,' says Ikey. 'Where the fuck are you going to go to?'

Mick realises he's stirred something that could go arse upwards.

'Hold on, hold on, I'm not saying they will get on to us, there's a lot of other Brummie bastards out there besides us lot, I'm just pointing out that we're not in the clear yet. We've got to be on our guard for at least another couple of months, watch what we do and say, keep everything as normal as we can. If we all do a runner like Barney says, they'll be on to us in no time. We've got to stay put and carry on as normal, no big spending, no nothing and then, slowly but surely, we can all piss off when we want to one by one. But if the law do come nosing around, we've got to be ready for them. We've gotta say nowt, no matter what they tell us. One wrong word could finish us all off. There's a copper and that Mordant bloke both dead, so we are all in deep shit if we get done. If the law does come nosing around, you've gotta forget what the rest of us might be doing or saying,' he points around for emphasis.

'It's what you're doing and saying that counts, nothing else, and that means keeping schtum, don't say fuck-all. Don't believe anything, anything, the coppers tell you. Keep your gobs shut and we'll be all right. We've got water-tight alibis. Stick to the story. We were in the Bartons Friday night, in the back room of the Castaway's last night, and will be up at the club again tonight. Get your missus to confirm that you came home late last night, pissed as usual, and you stayed in bed till mid-day today. Say nowt else to your missus. When the raid makes the news, she'll never think that you could have been involved. When you tell it like this, there's no-way any of us could have been doing a job over in Guernsey last night.'

Mick was right, I was finding it a bit hard to believe that we were in control of the whole island of Guernsey in the early hours of this same morning myself!

'Our stories have to match. So tell Friday night how it was until we left the Bartons and you went home. For last night you rerun what we did last Saturday, keep it to what went on in the club until we left.' He kills his roll up.

'When you get home, there'll be an envelope with betting slips in it. These are from the bets put on in your name yesterday. Tomorrow, pick up any winnings due to you, make sure the bookie remembers you when you pick up. Try to find out if anything unusual went on. There'll be a note in the envelope if anything was going on when your bets were laid. Talk about your bets, winners and losers, tonight at the club, so everybody knows what you won and lost on. Keep your slips, check the time the bets were put on, read the note and remember everything. If the law should check, you've got proof that you were in the bookies on Saturday.' He pauses and looks around.

'From now on we don't even talk about the job amongst ourselves if there's another bastard's earhole within a hundred yards of us. We never talk on the blower, no matter what.'

He points his finger at each of us in turn, including the girls.

'Schtum! Got it?'

'Schtum!'

'Schtum?'

'Schtum!' He went systematically around each of us demanding an acknowledgement.

Finally he smiles and says, 'We'll be all right, I can feel it in my water, now piss off home and get yourselves up the club, bring your missuses if you like, but don't make an issue of it, everything's got to be as normal.'

I could see that Tony was champing at the bit while Mick ran through the after raid plan as agreed before the job, a plan Tony had dreamed up. Tony was back home now safe and sound; it was his plan, so he felt he should be in charge again. 'Right, thanks Mick, as Mick says as long as we all stick to the plan as I set it out, we're covered. Remember on that first Sunday we got together, I said one of the main reasons I picked you lot to do this was because you can keep your traps shut when needed. We've just pulled off the biggest job in history, we've made fucking history, so we don't want to cock it up now by loose tongues or a bit of impatience. So, like Mick says, piss off home and get an hour's shut-eye and we'll see you all up at the club later. We might just break open a bottle or two of champers to celebrate the anniversary of D-Day.' He winks, draws breath on his cigar and beams at us, very full of himself again. As I've always said, Tony was a good spieler if nothing else, and this bit of bullshit certainly cheered most of us up.

Soon there was just Tony, Mick, me and the three ladies standing between the trucks. Still lying inside the trucks, however, out cold and huddled together like the babes in the wood, are the two bros recovering from the beating Dave and Barry had dished them. Funny how when you're in real pain the brain decides it's time to shut down, especially when you're knackered. Just in case they're not as out as they are making out, we go outside to decide what to do with them. It's agreed that the best option is for me and Mick to drive them back to their place in my motor while our girls go on to my place in Mick's motor. Once we've dropped the bros off, we sort ourselves out and get ourselves home too. It's also agreed that Mick and me would come back over to Tony's place first thing in the morning and sort the trucks and the loot out.

We woke the brothers who were out to the world. They squinted at us through bruised blood-shot eyes and winced with pain every time they moved. We more or less carried the pair of them between us to get them into the car, with them thanking us profusely for helping them to get home and, as they saw it, for saving their lives.

'Thanks Mick for stopping those two Cockney bastards. They'd have fucking killed us if you hadn't have stopped them, the crazy pair of bastards.'

'They'll wish they fucking had killed us when we get hold of 'em, they'll pay for this lot, the bastards, we'll cut their fucking bollocks off.'

They chuntered on and on like this until we dropped them off. They kept trying to draw Mick and me in but we said nothing. Their bravado and posturing was normal practice for any self-proclaimed hard men who have just taken a solid beating. But once we were on our own we started talking, fast and serious. It was turning out to be a bad show. On top of all the shit Mick had spelled out in the barn, we now had these two psychopaths vowing to sort out Dave and Barry as soon as they were fit and able again. Then there was the problem, or should I say problems, with Tony and Thelma. The way the brothers would see it was that it was Tony's fault that Dave and Barry had weighed in. They would not see that Percy's intent to rearrange Tony's Cannock Chase with his razor had anything to do with it. Then there's Thelma and Percy. Percy is obviously in deep, while Thelma is simply enjoying a bit of grumble and grunt on the side. Now these are not the sort of things you want going on backstage when you should all be keeping your heads down after a slice of hit-and-run. One thing, however, was clear. Dave and Barry had to get off the scene fast. The easiest thing to do was to give them a sizeable wedge now, and get them to sod off back to London to lie low down there until things began to look a bit better up here. With Tony, Thelma and the brothers, things were a little more difficult. There was bugger all we could do about that except spend as much time with them as we could so, when the brothers surfaced again, we'd hopefully be around to handle any of the sorting out necessary. And a lot of things were going to need sorting out.

13 Losing the loot

It was pushing nine o'clock when we arrived back at my place, so it was a quick cat-lick and scrape with no kip, before we're off to the Castaways. The girls drove while we at least got a bit of a break in the back. By the time we arrived at the club all of the lads, most with their missuses, were already there and were much the worse for wear because Tony's doing 'drinks on the house' for all and sundry. Nice way of keeping your head down, we thought, but in fact Tony had it covered with his D-Day Anniversary celebrations bull-shit. As everybody in the place was getting pissed out of their minds very rapidly, we decided that perhaps it was not a bad scene after all because, if any of the other lookers-on should be questioned by the law, none of them will remember anything of what anybody said or didn't say. We nevertheless told our lads that they shouldn't get so tipsy that they lose control of what their mouths are saying. We also told Barry and Dave of our plan for them. They saw the sense of it and they agreed to get off back to the smoke first thing the next morning, picking up a survival wedge at Tony's on the way.

We also noticed that just before the hour and the half-hour on the clock, Tony was diving into his back office. He was only away for a few minutes each time but when he came back he looked if he had lost a shilling and found a sixpence. At one o'clock, when the club was near enough empty, Mick and me followed him into the office. We found him with his ear stuck against the wireless listening to the Jack Jackson record show on Radio Luxembourg.

'What's all this then Tony?' asks Mick. 'We didn't know you were into this crap.'

'I bloody well ain't Mick,' says Tony. 'I've been listening to the news all night and when Auntie folded I switched over to see if this lot had anything. I'm telling you Mick, there something fishy going on. There hasn't been a fucking word about the raid, nothing, it's as though it never happened. Not a word, a hint, no nothing, now that ain't fucking normal.'

We took his point.

'Perhaps the news hasn't got out yet. We did a pretty good job of closing everything down.'

'Not that fucking well,' says Tony. 'It's been twenty-four hours now, if they'd have put a message in a fucking bottle and tossed it into the sea, some bastard would have found it by now. There's got to be something up, but I don't know what. We pull off the biggest fucking robbery in history and nobody knows it happened! The whole world should be talking about it by now. But what have we got? Nobody knows that it's even been done, let alone that it was us that did it! The bastards must be holding it back for some reason, but fuck knows why.' Tony was right. It was more than strange that there was absolutely nothing on any of the news programmes.

'Perhaps they're holding it back till they get the full picture,' offers I.

'Can't see it,' says Mick. 'They never do with anything else. Anyway there's nowt we can do about it except to wait and see what turns up.'

'We could put the papers on to it,' Tony says.

'You what?' says Mick and me in unified astonishment.

'We could let them know, anonymously, just a phone call or a pasted-up note, just to let them know, so they can follow it up and report it,' responds Tony, in all seriousness!

'Are you fucking barmy or something? What are you fucking on about? So they can report it, so they can fucking report it! I don't believe you. We don't do fucking anything. We don't get in touch with anybody, anywhere, anytime. The fewer people that know about it, the better it is for us. If it don't make the world news, that's fucking wonderful.' Mick stares at Tony in disbelief and Tony stares back at him in equal disbelief.

'The biggest robbery in history and nobody knows about it, what sort of deal is that?' Tony says. 'Some bastard is tucking us up good and proper and I want to know why.'

'Well this sort of fucking tuck-up we can live with,' says Mick angrily. 'It suits us fine. But it ain't gonna happen. It's still too early. Let's see what happens tomorrow but, whatever happens, don't you say fucking anything to fucking anybody,' he jabs Tony hard in the ribs with his fire-iron fingers to make his point clear. 'Fucking anybody! Got it? 'Cos if you do Tony, mate or no fucking mate, I'll cut your fucking tongue out before I blow your fucking brains out. There's no fucking way I'm gonna end my days swinging from the end of a fucking rope because you, or anybody fucking else, couldn't keep their fucking traps shut.' I think Tony got the message.

⌘　⌘　⌘　⌘　⌘　⌘　⌘

Although we were as tired as a rabbit's orifice, when we get back to my place we send the two girls off to bed so that we can pick this latest bit of shit out of the fan. At first we go round and round the houses getting nowhere and it's turning daylight before we finally came up with some basic defensive strategies based on what might, or might not, turn up.

Next morning, we sent the girls out to buy all of the morning papers. They split up and were under orders not to buy more than one from any one shop. While they were gone we listened to the news on the wireless. There was nothing about our do. When the girls got back with the papers, the picture was the same. Fuck all. Pages of crap about the Pope being on television in eight countries at the same time, which was something of a first in those days, but nothing, just nothing, about our do. It didn't add up. It was as if it hadn't happened, as if we had just dreamt it or made it up. We couldn't make head nor tale of it.

We tried to convince ourselves that perhaps the news hadn't got out of Guernsey yet but we knew we were spitting in the wind. A plane, a boat, a homing carrier pigeon, would have got out with the news by now. It didn't make sense, and it was scary. When things don't go as they should, there's a good chance that, as Tony implied, some bastard somewhere is pulling another set of strings. Or, using a slight modification to the old rule Dave had applied when he warned us about Mordant being a bit strange: if things ain't behaving normal, something somewhere ain't normal!

Mick and me drove out to Tony's place. He's obviously been looking out for us because he's down alongside and opening the door before we even stop the car.

'Well, what do you think now? It's not in any of the papers.'

'Have you seen all of them?' says Mick.

'Course I have. Well, most of them. I went out and got all I could this morning.'

135

'And all from the same shop?'

'Yeah,' Tony's initially confident reply descending into belated and embarrassed enlightenment.

'Bleeding dickhead,' says Mick scornfully.

We strode across the gravel drive towards the barn with Tony trailing at a jogging trot after us.

'Well, what do you reckon then?' Tony asks again.

'Well, first thing we got to do is to lose the trucks and the loot,' I reply. 'If the law finds them or the loot, we're in deep shit.'

We opened the barn doors wide and the trucks looked pleased to see us. I went round to the back of one of them and dragged out two of the ammo boxes. I checked the currency inside. It was all English. I tipped the bundles of notes in a pile into a corner of the barn and tossed an old sack on top to keep them in place. I turned to Tony.

'Dave and Barry will be calling in later. Give them that lot. Tell them to not go fucking mad with it and to keep in touch only as we agreed.'

Tony looked perplexed. 'What do you mean, only as agreed? Where are they going anyway? They're supposed to be working for me.'

'Tony, get it through your fucking head, with the amount we've nicked nobody is working for anybody anymore. All that's over and done with. And it's best if you don't know where they're going.' I look him in the eye. 'And don't try to fucking pump them because they'll tell you fuck-all, but they will tell Mick and me that you tried to pump them, that's for sure. The less everybody knows the better it is for all of us!'

With that, I climbed into the cab of the front truck, started it up and pulled out of the barn with Mick following on close behind in the other truck. When we reached the end of Tony's drive, I turned left and Mick turned right.

We met up later at Croxton, a village of a dozen houses and a pub on the road from Eccleshall to Loggerheads in Staffordshire. We drove on to an even smaller place just off the road called Arnhill where an old mate, Kenny Barker, and his missus had taken up pig farming. It was a good business to be in back in those days. Kenny had been a bit of a fly-by-night himself when we were kids but he couldn't cope with the uncertainty of a life of crime. So once he pulled enough money together to put down a sizeable deposit on a pig farm he decided to go straight, well, straightish. Kenny sees us turn in and comes out to greet us.

We explain to him that we want some stuff looked after for a few weeks, no questions asked, and that there's a five grand in it for himself. The offer of five grand sealed the agreement. Kenny moved a tractor out of one of his barns and we drove the trucks in. Knowing we are up to something, Kenny buggered off on the excuse of having to see to his pigs. The first thing we did was to sort out the paperwork we had taken from the Nazi vault and pack it into a kit bag. We then stuffed two rucksacks with English bank notes and pulled out a couple of tight fistfuls of notes to give Kenny as a down payment. After we'd sheeted up the trucks and locked the barn with our own locks, we got Kenny to give us a lift to Stafford station where we got a train back to Brum. By five o'clock we were back home having a cup of tea and a snifter of whiskey. The girls tell us that there's still been nothing on the wireless.

Tuesday and the rest of the week also draws a news blank. Mick and me spend our days at Tony's on the pretext of sorting stuff out and our nights at the Castaways just in case the brothers make a swift recovery and decide to do some breast-beating. Some of the brighter lads also notice the absence of news and collar us to find out what's going on, and to pick up some cash to tide them over. We tell them that they know as much as we do. Most don't like it because 'it ain't natural.' Tony tells them it's a government conspiracy to keep the world from knowing that we band of heroes have just pulled off the greatest robbery of all time. Tony's behaviour begins to worry all of us. He spends his time glued to the wireless or reading the papers. He gets more and more agitated each time there's no news, complaining that we are being cheated out of our celebrity status and our future place in history. We mostly ignored him but it was beginning to get through to us that he might just do something daft.

Whenever we were on our own at Tony's, Mick and me began to sift through the Nazi documentation stuff. The whole lot was a classic example of the Nazis' pre-occupation with getting the paperwork right. Everything that went in and out of that vault had been recorded in detail, every deal, every transaction, the names, the dates, everything. While the amounts of loot that had gone in and out was staggering, even more staggering was the complexity and dedication of the organisation behind it all. The primary business of this Merchant Bank was to look after Nazis on the run for war crimes and to finance the resurrection of the party.

But there was much more than just financial accounts. There were the names of everyone involved in the Bank's laundering network. There were details of how the money was distributed, of financing assassinations to silence would-be grasses, and hush money paid to those who could be trusted. The names included a substantial bunch of bastards at the top of the British establishment who had hoped for a Nazi victory. Not only had they supported the Nazis, they would have ruled Britain for them had they won the war. Among this bunch, one name in particular stood out. This bastard and his family were right at the heart of the so-called British aristocracy, bright blue blood right down to his bleeding piles. If the Nazis had won, this bastard would have been a willing puppet running the country for them. If word about their traitorous part in all of this had got out there'd have probably been a bloody revolution, and I mean bloody.

In the early fifties the old establishment were shitting themselves about the rise of socialism and the nightmare of a Russian-supported communist coup in the UK. It kept them awake at night. During the war the working class had been promised that if we won, and if there were any of them left, they would inherit a land fit for heroes. And what had they got? They got the socialist government most of them had dreamed of but their day-to-day experience of this was six years of hardship and severe rationing, and most couldn't understand why.

And now, to cap it all, the Conservatives and rich bastards were back in charge again. For sure, things were starting to get better for most, but not quickly enough for the pre- and post-war losers to be sure that they were not going to be shafted yet again. The argument was simple. If most of Eastern Europe and China had all gone commie, why shouldn't we? Wasn't the time ripe? King George had died a year earlier and his eldest daughter, Elizabeth, a bit of a kid, had been crowned as queen, so while the 'everybody's equal now' might be the daily crap being fed to the masses, nobody with any sense really believed it. But it was also obvious to all but the paranoid or fascist elite that the critical point of a commie-led revolution had passed.

That being said, it was, nevertheless, still possible that our stuff could generate enough distrust and discontent to re-ignite the dynamite. So we, Mick and me, had a dilemma. On the one hand we ought to grass on these bastards, and the big name in particular, so that they could be done for their treachery. On the other hand, this info had got to be worth a lot to somebody to keep it quiet, so why hand it over for nowt. More worryingly, these bastards might also be the reason that everything was being hushed up with the connivance of the powers that be. So taking all things into account, we decided that it was best, for the moment at least, to keep this particular stash of dynamite to ourselves. We also decided to set up some contingency plans just in case things didn't go exactly how we wanted.

⌘　⌘　⌘　⌘　⌘　⌘　⌘

It was two weeks later, on a Saturday night, before the Hammond brothers showed up at the Castaways again. Ernie's face still showed signs of a beating and Percy couldn't manage to do his usual swagger without a limp. But swagger in they did, straight up to the bar to stand with our bunch as though they had been drinking with us only the night before.

'All right lads?' says Percy, 'Anybody ready for a drink?' Neither of the brothers were noted for their sociability or generosity so most took up the offer, albeit warily. The chat revives and goes on; the horses, the dogs, who's shagging who, who's seen who. Getting onto 'who's seen who' prompts Eddie to enquire, quite sociably of course, about the whereabouts of Dave and Barry. The last time we had seen the brothers they were talking about the various forms of torture they were going to practise on Dave and Barry in revenge for the beating they had given them, so Mick and me leave it to the others to take up the question.

'That's a point,' says Ernie. 'Where are those pair of bastards? We ain't seen hide nor hair of them since the do.' Everybody looks around and shrug their shoulders.

'P'raps they've buggered off back to the smoke,' says Barney. 'Oh yeah, that reminds me, they said that I could have their share should they go missing or fail to turn up for the pay-out.' Everybody laughed except the Hammonds who simply smiled weakly.

'I bet they fucking did!' says JD. 'They'll show up soon enough when it's pay-out time. They're probably just keeping out of the way until things cool down a bit.'

'What's there to cool down?' says Tony sarcastically. 'There's fuck all happening!'

'Tony's right, it's really weird,' says Ernie and a range of theories as to why the raid has not hit the headlines are raised, and accepted or dismissed, with little in the way of reasoned argument.

After a time everything slides back to normal and so we withdraw to the back room where several three-card brag schools soon get going. Mick and me, playing as a team unbeknownst to any of the others, win some, lose some without any bastard fully comprehending that the ones we win are always much larger than the ones we lose. The bros say they're just going to watch but they are unable to hold back for long.

'Mind if we sit in?' says Percy.

'No skin off our noses,' replies Mick. 'The more the merrier and the more for me to take home.'

Percy and Eddie pull up a couple of seats. The game goes on and before long the losers are tossing in IOUs on the strength of the coming share out. It was just like what happened in the Ducks on the journey back home, nobody was really bothered about losing or winning, the usual aggressive fire of our games was missing. Percy finally snaps.

'This is fucking ridiculous,' he says. 'It's like playing Happy Families. Nobody cares a toss, tens, fifties, fucking tons, who cares, it's fucking pea-nuts. If we're going to play let's play for shares in our cut of the loot.'

'How do you mean?' asks Barney.

'Simple,' says Percy. 'Instead of a fiver, you bet a percentage of your share, one per cent, ten per cent, half, the fucking lot, it's up to you.'

This was good stuff coming from Percy, who was normally thick as two planks. The idea clearly sparked some of the lads off while some were not too sure if it was a good idea. JC and JD immediately decide that they want none of it and go off to the bar. As nobody else spoke out against it, Mick says, 'Well let's give it a go then.'

He throws me a quick glance before dragging on a roll-up to fire off a series of tiny smoke rings. The glance and the rings say to me, 'OK, let's take these two twats to the cleaners!' The deal was with me and there were seven in the game. Twenty one cards out of fifty two in each deal, so in just two deals if you're any good at handling a deck you know where to find almost any card you want, and I was known to many then as 'Wheeler dealer'.

Standard practice, I let things ride for the first few hands while I size the run of the cards up. Nobody's betting anything above one per cent. This allows me to see to it that the brothers have what they see as a run of luck and begin fancying themselves. The trap's set. All that I need now is for two of the lads to leave the game. I didn't have to wait long.

'I could do with a drink.' I said. 'Anybody else ready for one?'

'I'll get them,' offers Barney. 'I need a piss anyway.'

'I need one too,' says Ikey. 'I'll come and give you a hand.' And off they go.

This minor distraction is all I need to switch the pack for one, as they say, I had prepared earlier. It was a pack fully loaded for five players, to give one winner and two twats. I'm already dealing from the prepared deck as Barney and Ikey start to walk away. Spider who is sitting next to me, has a quick look at his hand and, without hesitation, chucks it in and goes to help with the drinks. Percy gives his the once-over and does a visible double take. If it had been a legit game, anyone with eyes to see would have known he picked up a killer hand. As it was I already knew that he was looking at a running flush; ten, Jack, and Queen of Clubs. Eddie clocks his hand and is also well pleased with his high flush of diamonds.

Percy opens up with five per cent. Totally idiotic as up to that point nobody had gone beyond one per cent, so he's broadcasting that he has a good hand. Mick, who hasn't touched his cards, looks taken aback. After some consideration, still leaving his cards untouched on the table, says, 'Well, just for a bit of sport then, I'll go five, blind.'

This means that Eddie has got to go ten per cent to stay in the game. He's uncertain but he must have got a hidden prompt from Percy and he puts in ten. It's down to me. I curse Mick.

'Bloody hell, Mick. We should have said nobody goes blind when we upped the anti!'

'Well, nobody did. So put up or shut up!'

I glower at him. 'I'm in, and I hope you've got bugger all.'

'Win some, lose some,' he smirks.

Percy, after some late-in-the-day melodramatic uncertainty, also goes ten and raises it ten. A quarter of Percy's share is now on the table. Mick still leaves his cards on the table.

'Ah, stuff it, in for a penny, in for pound, I'm still in. Blind,' says Mick.

With Mick staying blind, Percy's raise meant that Eddie had got to put up twenty per cent to stay in. Eddie realises that he needs to stay with Percy in an attempt to force Mick to open. I scan mine and, after due hesitation, toss them in.

'Prat,' I snarl at Mick. 'You deserve to lose, going blind on these stakes.' I push my chair back and stand away from the table. There's just the three of them at the table now, Mick, Percy and Eddie.

Percy stays in with twenty and looks to Mick. Mick appears to consider the odds and eventually picks his hand up. He looks at his cards without any sign of emotion, and puts them back down on the table.

'I'm in for another twenty,' he says.

Eddie is now beside himself with glee. He's absolutely sure that Mick is bluffing, so now all that he and Percy need to do is to bluff Mick out for one of them to win. 'Twenty,' he says.

Percy goes for the twenty without even pausing. The play goes round again and the brothers are getting uneasy and they add up what's on the table. With Percy still to play sixty-five per-cent of his share and ninety per cent of Eddie's share are in the game.

Percy stakes another twenty. Mick matches it and Eddie is out of the game.

Percy and Mick face each other. They each have fifteen per cent left. Percy breaks the stalemate. 'Let's settle it for the lot.'

'Sod off,' says Mick. 'You must have something pretty strong to go for the lot and I'm not ending up skint for a game of pissing cards.'

'That's unlike you Mick. Can't stand the pace?' He speaks out to the group around the table, 'This is something to witness everybody. Big Mick Tibbets playing a blinder till I call his bluff. Come on Mick, scared to make the big bet, scared you might lose? Can't stand the heat? Come on, put your money where your big mouth usually is!'

Mick looks sheepish. Percy taunts him.

'C'mon Mick, the lot, on the turn of the cards, or throw your hand in and stop pissing about.'

Mick takes on a resigned look.

'Now, you pushed for this, remember that, I wanted to leave it.'

'Come on, turn your cards for the lot or give me the hand.'

'OK. For the lot.' Mick says looking even more resigned.

Percy doesn't need a second telling. He bursts into a broad smirk and lays his cards out with a flourish, 'A running flush, ten, Jack, and Queen of Clubs! Sorry Mick but it looks like you've been well and truly fucked!' It was the best hand we'd seen all night, and he bursts out laughing, as much in relief as in jubilation. Mick says nothing; he just looks morosely at Percy's cards. Then he slowly picks up his cards from the table and clicks one down. It's the eight of hearts.

'Yahoo,' shouts Percy laughing out loud again, 'A pissing eight?'

Mick clicks another card down, it's another eight.

'A pair of eights, I can't believe it! You prat. I knew you were bluffing!'

Mick puts his final card down. It's another eight.

'Three of 'em actually,' he says. There's a moment's silence before Mick triumphantly smirks. 'Now who's well and truly fucked?'

A general clamour erupts round the table. Percy and Eddie are in a state of disbelief. Percy visibly starts to erupt.

'You cheating pair of bastards,' he bellows, clearly referring to Mick and me. 'Give me those cards!' He snatches the deck and spreads the cards across the table. His eyes rove over them like a maniac's, but there's nothing to see. All the cards that should be there are there and there's nothing unusual about the mix. His face goes as red as a blood blister. He begins hyperventilating. His fists clench and he lurches to his feet. Eddie springs up along side him. Next second their razors are out and they move towards Mick and me, presumably intending to do us some lasting damage.

'You pair of bastards, if you think you can fucking cheat me out of my share, you've got another think coming! I'll see you both in hell before you get a fucking penny of it!'

143

As they approach us, Mick suddenly pulls out a gun from inside his jacket. It's an old Smith and Wesson revolver, and looks the size of a cannon, and he points it directly at Percy's head.

'Back off you twats, go on, back off!' The brothers stop their advance. The other lads move back. 'Nobody cheated fucking nobody. It's just the way the fucking cookie crumbles. It was you that wanted to go for the lot, it was you that pushed for it, remember? I was ready to stop early but you wanted all or nothing. The way you were going at it, I thought you had a triplet of threes or at least something heavier than a poxy run. Everybody watched Ronnie deal, it was a straight deal. With all this lot watching how could it have been anything else. You gambled and you fucking lost. That's the way it is sometimes. If you ain't prepared to lose, you shouldn't play with the big boys. Now piss off home before I lose my fucking rag and do something I'll regret and you won't know about!'

Mick's surprise pulling of the gun certainly had a restraining effect on the brothers, but Percy chuntered on.

'I still think you fucking set us up. I don't know how, but you fucking did.'

'Stop acting like a fucking girlie, nobody set you up, it's what Brag is all about. If it wasn't for games like that, none of us would ever play it. It's win some, lose some. So just piss off and don't come back till you've calmed down and are ready to talk sensible, and then we might sort something out.' Mick voice was clear and authoritative. The brothers, wisely realising they were onto another losing hand, decided to call it a day. With their eyes fixed firmly on Mick, and the gun, they moved back, collected their coats and left.

As the door closed after them, there's an audible sigh of relief. Barney, in his own inimical way, has to open the post-mortem. 'Bloody hell, Mick, I thought you were going to blow his bleeding brains out. You'd have been disappointed though, 'cos he ain't fucking got any!' This opens a chorus of laughing.

Mick strides across to Barney. The laughing stops immediately. He puts the gun to Barney's startled head. Barney's face twists into a picture of surprise, bewilderment and sheer terror. Mick pulls the trigger. Click, click. The gun is empty. The laughing becomes more hysterical than before. Everyone is going on about Mick's cheek and the gullibility of the brothers. All we got from Mick was, 'Think I'm stupid? If your collar gets felt by the law you're in enough trouble carrying a gun, let alone a loaded one!'

The prospect of any more card games was dead and buried, so we ended up sitting around in small groups drinking and rattling generally. Eventually there's just Mick, Tony, Spider and me sat round a table on our own. Tony was still over-twitchy about the no-news scene.

'There's got to be something going on, it ain't natural.'

'We're with you Tony but there's nothing we can do about it.'

'I still think we oughta tip the press off, anonymously, see what they've got to say. Think what they'd make of what we did. We'd be bloody world famous without anybody knowing who we are!' Tony was deadly serious.

'Tony,' I say with emphasis, 'we've been through this a dozen times, we've told you, leave it alone. From our point of view the less people that know about it the better. Fuck knows why it's happening, but no news is good news. Get that into your brain once and for all!'

But Tony still won't have it, 'We might as well not have done it. We ain't spending the money and nobody knows we pulled it off. The world's greatest robbery and the world's greatest fucking secret!'

'We'll get to spending the money soon enough,' Mick counters.'

'The big thing at the moment is to stay clear of the noose and sort the problem of the brothers out.'

Mention of the brothers redirects Tony's concerns.

'Yeah. What are you going to do about those barmy pair of bastards? They're likely to do something really barmy after tonight,' he says. 'You don't know them like I do. There'll be fucking murder if they don't get their share.'

'We don't want their fucking share.' Mick says, 'We've all got more than we'll ever fucking need anyway. I just wanted to teach them a lesson. I'll sort it out with them next time I see them. If they're nice to me they can keep the lot, if they act bolshie, we might only give them half back.'

'Anyway,' I say, 'I'm knackered, let's call it a night.'

Tony and Spider immediately start tidying up and switching off the lights. When they've done, the four us go out together.

As we get to the door Spider tosses the deck of cards I had switched with him, before the killer deal, into a bin.

'Best get rid of the evidence,' he says.

Spider was not known for his happy disposition, but at that moment he was smiling from side to side of his bony face.

Tony stares at him and then at me.

He goes to speak but Spider stops him short.

'Mum's the word Tony, youse knows what I mean!'

⌘

The entrance to the Saints Bay 'Pill Box'.

14 Bad Losers

It was coming up ten o'clock on the Sunday night when the phone rings. It's Thelma, Tony's missus. She was crying and having difficulty in speaking.

'All right Thelma, take it easy darling. What's happened?'

'It's Tony, Ronnie, he wants to tip off the press, he wants me to do it. I've told him no, but he won't listen, we've had a big row about it, he's been knocking me about. I've got to be quick, he doesn't know I'm phoning you. I've never seen him so mad. Can you and Mick get over here quick? I'll try to hold him but I'm sure he'll do it before the night's out. Can you come over?'

'Soon as we finish, I'll get on to Mick and we'll come over. The stupid sod will get us all hung.'

'Thanks Ronnie, come as quick as you can.' The phone goes dead before I have chance to get anything else out of her.

I call Mick, tell him the scene, and within twenty minutes we're on our way to Tony's.

'The daft twat's living in a dream-world,' I say. 'I really don't think he understands the shit we're in. He thinks it's a fucking film or something, where the fucking heroes just disappear into the sunset and nobody cares a toss.'

'We can't trust him now, that's for sure,' says Mick. 'We're going to have to keep him under lock and key till he gets it out of his system. It's either that or we shut the bastard up once and for all tonight. I don't like it but there are no other options as I see it.'

I don't like it either but I nod my head to agree. We travelled the rest of the journey in silence. This was one contingency we hadn't planned for.

Tony's place was all lit up like a Christmas tree when we got there. We dashed up the steps and rang the bell. We heard Thelma's heels clatter their way down the hall stopping as she opened the door.

'Ohh... Thank God you've come, he's in here.' and with that she went off at a trot clattering back down the hall before Mick and me have a chance to say anything or get a feel for the situation. She dived through a door to the right and we followed. Tony was in there all right, tied and bound to chair. He was gagged and his face was covered in blood. Alongside him, tied to another chair, was the motionless and blood-drenched figure of Spider. There was a dark red pool of drying blood around his feet with what looked sausages scattered in it. My mind had just taken in that these lumps were chopped off fingers, Spider's, when I was whacked hard on the back of the head by something solid and heavy. As I went down, I caught an image of Mick's body falling together with mine. Repetitive blows to my head and body, allied to the sound of dull thuds pounding into human flesh, informed my hazed brain that I was getting a solid kicking from somebody. The kicking eventually stopped. Above the roaring sounds of my own breathing and heart beat I could hear Thelma crying and Mick groaning.

'Right, you fucking pair of cheating bastards. Don't move and don't say anything unless we tell you to.'

I recognised the voice. It was Percy's. I turned my head to look up and saw Eddie pointing a gun in my direction. A boot thudded into my gut.

'What did I just fucking say? You don't move, you don't speak, you don't do anything unless we tell you!'

Eddie strutted around us like an arrogant rooster while Percy searched us for weapons. I had nothing but Mick had his Smith and Wesson. When Percy found it he couldn't resist smacking it, side on, hard into Mick's face. He checked the gun and found that it was fully loaded this time. His response was to kick Mick again.

'Bastard! Right, you, Ronnie, up. On to that chair and no fancy stuff!'

I can actually remember thinking, 'what is he on about? No fancy stuff?' I could hardly stand up let alone start any 'fancy stuff'. I dragged myself to my feet, staggered to the chair and near fell on to it.

'Right, hands behind the back of the chair.'

I pushed my arms around the back of the chair and felt a pair of handcuffs putting paid to any hopes I might have had of some fancy stuff in the future. By the time my head and eyes returned to normal service Mick was facing me in a similar situation. Percy was standing close to Mick, and Eddie was still covering us with a gun.

'Not so fucking big now, are we?' Percy emphasised his point by smashing his arm into Mick's face. 'Not so fucking clever now are we, you cheating pair of bastards?'

148

And he re-emphasised his point with a blow to my face too!

'We told you, nobody cheated anybody.' I speak as if I've been to a dentist and had half of my teeth pulled out without the luxury of an anaesthetic. My words drizzeled in a shower of blood and spit.

'You lying bastard!' Percy shouted into my face and gave it another forearm smash. He moved to Spider and dragged his head up by the hair. Spider's throat had been slashed and both of his eyes had been gouged out.

'Before he kicked it, this little prat told us how you did it, you must take us for a right pair of dickheads. All had a good laugh afterwards, did you? The Hammonds, a right pair of dickheads. Well, you ain't laughing now are you? We ain't such dickheads now are we?'

'It was a stupid game, we were going to tell you, we didn't want your share, there's more loot than any of us could handle, what would be the point of nicking your share? Next time we saw you we were going to tell you. Straight up Perce, ask any of the lads.'

'Oh! You were were you? Going to give us your share as well I suppose, just for old time's sake? Percy whined sarcastically, ' "Straight up Perce, ask any of the lads". You really must take us for dickheads!' With that he let go of Spider's head. It dropped deep into his chest. An eye ball slithered down the congealing blood on his face before gently slipping off to hang from a silvery string-like membrane. Percy gave me another smash to my face. My head reeled from the force of the blow which nearly knocked me and the chair I was tied to over.

'We'll show you who's the bleeding dickheads. We're not just taking our share back, we're taking the fucking lot and we'll be out of the country with it by the end of the week. So, all we need from you now is for you to tell us where is it?'

Bingo! Just as I'm thinking we've got no cards to play, Percy gives me one.

'Where's what?' I ask

'Where's what!' Percy screams in my face. 'The fucking money, the trucks, the fucking gold, you twat.' He's besides himself with rage. 'Where's fucking what? I'll show you where's fucking what in a minute.'

'As far as I know it's still in the trucks in the barn out the back.'

Percy rolls his eyes in mock disbelief. He goes over to Tony and pulls his gag off.

'Now this great turd told us that you've taken both trucks off somewhere, but he claims he don't know where.' His tone was sarcastic and deadly. 'Isn't that right Tony?' Tony's swollen face shows signs of agreement. 'Unfortunately we didn't believe him, and this proved to be particularly unfortunate for little Spider here. So now we're going to do to him, what we did to Spider, until you decide to tell us where the trucks are. Comprende?'

I stare back at him, not really in defiance, more a case of not being able to think of anything better to do at the time.

'And if Tony decides to give up the ghost before you tell us, we do the same thing with him.' He gives Mick a kick. 'And if you still haven't told us when he sprouts wings, last but not least, we start on you.'

Tony shrieks across at me. 'For God's sake tell him Ronnie, please Ronnie just tell him, please Ronnie, please.'

My mind's racing about as if it's inside a pin-ball machine which is giving out random flashes of hope, only to be quickly extinguished by dark reason. I know if I tell him we're all going to be dead meat. If I don't, we'll probably end up the same way, but get there a lot more painfully. I look across to Mick and Percy cracks me in the face again.

'You don't need to look to him, it's you I'm fucking asking, not him. You can look at him after we've finished with Tony unless, of course, you decide to tell us what we want to know.'

'Please Ronnie, please don't let him touch me Ronnie please!'

Tony is pleading with me, imploring me. I'm in the shit as to what to do. I know the moment I tell them, we're goners. So too is Kenny, a good mate, innocent and snug and happy with his pigs, and his missus, and the trucks stashed away safe and sound in his barn. I decide to play for time, although I know that it's probably pointless. But if you don't try.....

'OK Percy, just hold on a minute. We, you, don't need all of this.' I try to sound sincere and co-operative, as if I'm talking to a mate. 'Look, I can't really tell you where they are but I can take you to them. You'll never find the place on your own. It's right in the middle of nowhere. It's no good me just telling you where, I'll have to show you.'

Percy smiles and pulls out his razor.

'I tell you what Ronnie, you try telling us where it is and we'll decide whether we can find it or not. How does that strike you?' He moves to stand behind Tony who is screaming at me.

'Please Ronnie, please, just tell him Ronnie, for God's sake, please.'

Tony kept pleading, begging me. I tried to ignore him, along with Mick, Spider, and Thelma and try to focus solely and completely on Percy.

'It's not that easy, Perce,' I say, still trying to sound matey. 'Honestly, on my mother's deathbed, and all that shit, I can't tell you but I'll show you, no trouble. I'll take you straight there. We covered them up so well no-one would find them from even a yard away, even if they knew where to look.'

'So, you're not going to tell me. OK. Right? Well that's OK by me, is that OK by you Tony?'

He breathes on the razor, warming and wetting it, for a smoother, sharper cut. He stoops towards Tony. Tony screams and writhes in the chair. 'Ronnie, for Christ's sake Ronnie, tell them!' Percy takes hold of one of Tony's fingers.

'Stop, stop, I can't stand any more of it.' It was Thelma, holding her head between her hands and shrieking at the top of her voice. She throws herself between Percy and Tony. 'You said you wouldn't touch him, or kill him, you promised, you promised. Please stop, Percy, stop, it's gone too far. I'm sick of it all. The blood, the screaming, the killing, I just want it all to stop. Please Percy, please.' Percy steps back, in surprise as much as anything. Thelma throws her arms around Tony and tries to untie him. 'I'm sorry Tony, I didn't want this, I'm sorry, please believe me Tony. I love you Tony, I'm so sorry, I'm so sorry.' She begins kissing Tony's blood splattered face as she is trying to untie him.

Percy is aghast. 'What the fucking hell are you doing? What's all this shit, 'I love you Tony'? You said you loved me, not this piece of shit!'

'I'm sorry Percy, I didn't expect any of this to happen, just let them go, please Percy stop, let's forget it ever happened.'

'Forget it ever happened, you little tart, you fucking little tart, get out of my way.' He grabs Thelma and throws her bodily several yards across the room.

'Now stay down there till I say you can move.' He moves back to Tony and raises his razor. Thelma instantly jumps to her feet and starts to run screaming towards him. Percy drops the razor, grabs Mick's Smith and Wesson, and shoots Thelma through the forehead at point blank range. Thelma's head explodes into a shower of blood, brain and bone fragments. Percy catches most of it on his face. He's shocked and disgusted and tries to wipe the blood and other bits from his face and lips. He begins raving at Thelma's motionless body.

'You dirty fucking slut, look at this fucking mess all over me, you fucking slut. See what you've made me do, preferring this arsehole to me. You fucking asked for it, you should have kept out of it, it's your own fucking fault, it wouldn't have happened if you'd have kept out of it!' He throws the Smith and Wesson at her body in total anger and frustration, still scraping at his face to clean the mess off.

Tony is screaming relentlessly. Eddie walks across to him and put his gun against the side of Tony's head.

'Shut up or I'll shut you up once and for all.' Tony fell to involuntary quiet groaning.

Eddie turns to me. 'Right , we've had enough pissing about. I'm going to count to three and if you haven't told us straight by then, I'll put a bullet right through this bastard's brain, then I'll do Mick and then I'll do you after shooting you in the bollocks first. You understand what I'm saying, no more bull-shit, no more going around the fucking houses, just tell us where it is. OK?' He puts his finger on the trigger. 'One.... Two....'

He never got to three. A mega-storm of breaking glass, rapid gunfire and armed men dressed in black burst into the room through the French windows. Eddie was ripped apart by a volley of bullets which pounded into his body until it was only their impact gave it movement. Percy made a lunge for Mick's Smith and Wesson lying on the floor but, as he grasped it, his hand was crushed by an army issue boot and his head smacked with a heavy rifle butt. The intruders had to be a commando squad, dressed and fully equipped for an operation into enemy held territory. I'd seen their like in training many times but I'd never seen them in action at first hand before.

It was an impressive display. There were about a dozen of them and they spread out silently around the room like a pack of hungry wolves on the scent of a prey. Two hauled Percy to his feet and wired his hands behind his back. Two more checked that Eddie was well and truly dead. There was no need to check out Thelma. The rest, backs to the walls, were on concentrated surveillance duty. Throughout the manoeuvre, and even now, not a word was spoken, they communicated only by hand signals and head movements.

The action ceased as suddenly as it had begun. Peace reigned once more. Mick threw his head back and laughed.

'Well fuck me, saved by the fucking bell!' He continued to laugh on in a state of complete disbelief. Tony was sobbing his heart out, poor sod. I simply sat there mesmerised by this wholly surreal incident. Somehow we had cheated a certain and painful death at the hands of the brothers, but now what? Who were this bunch? How did they get here? More to the point, why were they here? What did they want? What were they going to do, with us? I hoped to fuck that I was right about them being commandos! But at that moment I couldn't have cared less. We were still alive and, undeniably, there was a new game in play.

After a few further minutes of silence and inactivity, a smallish, somewhat slight bloke comes in through the French windows the masked intruders had shattered in making their grand entrance. He was dressed head to toe in black too but his outfit was a civvies suit, overcoat and regulation trilby. He walked slowly round the room, pausing now and then to scrutinise us each in turn, first me, then Mick, Tony, Percy and finally the inert bodies of Spider, Thelma and Eddie. The living among us looked back at him just as keenly. He doesn't say a word. Eventually he nods to the blokes holding Percy and they haul him out. He gives another nod and Mick and Tony are carried out wholesale, still bound to the chairs. The bodies of Spider, Thelma and Eddie are left where they fell. Another nod and the rest of his masked bunch leave so there's just him and me left. He throws his trilby down on a chair before pulling another one up to sit facing me.

He's a calm confident little bleeder and only in his early twenties. He reaches inside his fitted overcoat and pulls out a gold plated cigarette case. He opens it and selects a cigarette which he puts to his lips. He searches for a while in the pockets and folds of his layers of clothing eventually pulling out a gold plated cigarette lighter. He lights the cigarette, blows the smoke towards me and looks about the room. For me this was all poor quality amateur dramatics. He knew where his lighter was. You only needed a minute with this bastard to know that he was too precise to mislay anything, least of all a well-used lighter. The fag, lighting it, the looking about, shit, Mick and Tony were Oscar winners compared to this idiot.

'So Mr Wheeler,' he says, finally deeming to speak, 'tell me where they are?' He spoke quietly without any discernible accent.

Despite my physically battered condition I just couldn't resist the obvious answer.

'Where's what?'

A hint of a smile flickered on his pursed lips. He looked at me directly.

'Don't play games with me Mr Wheeler. I'm not a good loser, so please don't play games with me. Where are the two lorries containing all the souvenirs that you and you colleagues brought back from your little expedition to Guernsey?'

'Guernsey? When was that then?' I ask in a voice exuding total innocence

'Please Mr Wheeler,' he says raising one eyebrow.

'Well that's for me to know, and for you to find out.' A taunt retrieved from childhood but it felt appropriate. The bloke was clearly not amused.

'Oh yes, I'll find out Mr Wheeler, have no doubt about that. I, or should I say we, have at our disposal more exquisitely sophisticated techniques to extract information than the barbarous methods employed by either you or your associates.' He paused. 'And they never fail. Now, I ask you again, forget the lorries, I want to know where have you hidden what you and your colleagues stole from the island of Guernsey on the night of the fifth of June?'

'Guernsey? On the fifth of June. Not us mate, we were up the Castaways Club, ask anybody. We can prove we were there. Anyway I haven't heard about any job being done on Guernsey, there's been nothing in the news as far as I know. So, what's this lot all about?' I ask feigning surprised incredulity which unfortunately cut no ice with the bastard.

'Yes, you're right, the raid hasn't been reported in the newspapers or on the radio, which is very, very unusual. So whatever you stole Mr Wheeler, it must have included something of great importance to someone of great importance. The other fact that leads me to this conclusion is that my department has been instructed to handle this operation rather than the normal law enforcement agencies. What this means for you is that you have no recourse to the normal protections the law offers such criminals as yourself, for example, you do not even have the right to a fair trial. Am I making myself clear Mr. Wheeler?'

'Well I'm starting to get the picture.'

'Good. Let me paint in a little more of the picture for you.'

He drew out a leather bound notebook. He opened it and ran his eyes up and down it.

'My department were allocated to this operation during the early hours of Monday the seventh of June. I flew to Guernsey the following morning, courtesy of the RAF. When I took over the operation, a total security blackout had been ordered and was already in force. From information gained in a number of interviews, I was able to conclude quite quickly that, on the night of the fifth and sixth of June, a group of ten men and three women robbed nine of the island's banks and looted a number of its Jewellery stores. In the course of the robbery,' he paused. 'I prefer to see it more as a vicious and barbarous raid because during the course of the robbery the raiders shot and killed one police officer and seriously injured another. They also physically mutilated and killed the manager of one of the Banks. All but two of the men spoke with quite distinctive Birmingham accents. The accents of the other two were less distinct but may these have been from the London area. During the raid one male was referred to as 'Percy' and another as 'Dave'. My brief was to identify and follow each member of the gang, without arousing any suspicions on their part, until I had ascertained the location of every last item that had been stolen in the course of the raid. Within five days I had the names of every one actively involved and since Sunday the thirteenth, an appropriate date don't you think, I have had men trailing each and every one on that list of names.' He took out a photograph and held it for me to see.

'Here is a photograph of your grand departure from Weymouth.' Although my eyes were nearly closed from bruising, I could see that it was a picture of Gert going into the sea at Weymouth with Tony stood on the bow doing his saluting Major impression. Even in the shit I was in, I couldn't help smiling inwardly.

'It's a good photo of Tony,' I said. 'Where did you say it was taken?'

'I said let's not play games Mr. Wheeler.' He did not smile and the coldness of his response killed any covert smiling in me.

If what this bastard had just said was true, he, or his lackeys, had probably been looking in as Spider was tortured to death and while Thelma had her brains blasted to smithereens. He hadn't even mentioned that they had died under his watch. His demeanour and attitude told me that he didn't care a toss! Whether people lived or died was obviously of little or no importance to this bastard. He was playing to some set of rules without question, doubt or regret. What really got up my nose too was that the bastard talked and sounded like a bloody tax form, and I hate tax forms! I realise that I, we, use the term 'bastard' perhaps too freely, but at that moment and forever after this man was for me the ultimate bastard. I hoped I would live to see him die more slowly and more painfully than Spider and Thelma had died. I decided that he was devoid of feeling for human life and so, given the chance, I would some day test his feelings for his own life as I coaxed his body to death.

He continued impassively. 'I want you to tell me, now, the precise location of everything you collected during your stay on the island.'

'Suppose I do, what do we get out of it?' I asked, working on the principle of nothing ventured, nothing gained.

'What do you get out of it, Mr. Wheeler? Something worth more than all you have stolen in your entire life. What you may get out of it, Mr. Wheeler, is a chance to stay alive, and perhaps each and everyone of your friends too. This is an opportunity for you, and for them, to live for another day.'

'Only a day, hardly worth the effort.' I replied gaining in confidence. I decided to find out who I was playing against and what sort of hand he was holding. 'Anyway when I'm playing games I like to know the strength of the opposition. So who the hell are you and your balaclavered mates and who the fuck are you all working for?'

'Firstly, you may refer to me as George, that's all that you need to know at this moment. Secondly, we are not playing games even if you prefer to regard it as such. And finally, please, there really is no need for such foul language.' He spoke contemptuously brushing some imaginary dust from his sleeve to demonstrate his 'holier than thou' virtues.

'Right George.' I hid my seething disgust of the bastard. In a straight fight I could have slaughtered him with one hand tied behind my back, and here he is treating me like a fucking school kid. 'So let's start again then. If I tell you where the money is, then what?'

'While I'm not quite sure what it is that I'm after Ronnie.' He paused as the hint of a smile touched his lips in an artificial show of blossoming friendship. 'I hope you don't mind me calling you Ronnie, but I feel that we getting to know each other rather well and so I must tell you that I am very confident that the recovery of mere money, however large that sum may be, will be of minor importance to my superiors. I have to have everything you and your colleagues took, you understand that, everything, no matter how small or insignificant it might appear to you or anyone else.' He fell silent, waiting for my reply. I surmised that letting me know that he knew my name was an attempt to convince me that he knew a lot more than he did. So I decided it was time to lay down a card to open his hand up a little.

'Did you know that one of the Banks was funding top Nazis on the run?'

'You're not starting to play games with me after what I just said are you Ronnie?' He sounded impatient. Clearly he would not get far in a high stake card game.

'No! I'm being very serious. Did you know?'

He took some time to answer.

'No, I did not.' He paused 'And what might have led me to think that?' George looked quizzically at me and I was pretty sure that he wasn't play acting.

'You must have seen all of that Nazi stuff in one of the Merchant Bank's two vaults?' I scrutinised his reaction intently.

'Nazi stuff? No. I can assure you that I did not see anything of that nature. I did note that it was unusual for such a small Bank to have two vaults, and that one of them had been so cleverly concealed that it is likely the robbers, you, had inside information about it. We nearly missed it ourselves. So what is this nonsense about Nazis?' There was not a blink or the slightest hint that he knew what I was talking about. He either didn't know or he was a bloody sight better card player than me!

I ignored the question and asked him another. 'And what did you find in that concealed vault when you eventually opened it and got to see inside?'

'Nothing of any significance. It was in this respect as empty as the other vault.'

'So, please bear with me George while I do a recap. This job happened, you say, over the Saturday night Sunday morning but it wasn't until the Monday morning, a whole day later, that your department says it got wind of it. Another day passes before you are put in charge and you fly over to Guernsey. By the time you get there the concealed second vault in the Merchant Bank was closed and, when you finally managed to open it, it was starkers. And nobody, not the police or anybody, indicated anything to make you think that it was not exactly how the thieves left it?'

'Yes, that's a relatively accurate, if brief, summary of events up to that point. Now, what is your point?'

Perhaps somewhat irrationally, I was convinced that George wasn't lying. Assuming that he wasn't, I tried to weigh up this sequence of events alongside what I knew. It seemed likely that when the Island woke up to the aftermath of our raid, somebody tipped off somebody important very, very, quickly that the Merchant Bank had been done over, and that the secret vault and the laundering operation had been discovered, and emptied! This had to be before anyone not involved in the cover-up had a chance to see the stuff. It followed that the informer had got to be one of the local police, quite likely a senior officer. Then somebody, probably the same person, had sufficient clout to organise an immediate and secret clear out of the Nazi vault and for it to be closed and hidden again. It had to be at the moment of discovery because if any non-involved witness had mentioned anything about it to George, it was highly unlikely that he would have forgotten something as unusual as that.

When the news finally reached the mainland, and that took a full day in itself, it took another day before George was put in charge of the operation. Then someone put George, a bit of a kid still wet behind the ears, in charge. Why? Finally, an important somebody, or, more likely, a group of important somebodies, somewhere, had enough influence to enforce a total news blackout. Consequently it was pretty reasonable to assume that only a very small group of co-conspirators had any awareness or knowledge that the Nazi money-laundering operation had been discovered. My link to this probably small group of bastards inevitably lay through, and only through, George. Their orders would have been passed down however many links there were in the chain until they landed on George's lap. Conversely, any reports from George would pass back up the chain to those master-minding the operation. If the aim was to keep it all quiet, there wouldn't be too many links in the chain. If you are hushing something up, the fewer that know anything, the better.

'Can I ask you something George? For this job, are you reporting back to your normal next-in-line, or are you reporting directly to someone right at the top?'

George puffed up like a peacock. 'I can assure you Ronnie, the top, the very top. Why do you ask?'

'No matter,' I replied and continued with my mental ruminations.

There were two facts which told me that whoever they were at the 'top', they had frightening powers and were prepared to use them ruthlessly. Firstly, the murder of two prominent islanders had been covered up with apparently no repercussions. Secondly that a bunch of their foot soldiers, acting under orders, simply watched while one of our mob was tortured to death and another shot through the head. With this sort of power, they would be able to order our immediate execution whenever the fancy took them!

But we were still alive. This meant that they were fearful that we had something that could cause them major grief should it become public knowledge. As long as they continued to believe this we were relatively safe. Once they decided we were not a threat to any of them, we were undertaker's merchandise. If I was right, they needed to be brought into the game. It was time to play another exploratory card. 'What if I told you that I recently established a direct mailing line to Simon Wiesenthal?'

Simon Wiesenthal was a Jew who had survived the Nazi Holocaust. Eighty-nine members of his and his wife's families had not. After the war he founded the Jewish Historical Documentation Centre which was dedicated to bringing Nazi war criminals to justice, wherever they were and whoever they were. He had published a well-known book, 'Head Mufti: agent of the Axis' and I happened to have read it and to know what the bloke was about.

'Wiesenthal? The Nazi hunter?' George seemed genuinely surprised.

'You're a bright lad, George. So you'll know that he's set up this centre to catch the naughty Nazis and their mates who escaped at the end of the war. Anyway, no disrespect intended George, but I suggest that you report this tit-bit of information to your man at the very top before you do something that might nip your blossoming young career in the bud.' I had decided that young George was an ambitious, unscrupulous, company man for whom career advancement, rather than any moral viewpoint, would totally determine what he would do or wouldn't do. This hint that a slip-up on his part might disrupt his career prospects got the desired impact.

George looked at me so as to signal his distrust. He hesitated for a few moments before calling in one of his men.

'Watch him carefully. Do not speak to him nor let him speak to you. If he speaks or tries to speak, hit him, hard, so hard that he can't or won't dare to speak again. Is that clear?'

His hardman shunted to attention and saluted to acknowledge the order. George left.

I had fallen asleep by the time he returned so I have no idea how long he was gone. I was wakened by a rough unlocking of the handcuffs which held me to the chair. The physical relief was enormous. My arms slid forwards. They were totally numb. I tried desperately to move them, to revive some circulation, some feeling, anything. Only vague reminiscences of muscular contractions gave me hope that I would ever be able to move them again.

'Right Ronnie, it's getting late. We all need some sleep so you will be given a bed in one of the rooms here. The room will be well guarded and there are guards and dogs patrolling the grounds, so please do not attempt anything foolish. We'll talk again in the morning.'

'What about Mick and Tony?'

'They will be spending the night here with us too. You may be able to see them in the morning if you continue to co-operate. For now,

good night and sleep well. We have a busy day ahead of us tomorrow.'
He could be a sarcastic bastard.

With that he turns tail and clears off, leaving two of his armed
lackeys to put me to bed.

⌘

The Radio Mast and Sheds.

15 Ten Days to High Noon,

It was well past nine o'clock the next morning when I was hauled from my sleep to bathe and feed. When I looked in the mirror my face was not a pretty sight. It was swollen badly and covered with black and blue bruising from Percy and Eddie's attempts to realign my facial geography. I could barely see out of my left eye and my mouth and nose were so disfigured that I deemed it wise not to even attempt to shave or brush what teeth I had left. My arms had regained some of their former dexterity and so at least I was able to dress myself in the set of clean clothes which had been left for me. After painfully munching through a full English breakfast I was taken to a room where George was sitting alone at a table. He pointed to a bare wooden chair and I was sat down on it. He nodded to my two minders and they left.

'I trust that you slept well Ronnie.'

'Yes thanks.'

'And you've had a good breakfast?'

'Not bad, but no champagne. I do like a drop of champagne on these occasions, helps kill the bacon fat you know.'

'Yes, I'll make a note of that, but I particularly wanted you to have a clear head this morning for a little chat.'

'And what might that be about then?'

'You never stop playing games, do you Ronnie? Even when the game is lost.'

'A game is never lost until they're shovelling the dirt over you and you're the only one who doesn't know.'

'Be that as it may, but while you have been asleep there have been some developments that you ought to know about. Majorie and Mavis, your good wife and her sister, have joined us here at the Hall. We really didn't want to leave them alone worrying about your safety and whereabouts. Similarly we didn't want you to be worrying about them or their whereabouts. Now that they are here, their safety and well-being is entirely in your hands.'

So George is getting into position to turn the family screws if and when necessary. I had prepared myself for this play so I tried hard not to let my face show any sign of emotion, not too difficult given the physical bashing it had taken.

'Well thank you Georgie, it's nice to know that you want to keep us all tucked up snug and warm in your tender care. Are any more of our mates coming to join us?'

'Not for the moment. We think that they're better left to their own devices, to do and go where the fancy takes them. Naturally we are monitoring what they do and where they go, just to make sure that they come to no harm, and to see where they might unwittingly lead us.'

'I've got a lot of mates.'

'Of course you have Ronnie, we're just monitoring those that are of particular interest to us.'

'Such as?'

'Let me see now. Lets start with the so-called Aston Villains 'mob'. Firstly there's Ernest Roberts and his two associates, Terrence Isles and Michael Barnsley, known as 'Ikey and Barney'. This trio of miscreants spend most of their time meandering between the snooker hall, the pub and the Bookies' runners on the Kingstanding circle. Then there's John Cooper and John Davies, known as JC and JD. They prefer to while away their hours in and around Lozells, while Bertram Bates and Stanley Leach seem to flit between Small Heath and Witton having their hair styles and sexual depravations attended to. Shall I go on?'

'Yes, I think so, we don't want to miss anybody out do we?' I wanted to see if he was bluffing. It was a good call. His response told me he was. He'd never make a good card player.

'Some other time perhaps. For the moment there are more important matters I want to discuss with you.'

No mention of Dave and Barry. So while he knows these two exist, he'd even mentioned Dave by name in our exchange yesterday, he doesn't know exactly who they are or where they are. He continued.

'Towards the end of our little chat last night you mentioned Simon Wiesenthal. Why was that?'

'Something to talk about I suppose. Don't know the bloke myself, but I've heard that he's does a good job nobbling Nazi war criminals and those who collaborated with them. Anyway, Mick and me decided to bequeath him some documentation we came by recently that might be of interest to him in his task. It will be passed on to him if either Mick or me, or the both of us, end up playing cards with the grim reaper and lose. Dead I mean, you can only bequeath stuff when you're dead you know.'

I cursed myself. I was getting a bit too cocky. Perhaps that was George's play, but I felt that I had played a surprise trump card far to early.

'Yes, of course.' Said George, stroking his chin in a gesture that was far too old for his young years and which I found incredibly annoying. 'That's very interesting Ronnie, but, for argument's sake, how will this bequest be fulfilled should, heaven forbid, you or Mr. Tibbets meet an untimely or unexpected death?'

'All sorted,' I answered as cheerfully as I could given the situation. 'As soon as news of our deaths, one or both, reaches certain people in Switzerland, they send the documents on to Wiesenthal. He's based in Linz, don't you know. Hitler's home town. How's that for rubbing the Nazi's noses in it?'

George ignored the question. 'Yes I see, but what if, just for example, news of your death doesn't make the headlines or get to Switzerland? And why should it? You're hardly news-worthy. So let's imagine, just for example, that you both simply,' he shrugs his shoulders, 'fade away, you simply ..... disappear.'

'We covered that eventuality too. We have arranged that these folks in Switzerland are to send the documentation on to Wiesenthal if they don't get the right code word from either Mick or me at very specific intervals.' I exuded a concerned attitude. 'It's going to be a great responsibility for us, you know, sticking rigidly to the agreed schedules, remembering the codes and everything, because what's in these documents could cause a lot of important trouble for a lot of important people, and Mick and me are not ones for stirring up important trouble for anyone important, unless, of course, we're forced to.'

'Then why don't you entrust them to someone else?'

'Oh no. We couldn't do that. You see they're like an insurance policy. If we give them up, it's a racing cert that we'll end up dead, all of us probably. If we hang on to them, we might still end up as dead, but at least the insurance will have to pay out.'

George fixed me with an accusing gaze. Quite suddenly he clicks his fingers. A lackey comes to the door.

'Bring Mr. Tibbets in please.'

A couple of minutes later Mick is brought in. He's in much better nick than when I saw him last. Apart from his face, which bore a strikingly blue and purple resemblance to mine, he's looking unusually smart, hair combed, shoes cleaned, all spick and span.

'All right Ronnie,' he beams soon as he sees me. 'You're looking good.'

'All right Mick, you're looking pretty good yourself.' I beam back and wink

Our heartfelt pleasantries didn't go down too well with George.

'Please sit down Mr. Tibbets,' he says curtly and points to a chair alongside mine. Mick sits down on it and his two minders leave. 'Now tell me Mr. Tibbets, without any help or prompting from Ronnie here,' he gives me a warning glance. 'What do you know about Simon Wiesenthal?'

George's eyes flitted between each of us as he listened to Mick basically recount the same story as I had just fed him. Without so much as by your leave, George suddenly claps his hands and four heavyweights come in and he tells them to take us back to our rooms. He was acting like the fucking Gestapo, as if we were totally under his control, which obviously we were, but he was rubbing our noses in it and that got me angry. To me he was an arrogant little wet leg who needed to be brought down a peg or two, and I was going to give it a try. I yelled at him mad with anger. 'You bastard, you let your men stand by and watch Spider being tortured to death and do fuck all to stop Thelma getting her brains blown out.'

I made a dive for him but two of his heavyweight minders got hold of me before I could grab his throat or even land a punch. He recoiled backwards, clearly he was not used to being at the receiving end of physical violence. To give him his due though, he regained his composure pretty smartish once his blokes were nigh on breaking my arms up my back.

'You must learn to control yourself Ronnie. We were overtaken by events, as you yourselves were. Mr. Webb was dead before my men were able to contact me for authorisation to act independently, and

Percy Hammond killing Mrs. Day, in the way he did, had really not been anticipated by anyone at that point; a misjudgement made, I suspect, even by your good selves. It's worth remembering, however, that had you told the Hammonds what they wanted to know, she might still be alive and well today. I assumed that you would tell Hammonds what they, and I, wanted to know before anyone else got hurt. Had you have done so, then my men could have acted. Unfortunately, I underestimated your tenacity and, unfortunately, I also underestimated Percy's impetuosity.' He waved his hand and his storm troopers began to manhandle us out of the room.

Realising that this could be our last chance to communicate directly with each other, Mick called out to me, 'Ronnie, I'll keep totally schtum, you do all the dealing from now on. And don't let the bastards pull any stunts!'

This was a sound move on Mick's part. The best deals are always achieved by one bloke running the show, making the bids and rejecting the offers. More than one and you're into going backwards and forwards to each other, 'shall we, shan't we? What do you think? I dunno, what do you think?' It goes on and on. It's kids' stuff. The opposition see it, play on it, and screw you for it. Leave it all to one who can be trusted and accept whatever he manages to achieve with approval or good grace.

Back in the seclusion of my room, I decided that if I ever got out of this shit, I would some-how get to kill this unfeeling servile servant of the hidden establishment. It was him, and blokes like him, that kept them hidden and in positions of power. I also decided that, given the circumstances, both Mick and me had played our prepared deck as well as could be expected. I laid down on the bed feeling relatively well pleased and began preparing for the next round. I had kept some trump cards and aces back and felt-well placed, but the game was still far from over.

⌘   ⌘   ⌘   ⌘   ⌘   ⌘   ⌘

It was some hours later before I was hauled back to face George again.

'I trust you have regained your normal composure now Ronnie?'

'That was me behaving normally George, believe it. Calm, cool and collected until something, or somebody, upsets me, then, before you know it, there's all hell to play.'

'I'll try to remember that,' George replied taking the piss.

'It will pay you to.'

He smiled contemptuously. 'Is that a threat Ronnie? I do admire your gall Ronnie, albeit misplaced. Anyway, I want you to control your little temper tantrums for a while so that we may discuss things like civilised people. Are you able to do that?'

I didn't answer the patronising bastard. He took my silence as reluctant compliance.

'Good.' He spoke to my handlers, 'Leave us now but stay near in case I have need of you.' This seemed a strange move on George's part. Why was he risking being left alone with me? Easy, to be alone with me. None of his men had been present during any of our previous discussions. He, or whoever was pulling his strings, didn't want anyone who didn't already know of our jaunt to find out about it. They were afraid of any news of it getting out. I didn't hold many aces but at least I was getting to know and understand the hand George was having to play with.

'Now, Ronnie, back to the business in hand. I discussed our little chat with my superiors, but unfortunately your fairy story about Nazis and Swiss contacts fell, shall I say, upon stony ground. They feel that the story is merely the product of a desperate, albeit fertile, mind. I am afraid, therefore, that I have been ordered to hand you, your wife and your other friends over to some of my less civilised colleagues to extract the information my employers need from you.'

'Fair enough,' I say. 'Let's just hope for the sake of who ever is in control of this fiasco that I am bluffing. Funny though isn't it that Mick is suffering from the same delusions as me? Anyway, just get on with it if you're going to, at least me and the others will die with the satisfaction of knowing that we'll have spiked the Nazi bastards who betrayed our country, and still are, while living of the life of Riley off the backs of those they despise.'

'Ronnie, Ronnie.' He tried to feign exasperation. 'All this childish stuff about Nazi collaborators and traitors hiding under the bed doesn't become you. Look, I don't want this to happen any more than you. If only there were some way you could prove to me, to my superiors, that there is some truth in what you say then there's just a chance, only a chance mind, that I might be able to persuade them to spare you, your friends, and indeed your good ladies, any unnecessary, and perhaps prolonged, suffering.'

'I can do that easy enough, but you probably still won't believe it. So that's that then.' I stood up as if I was going to leave. I was giving him a master class in the art of bluff and counter-bluff.

'Wait, wait. Just sit down for a moment Ronnie. Why don't you let me decide if it will be sufficient?' He gestured for me to sit down and I complied showing due reluctance.

'Well I can't prove it just like that, it will take time.' I paused in apparent thought. 'Things have to be put in place. It will take few days at least.'

'Mmmm,' George stroked his chin again in an equally fine display of apparent deep thought. 'How long is a few days?'

'A week should do it, providing you do as I ask and everything works as it should.'

He continued to stroke his chin while drumming the fingers of his other hand on the table. This was indeed a gold medal display of 'deep thought'. He stopped and clasped his hands before him.

'Before I could agree to such a proposal, to prevent any fudging or possible dispute from either side in the event of non-compliance in the future, I need to have a quite specific day and time before or on which you will produce your 'evidence'. You have suggested one week. So, to avoid any future request from you for more time I am prepared to extend that time scale to ten days. I suggest that we agree a deadline of mid-day, that is noon, on Thursday the thirtieth of June. By that time you will have presented me with evidence that fully substantiates your story. You will have no second chance. Can you agree irrevocably to this proposal?'

'Ten days should be plenty enough, but first I have some conditions.' I'm riding high on the way things are going and, so working on the principle that if you don't ask, you don't get, I try what even I thought was an outrageous punt. 'I want you to let me and Marg be together while we wait for the proof to arrive and for Mick and Mavis to be together too.'

'I hope your request is not what this is all about Ronnie, just gaining a little time to be with your wife, because if it is, and you are just messing me about, Ronnie, I swear to God that I won't have to get someone else to loosen your tongue, I'll do it myself!'

'You agree then?'

'Before I consent Ronnie, I must give you some friendly advice. Once my employers have entered into an agreement, albeit through me, or indeed anyone, the conditions are absolute and binding to the letter. Their rule is 'nothing in moderation'. No changes or deviations, no matter how slight, will be acceptable. It is the only way that our bond is universally accepted. If we agree, you must understand that, no matter what the cost to either party, there will be no second chance to re-negotiate what is a binding contract, in any way, once the deadline has been passed. You understand?'

'Perfectly.'

'It is agreed then,' he said. In response, I held my hand out towards him to shake on, and so seal, the deal. He declined to take it.

'It is not necessary to shake hands. It is a moronic and futile ritual intended to secure loyalty and compliance from those who cannot be fully trusted. Am I not to trust you Ronnie?' I withdrew my outstretched hand. 'You have until mid-day on the thirtieth. Until then, you and Mr. Tibbets will enjoy the company of your good ladies. Now what do I have to do to set the wheels in motion to get this proof?'

'You must put an announcement in the "Situations" column of the London Evening News. It must read exactly as I say it.'

George picked up a pen and pad.

'Communications manager, put that in bold, wanted to initiate links with small Swiss company dealing in gold and foreign currency. Early reply urgently required.'

'Is that it?'

'Yes. Run it every night until we get a reply.'

'But there's no contact address or phone number for a reply.'

'So only the people who have been looking for it will apply.'

'And how will they apply or reply?'

'They will eventually reply through the "Lost and Found" column in the same paper. There will be an announcement that someone has recently found a brief case full of documents which they will be returning to an address in Linz, via Geneva, if they are not claimed beforehand by the rightful owner. Words to that effect anyway.'

It was some time before George replied. He looked me up and down, he stared at his note pad, the ceiling and out of the window, he pursed his lips and finally he spoke.

'I must remind you, Ronnie, of the conditions underpinning any agreements we enter into. Should this be simply a ploy to gain time, you and your close associates will not be given another chance whatever the consequences. The lid has been held on this thing for far too long for you to play cat and mouse games with us. If this is a fool's errand, it will be your last.'

'Fair enough. Now do I get to see my missus?'

'She will be brought to your room.' He waved his hand and his minders came in to take me back to my room.

A few minutes later Marge joined me and, after some quick reunion pleasantries, we made up for lost time with a closer reunion celebration on the bed. Further along the corridor, although I didn't know it then, Mick and Mavis were enjoying similar conjugal delights!

16 Wheeler's Deal

The next day, a copy of the previous day's Evening News, late edition, was delivered to our room. In the 'Situations' column there was an advertisement for a 'Communications manager', just as I had directed. To have got the ad published in what must have been just a few hours was another small reminder of the power and influence of the organisation at George's disposal. We were also given a printed time-table for our day, including meal times, when we would be allowed out of our room to take exercise and fresh air in the grounds, and even bloody lights out and wake up! From our room, we would sometimes see Mick and Mavis strolling in the grounds, so they were obviously enduring a similar prison programme as us. We never caught sight of Tony but decided that he would be somewhere in the house recovering from the terrible beating he'd taken from the brothers.

From our point of view though, apart from actually being interned against our will and the early lights out bit, it was like being in a first class hotel. Marge and I could have almost anything we wanted, including high-quality booze. We decided to go easy on the booze, however, as we thought that the purpose of it, like the relatively benevolent regime, was probably intended to loosen our tongues. We viewed everything with suspicion and never spoke about the raid while in our room. Although we searched high and low for a bug, we were never able to find one. We never-the-less concluded that the safest strategy was to assume that there had to be one somewhere. The thought of people listening in to everything we said or did had the unexpected bonus of the heightened passions inevitably aroused by necessarily silent and surreptitious love making!

It was late evening on the following Saturday when I was taken alone to see George again. He was sat at the same table as our last meeting and I was directed to the same chair in front of it. He was holding a copy of that evening's News.

'Hello again Ronnie. I trust that you are well and that everything has been done to make your stay with us as comfortable as possible.'

'Nearly as good as the Hilton,' I replied sarcastically.

'Good,' he replies without so much as a blink. 'I have something that you might be interested to see.'

He pushed the newspaper towards me for me to see. 'Look under "Lost and Found", I think that the third or fourth item down may interest, perhaps even surprise, you.'

'I know where to look.' What I read, however, was not what I was expecting and it caused a brief moment of panic. 'Brief case documents lost. Owners now resident in SA, no further contact possible'. I read it and re-read it. My initial instinct was to scream out 'the bastards', but somehow I retrained myself, controlled my usual instantaneous anger. The stakes were too high to blow it in a fit of vengeful pique. I mentally forced myself to slow down, to think calmly, to work it through rationally. I put the paper back on the desk and pushed it back to George as though nothing was amiss. A golden rule of mine is that if you don't know what to do or say, do nothing and say nowt. So I remained silent. The silence paid off and George was wrong-footed.

'It isn't quite the message you were expecting, is it Ronnie? It seems that your contacts may have taken themselves off to SA, which is presumably South America. And they say there's honour among thieves. Now where does that leave us and our agreement?'

Although he was shaking his head in empathy there was a slight hint of triumph in George's manner. Why? I was devastated and so should he be, but he wasn't. Even as dim as I thought he was, he must have worked out that loss of contact with my contacts could mean that the materials he had been ordered to retrieve would remain out there, beyond his or my reach. The ultimate consequence of this was that they could end up anywhere and with anyone. He should be as concerned as me, if not more so. This realisation brought my mind back on course.

The situation was that George knew that he hadn't got tabs on two of our lot, Barry and Dave, although he knew that one was called Dave. He had probably worked out that I, we, were dependent on these two to activate the release of the documents to Wiesenthal if and when we decided the time had come. I reasoned that George had played a dummy card. If I believed that our two had reneged on the deal and had simply cleared off with the loot leaving the rest of us to face the music, I might seek redemption by telling all.

What he didn't know, however, was that although Mick and me had a lot of faith in our two recently acquired London mates, we hadn't known them long enough and we didn't know them well enough for us to let our lives depend simply upon any loyalty they might have developed for us. They were two lads we had done a job with, not necessarily trustworthy mates. So when we set up our escape and survival contingency plan we arranged for Kenny up in Arnhill to take one of our trucks which we had loaded with paper currency to Switzerland. Once there he deposited the whole lot into an account Mick and me had opened in one of Switzerland's small high security banks. The gold, jewellery and the remainder of the cash remained stashed in the other truck and stayed in Kenny's shed. We then set up a variety of accounts for each of the lads, one of which would drip feed Barry and Dave's share of the haul over a period of years into an account of their choosing. The feed would only continue if they did their duty by us, which was to respond to the schedule of contacts Mick and me had drawn up. With such enormous wealth at stake in the long term they would be unlikely to abandon us and bugger off to South America, at least not within the first few years!

A key part of our deal was that if we ever had to contact them via the London News, they must bugger off to Spain post-haste. Once in Spain they could live the good life on their continuous pay-out with no chance of extradition! I decided to play a blind card to parry George's dummy.

'Now who is playing games? Do you honestly think I'm stupid enough to fall for this childish stunt?' It was a considered gamble and I feigned anger. I took another gamble. 'The real reply was in last night's paper wasn't it? I'm telling you straight George, if you don't want the stuff getting out, you had better start dealing from the top of the deck right now!' The gamble paid off!

'OK! OK! Ronnie, calm down, it was just another way to make sure you're telling the truth. OK?' I nodded to indicate reluctant acknowledgement.

'So you have proved that you have established a system of contacts to forward something or other on to people such as Wiesenthal for some purpose. What I don't know is the exact nature of the materials you claim to have. For all I know you may not have anything that is of interest to my superiors. I need to know, perhaps see, what it is you claim to have. Can you do that for me?'

George was a trier, an inept one, but a trier all the same. Did he really think that, given our situation I would show him what we had? Maybe. I thought a surprise play was due.

'Much more easily than you would think George. Follow me.' I got to my feet and headed for the door. I opened it but a couple of heavyweights blocked my way. George waved them back. The trio followed me out of the house and into the nearest of Tony's barns. I went to one of the corners, brushed aside a pile of old wood and told George to get one of his lackeys to dig there. In no time at all, he had unearthed a steel ammunition box. He lugged it back to George's interrogation room, dumped it on the desk and left. George opened the box. In it were dozens of high resolution photographs of the most damning documentation we had taken from the vault. George began to scrutinise them one by one. 'And that's just some of the juicier bits,' I said.

George nodded and continued to pore over them in silence. Occasionally his lips would purse, or his forehead crease to a frown. I tried to imagine whose names he was either recognising or discovering in the 'who's who' of British traitors I had presented him with. Those linked to Windsor-Simpson circle perhaps? John Amery's connections? Top brass in the Tory party, some right at the heart of the Government? Prominent members of the international Catholic Church? Wodehouse, Metcalfe, Ramsey, Becket, Halifax or his puppet Bryant? Promoters of the traitorous 'British Free Corps'? Or perhaps he was looking at the names and locations of some of the top Nazi criminals still on the run? I could only speculate, but it did make me appreciate the number of English top dogs and fat cats at risk if the documents we had ever got into the limelight. George kept going for the best part of an hour before he spoke to me again.

'I have to commend you on your foresight and initiative Ronnie. You seem to have thought of everything. I am genuinely impressed at the precautions you have taken without, I presume, necessarily knowing that anyone was on to you. Did you know we were on to you?'

'Not for definite, but when there was a total news blackout, Mick and me concluded that for us, no news was bad news, and so we decided we ought to take out some insurance.'

George nodded with, I felt, begrudging appreciation. He looked at his watch.

'It's getting too late to do anything now. We will talk in the morning. Goodnight Ronnie.'

Before I have a chance to answer, he snaps his fingers and the heavyweights entered and took me back to my room, and to Marg.

⌘   ⌘   ⌘   ⌘   ⌘   ⌘   ⌘

Immediately after breakfast next morning I was taken back to George's room. George did not beat about the bush. He told me that his job was to ensure that none of the documentation we had would ever be made available to foreign governments or made known to the British electorate. I replied that my job was to ensure the health and safety of my crowd, and that meant each of us staying alive and out of prison. And this could only be guaranteed as long as either Mick or me retained complete control over if or when the documentation was released upon an unsuspecting and vengeful world. George's opening gambit was that this was impossible, and followed up with a series of testing and then blustering threats. These were easily parried. Provided I kept my cool and refused to shift on this key point, I had not just a strong hand but a winning hand. These negotiations would not have been taking place if I had anything less!

Having failed with the stick approach he tried the carrot. He even offered me a well paid 'job' in his 'department' which he said was some sort of covert cell buried in one of the Intelligence services. He praised me up no-end. He said I had all the skills and abilities they were looking for, able to think and plan head, to operate effectively under stress, to develop strategic policy, a leader of men, Hallelujah Hallelujah, bull-shit, bull-shit! And in return, all I would have to do was hand over the original documents!

To even consider that I might be taken in by this crap shows that in truth he thought that I was some sort of dickhead, because only a dickhead would hand over the only thing that was keeping him and those closest to him alive. Mick and me had long adopted and rigidly stuck to what we called the 'Inca Principle'. The story goes that when the Spanish conquered the South American Incas, one of the Inca chiefs offered them a room filled with gold if they would let him live. The Spanish naturally accepted his generous offer but as soon as he gave them the gold, they killed him and, for good measure, all the rest of the Inca chiefs too! I thought it timely to relate this little tale to George, although he didn't seem at all impressed with this tit-bit of European imperialist history.

The 'game' played on for two days solid. The only breaks were for food, sleep, toileting and George's frequent need to contact his 'employers' for guidance as to the latitude available to him. While he was going backwards and forwards 'consulting', I was able to negotiate alone. Each time he 'consulted', he unwittingly gave me valuable information about their lines of defence and attack. As my armoury improved, so the 'consultations' became even more frequent and my hopes for winning the game rose.

I arrived on the morning of the third day expecting to continue the negotiations. George, however, without ado handed me a single typed sheet of paper. It was headed, 'The Agreement.'

'Here is our proposal for an agreement. Read it carefully and tell me if you accept the terms and conditions set out therein in their entirety and without exception.'

The paper set out, in very precise and unambiguous terms without any unnecessary legalese or jargon, the agreements George and I had provisionally reached over the previous two days. There should be no misunderstandings on any one's part as to exactly what they meant and what they required from each party.

'There's no mention of Percy?' I put it as a question rather than a statement of fact.

'I think it best that Mr Hammond is not referred to in any way in the agreement.'

'Well he'll have to be dealt with, he's the proverbial mad dog.'

'That he is and I assure you, Ronnie, he will be dealt with. You will just have to trust me on that one. Do you find the contract acceptable otherwise?'

'Yes, given our situation I can't complain.'

'Do you think that the conditions will be acceptable to all of your colleagues?'

'To be honest George, they don't have a choice. If they don't like it, we can strike their names off the list, and they can deal with you and your masters on their own.'

'You should have been a politician Ronnie, you would have gone far. I will assemble your associates here tomorrow at two o'clock and you can present it to them.'

⌘   ⌘   ⌘   ⌘   ⌘   ⌘   ⌘

The next day at two o'clock precisely, Marg and I were taken to the 'Terrace Lounge' where Tony had first put the plan to us all those months ago. All of our mob were there. Mick and Mavis on the front row with Tony alongside them looking a lot better than when I saw him last. He even managed a smile. A banter of light-hearted greetings broke out. George stood silently at the front until it had subsided. He explained precisely and concisely why they, we, had all been rounded up and that I was to propose a contract to them which they could agree, or not agree, to enter into. He emphasised there could be no half-way houses or amendments; it was a case of take it or leave it. With that, he abruptly left the room, leaving me in charge.

As he left, a noisy hubbub filled the room and I had to quieten everyone down before I could begin.

'Firstly lads, it's good to see you all again, although it's a pity it isn't under happier circumstances. Now this place has got to be bugged, so don't mention anything or, more importantly, anyone I don't mention from here on in. OK?' Surprisingly, there's no back chat or barracking.

'So let's get down to business. You know we've been rumbled big-time otherwise you wouldn't be here. You probably also know that getting rumbled for what we pulled off spells big trouble. Forget the amount we nicked, the big trouble comes from the two blokes killed by the Hammonds during the job, the copper and a bank manager. Now just because none of us actually did the killing doesn't mean that our necks are not in the noose. The moment Percy shot that copper, in the eyes of the law, just from being there, we are all guilty of premeditated murder. So, if any of us, and I mean any of us, get out of this alive, that in itself is a fucking great bonus. Keep that firmly in mind while you're listening to what I've got to say.'

I'd never known our mob be so quiet and attentive; even Barney

177

wasn't tossing in his usual two-penny's worth. I went through how Mick and me had brought back the Nazi documentation, and how we had set things up so that we might have a bargaining tool to save our necks if things went horribly wrong. It was as well we did, because I had been able to use the stuff to do just that. I had reached an agreement with George and provided they accepted it and stuck rigidly to it, we should all be able to live out the rest of our mortal lives in relative comfort. They were each given a copy of the contract setting out the details of the agreement. In order to acknowledge their acceptance of the terms in full, they were to sign it.

The basic terms were fairly straight-forward. They would be allowed to walk free but they must not make contact in any shape or form with any of the other signatories to the agreement. The exceptions to this were me in relation to Marg, and Mick in relation to Mavis. We could all engage in any legitimate business activity of our choosing, but we must cease all criminal activity. We must not reveal or discuss any aspect of the Guernsey raid with anyone, at any time, anywhere. Within three months, we must move to live beyond Birmingham's city boundaries and not within twenty miles of another signatory. We must never leave, or attempt to leave, the country.

In return, besides staying out of nick, we would each initially receive an annual income of five thousand pounds per year, subject to tax, until the deaths of both Mick and me. This money was to come from the cash we had already deposited in the Swiss Bank. This income would be reviewed every five years and adjusted, if and when necessary, in line with inflation. Everything else we had taken was to be returned. This included what currency remained, the gold bullion, all contents of the safe deposit boxes and the jewellery, so joyously thrown into the back of the Ducks, prior to our departure from the island. On completion, our homes would be thoroughly searched. Should anything be found that had not been handed over or declared prior to the search, no matter how small or insignificant, it would be considered as a breach of contract with one inevitable consequence: death! The word used in the contract was 'elimination'. It was a blatant euphemism for execution. Despite this terminal clause, however, it was a bloody good deal and showed just how far the powers that be will go, or what they will sacrifice, to protect their own backsides.

'What if we take no notice once we're out of here and just do a runner?' It's no surprise that it was Bertie Bates who asked the question.

I refused to answer it because George said that it was imperative that he would deal with that anticipated question himself later. At this point, and very timely, he walks in followed by two masked heavies carrying Percy who is bound bodily to a chair. George stands at the front and the two heavies dump Percy and the chair up there too. They stand either side of him. Percy breaks into a smile when he sees us, a very un-Percy like reaction.

'All right lads, fancy seeing you lot here!'

George takes over before anyone can respond.

'I will answer the last question you put to Mr. Wheeler, Mr. Bates, by way of a practical demonstration, using Mr. Hammond here as an example. Unfortunately, Mr. Hammond cannot be party to our agreement. This is primarily because it was he and his brother Edward who murdered two people in cold blood during your raid and badly injured another. Murder is one of the few crimes in our society which carries the death penalty. It is a crime which our state cannot condone or show any quality of mercy. Consequently, Percival Hammond has been condemned to die in a manner appropriate to his crime. Do you have anything to say Mr. Hammond before the sentence is discharged?'

Percy looked at George in total bewilderment.

'Bollocks you stupid bastard. You can't do fucking anything to me here.'

'And that is all you have to say Mr. Hammond? This is your last chance.' George said quietly.

Percy, totally misreading his predicament, snarled back at George. 'What else is there to say you prat?' He then looked to us and shook his head in mock disbelief.

'So be it,' said George, and nodded to the two heavies on either side of Percy. One moved behind Percy, put one arm around Percy's chest and pulled his head back by the hair. The other heavy moved in from the side, pulled out what looked like a fifteen-inch bayonet from a scabbard on his belt and, with a single sweep, slashed Percy's throat from side to side. His blood gushed out in pulsating torrents. The girls screamed out in horror, while me and the lads shouted out involuntary and undirected abuse in complete surprise and agitated shock.

The heavy let go of Percy's head which slumped forward so that his blood spurted downwards over his own body and, presumably for a few moments at least, before his own still-conscious eyes. George watched impassively until Percy's blood-drenched body ceased convulsing in the chair. What we had witnessed was a clinical re-enactment of Percy and Eddie's slaying of Adrian Mordant. Apart from the quiet muted sounds of the girls crying, the room was charged with the electrifying silence of shock.

'There is the answer to your question, Mr. Bates. Should you 'do a runner' as you call it, should you run to the furthest corner of the world, you will be hunted down like a dog and executed like one. Why? Because, technically, you are all guilty of murder and should rightly be hanged by the neck until you are dead. Because of the agreement I have made with Mr. Wheeler, and perhaps with yourselves, by tomorrow you will have an opportunity to escape this particular fate. Should you not accept it or should you not adhere rigidly to the conditions laid out in it you will be eliminated without a trial and without delay.'

'You can't just go around killing people as and when you like,' Bertie retorted, on his feet and pointing aggressively at George. 'Somebody somewhere will begin to notice and start to ask questions and seek answers.'

'Unfortunately I can and I do, Mr. Bates. And the circumstances of any deaths I authorise will never, I can assure you, arouse the suspicions or concerns of anyone in authority. Would you care for another demonstration Mr. Bates?'

Bertie paled and sat down. George scanned the rest of us and it was clear that no-one was going to argue. He moved away a little to avoid the spreading pool of Percy's blood and continued with his spiel.

'You will all be staying here with us tonight. Spend your time this evening mindfully considering the terms and conditions of the contract that has been put before you. With your breakfast tomorrow, you will be give a copy of the morning edition of the Birmingham Post. In it you will find a news item concerning the deaths of Percy and Eddie. I suggest that you digest that news as carefully as you will your breakfast. With that prospect gentlemen, and ladies, we will all adjourn to our quarters for the night. I'm afraid that some of you will be billeted in tents but as ex-soldiers I am sure that won't stop you getting a good night's sleep. You will meet again in this room at ten a.m. tomorrow and I will join you at ten-thirty. Until then I bid you all goodnight.'

And with that, George strode out of the room followed closely by his two masked heavies carting out Percy's blood-drenched body, still strapped to the chair, with them!

⌘ ⌘ ⌘ ⌘ ⌘ ⌘ ⌘

The next morning, as promised, a copy of the Brummie Post was served up with our breakfast. I flipped through the pages until I spotted a minor headline on one of the inside pages, 'Brothers die in tragic accident'. This would be it. It reported that a car had 'plunged into the River Seven near Bewdley late on Sunday evening. An eye witness to the accident said that the car was travelling at high speed when it failed to make a turn at the town's main bridge. The car crashed through a fence before flying several yards out into the river. It sank immediately on impact. Police frogmen located the vehicle latter that day and found the bodies of two men still trapped inside. The men were two brothers, Percival and Edward Hammond of New Town Row, in the Aston district of Birmingham. An autopsy found that both men had very high levels of alcohol in their blood at the time of the accident. It is believed that Percival was driving the vehicle. A police statement said that an inquest would be held but it was believed that two deaths were the result of a tragic accident. Relatives have been informed.' End of story!

So that was it. George and his soldiers riddle Eddie with bullets, cut Percy's throat from ear to ear and their deaths are reported as a road accident with no questions asked. There was even a bloody eye-witness! Another thing struck me. To have been in time to be reported in that morning's edition, the story must have been with the Post well before Percy had uttered his final farewell; 'what else is there to say?' George had demonstrated that he could have anyone killed, anywhere, anytime, and no-one would or could cause a fuss. He could also have any death reported and recorded exactly as he wished. He had already told me, for example, that Thelma's death, Mrs. Day as he called her, would be decreed the result of a coronary attack following an accidental fall. Because of his insignificance, Mr. Webb's passing would not be reported but it would be recorded by the coroner's office as 'death by misadventure'. George had also demonstrated, beyond any reasonable doubt, the ultimate power of an ultimately corrupt group within an acquiescent establishment.

As ordained by George, we all met again in the 'terrace lounge' at ten o'clock. Everyone had an opportunity to have their say about the agreement and the significance of Percy's execution and the legal cover-up. In the brief half an hour we had to discuss it amongst ourselves was unanimously conceded that, given the circumstances, the deal on offer represented a major achievement on my part. It was therefore concluded that everyone should sign their acceptance of it there and then so as not to risk any last minute retraction by George because of prevarication or protracted negotiations on our part. At ten thirty prompt George joined us. He just walked in without so much as a by your leave, kiss me arse or bugger you. It was just another way of ramming home his current dominance and control over us.

'Good morning ladies and gentlemen. I trust that you have all slept well and have arrived at a conclusion regarding the proposed contract. So to business, has each of you reached your own individual decision?' He was a condescending bastard.

I stood up and handed him the signed agreements which he took from me. This seemed to surprise him. I suspect that he had assumed that we could not have reached a unanimous agreement in the short time given to us.

'Is this everyone?' he asked.

'Yes, it is. We have all signed and accepted it without reservation.'

George smiled with that smirk of triumphalism he was prone to.

'Good.' He turned to address everyone. 'There now exists a binding agreement between my employers and yourselves. My department will ensure that each party will adhere to the terms of the contract rigidly and steadfastly. I must remind you that the consequence of any non-compliance on your part, no matter how small, will not be tolerated and will result in an immediate order to effect your elimination. I, personally, look forward with great anticipation to receiving or giving such an order. In my personal view, every single one of you is guilty of heinous crimes which, in more normal times, would result in your being hanged by the neck until you are dead. You have unfortunately, but hopefully only temporarily, escaped such a fate. In assurance of this, you will live under life-long surveillance and monitoring by my department. For practical reasons this cannot be continuous, that is covering every minute of every day, as I would like. It will, however, be systematically randomised so that, should you become aware of being observed, you will not be able to identify a discernible pattern and hence attempt to act accordingly. I can assure you that neither I, nor my successors, will show any mercy or leniency whatsoever.'

He paused and looked at each of us in turn. 'Personally I despise each and every one of you, most particularly Mr. Wheeler and Mr. Tibbetts who have conspired to secure your freedom. In one hour you will be free to leave, at ten minute intervals, in the alphabetical order of your surnames. You will each be accompanied by two of my men who will collect any item from the raid, no matter how insignificant, you still have in your possession. To avoid arousing any suspicions in the short term, you will all attend the funerals of Percival and Edward Hammond. They are to be cremated at two o'clock on Monday the fourth of July at Perry Barr crematorium. The story you will tell to your so-called friends and any mourners is that you have won a large sum on the football pools as a syndicate and, consequently, you will be moving house as soon as possible. With that being said, there is nothing to add or discuss. In anticipation of us meeting again, I wish you au revoir.' With that, as was his way, George strode out of the room looking neither left nor right.

Given no real chance to speak to each other we were shunted back to our rooms, no good-byes, no escape celebrations, no nothing. An hour later Bertie Bates left with two henchmen, and the rest of us followed at ten minute intervals, with the euphoria of escape subdued by a foreboding of the future and the impending loss of life-long friendships.

17 An Open Prison

Our story should, or could, have ended there, but inevitably time and fate, those two uncontrollable, unmerciful collaborators, again conspired that it would not be so. It was less than three years later, on May the fourth, nineteen fifty-seven, that Ikey and Barney were the first to experience the fatal consequence of violating the terms of the agreement and defying George's explicit and dire warnings. Sod's law had decreed that Aston Villa were to play Manchester United in the FA cup final at Wembley and, somehow, these two loveable bastards had managed to get tickets. It was something these two avid supporters of the good life and Aston Villa could not miss and I reckon they just decided to take a chance. Villa won the cup by two goals to one after Peter McParland nutted the United keeper, Ray Wood, early on and put him out of the game. But the lads barely had time to enjoy a post-match victory piss-up before they were allegedly involved in a street brawl with rival fans and were so beaten up that they died later from their injuries. The police never did manage to arrest the other parties involved or indeed find any witnesses of the incident. The initial interest of the press soon faded and they became another fable in the catalogue of unsolved killings.

I learned of their deaths from George by telephone. He explained that even before the cup final, Ikey and Barney had been seen out and about together as if the agreement no longer existed. Through a range of mutual contacts I knew this to be true, and had even asked a close associate to remind them that they had certain obligations to fulfil. Apparently to no avail. George told me that their contract had consequently been terminated. I flew into a rage but George had a winning hand. He had stuck rigidly to his side of the bargain. Consequently, what had happened was entirely due to Ikey and Barney's violation of the contract. They were not even attempting to hide their jaunts out together. It was as if they were either testing George's will or flaunting their rejection of the contract. If George had not acted as per the agreement, then why should any other of the signatories feel bound by it? His case was that, given these circumstances, neither Mick nor I had any justification under the terms of the contract to initiate the release of any of the incriminating documentation.

Logically I had to agree, but I welled up in deep anger and frustration. As I put the phone down I speculated as to which of the lads would be next. My fatal prediction was that it would be Stan Leach and Bertie Bates. They were two more of life's great chancers, the mischievous goblins I had watched looking back through Gert's mirror outside the J&S jewellers. And so it was, despite the fact that whenever an opportunity arose I sent them blunt reminders of the terminal terms of the contract. It was all to no avail, and on the eleventh of January nineteen sixty-one I had another phone call from George. He explained in great detail why the contract with Stan and Bertie had also been terminated.

Perhaps buoyed up by the revelries of Christmas and the New Year, they had been out on the spree together and crashed their car on the way home and had died from their injuries. Naturally they were both found to be drunk, and an unchallenged coroner's verdict a couple of weeks later recorded their deaths as accidental. Their passing was largely ignored by the national and local media, which was primarily concerned on that day with an announcement by British Rail that it had ordered an enquiry into why the Queen's train had broken down and had delayed her by more than an hour! How terrible for her! I wondered if, after sending my condolences to Stan and Bert's distraught families, I should register my deep sorrow to the Queen for the terrible inconvenience she had suffered. But George had made his point.

Although others of the raid's Villains died at various intervals over the coming years, I do not think they were slaughtered on George's orders. Tony, poor bugger, never really recovered from the effects and consequences of the Hammond's torture session and went out of his mind. He ended his years in Rubery Hill Mental Hospital which is on the outskirts of Brum. George allowed me to visit him on three occasions. During these visits he talked incessantly about the raid, the deaths and the mutilations. He did so with the detached air of an uninspired history teacher, complete with unrealistic exaggerations designed to excite or impress his disinterested, mostly mad, listeners. Apparently he talked of little else to the other inmates and staff, who viewed his stories simply as symptoms of his madness. There was no danger and so George let him live. He unexpectedly committed suicide in the early hours of Sunday the sixth of June, nineteen sixty-five. He slit his own throat. It was eleven years to the day and almost to the hour of Adrian Mordant's death. George allowed both Mick and me to go to the funeral, provided we stayed apart during the proceedings.

The remainder lived to reasonable old age in relative comfort and died off naturally one by one. The income we received meant we didn't need to work but most of us found life intolerable without ambition or purpose, and so we occupied ourselves in various business enterprises. I threw myself into my transport business and Mick did likewise with his industrial cleaning venture. Such was our success, that the income from the raid became little more than pocket money for either of us. John Davies went into the wholesale haberdashery trade and did well, while his mate John Cooper dabbled in farming but didn't make much money doing it. Ernie Roberts spent most of his time at the dog or horse tracks backing losers, and gave away the rest of his money in dubious card games. Although he was nearly always skint, a rare experience for him when Ikey and Barney were his accomplices, he was probably the happiest of the lot of us left alive here at home. Dave Treadwell and Barry Whittemore remained in Spain drawing their cut, living the good life and reading the adverts in the London Post. The last ad they, or one of them, put in for Mick or me was in June, nineteen ninety-seven. My Marg died two years ago from a cancer.

You might think from this brief review of how we all fared that I would be well pleased with my 'achievement' of nailing the deal. Initially, the others in our mob, despite a few niggles, were over the moon. But for me, right from when we first discovered the documents, it grated greatly that the guilty British establishment bastards fingered in them were never brought to trial or punished for their collaboration or treason. With the passing of time this feeling of guilt, that we had not made the evidence to convict them known, grew. I began to feel that in keeping schtum I was no better than the collaborators and traitors themselves. Keeping the evidence quiet was also in effect aiding and abetting the Nazi criminals still on the run. An example of this was when the Israelis finally got their hands on Adolf

Eichman, an arch Nazi criminal, in nineteen-sixty. Although I was delighted with the news of his capture, I also felt ashamed that had we released our documents back in nineteen fifty-four he might have hung from a noose that much sooner.

But George had cleverly trapped me within the contract. I could not release the stuff to resolve my own personal feelings of guilt, for to have done so would have meant the death of Marg and of all of those I still think of as 'mates'. It also became obvious that as the years slipped by, with every death of an unexposed British traitor or collaborator, our 'evidence' became less relevant and less valuable.

By nineteen seventy-three, West Germany had been admitted to NATO, the EEC and the UN. Everyone, except the Israelis and Russians, wanted to forget the war, and particularly the terrible horrors of Nazi war crimes. It was a time to forgive and forget for those who had little, personally, to forgive or forget. Those of us who could remember and, because of that, refused to forgive or forget, were regarded as bitter, old, revengeful men, out of time and out of place. It seemed more and more likely that as the years passed into decades, few would have taken a blind bit of notice, even less cared a toss, if we had have released the documents. The only consequence of their release would have been our funerals.

George rang periodically to remind me that the contract still held good. Every five years, on the first of April, he would tell me what the indexed-linked increase to the pay-outs was to be. When I couldn't understand why he persevered with the deal, I tried to negotiate bringing it all to an end but he would have none of it. The bond must be honoured to the letter, without let or hindrance. There was no question of 'getting out' either for those on his side or for those on our side. It was a situation of 'till death us do part'.

With every passing year, I realised more and more that we were prisoners in an open jail. I longed to see the world. To see New York, Las Vegas, Paris, Sidney, any doss hole as long as it was somewhere out of the UK. Not being able to go, made me desperate to go. Similarly I wanted to contact old mates, actually go into old haunts, but I could not.

I also began to question if we would have all gone to feed the hangman's noose anyway. At the time the public outcry over the topping of Bentley the year before was still going strong, so would they have dared to hang so many of us who hadn't actually committed the murders, especially in view of the number of Nazi collaborators, traitors and criminals we would have exposed? I don't know, but probably not. What was hardest for me to accept was that I was the only one who had been actually there when both of the murders had happened. Mick had been there when the brothers did for Mordant, but I was the only one who was in at both killings. So, apart from the brothers, Mick and me were the only ones who might have come face-to-face with the hangman. The others would have served a few years in nick and been free thereafter. Ikey, Barney, Stan and Bertie might have lived to a decent old age. Even Mick and me might have got off with jail. We might even have become celebrities, making a fortune selling our stories, who knows? Would that have saved Tony from going mad? And for fuck's sake, to top it all, Mick and me were the only ones who even knew about the Nazi documentation, let alone know what was in it. So in reality, the others weren't even a possible threat to George and his masters.

The more I thought about it, the more I realised that George and his masters had out-played me. For me, that thought in particular was not a happy one, nor was the thought that I had unconsciously saved my own skin by unwittingly sacrificing the others. And recalling what Mavis had said to me at Mick's funeral, only a few days ago, made me even less happy. 'I know you pulled off the deal Ronnie and that we all agreed it, but I sometimes think we'd have all been better off to have done our time, at least we'd have all gone down in history like Tony wanted and had something of a life when we got out. That bastard George squeezed the life out of Mick, out of all of us for that matter and out of what we did.' Mavis was right and I have decided to fulfil my promise to her when I said, 'I'll see what I can do'. It would be like old times; it would revive the grey matter, and it would be a great way to go!

188

18 The End Game

15 May, 2001.

On more-or-less finishing writing our story, my hatred for George and what he represented, so long repressed, so long matured, erupted. Perhaps it was writing this, recalling what we did, reliving it in such detail, analysing it and thinking it through step by step, I don't know, but I resolved to see if I could get some recompense for the lads who died. I needed to make contact with George. I phoned Mavis.

'Hello Mavis. It's me, Ronnie.'

'Ronnie? What's the matter? You know we're not supposed to get in touch with each other.'

'I know, but remember what I said at Mick's funeral, sod it.' I paused before continuing, as if I was uncertain about what to say. 'Mavis, I've been mulling over what you said at the funeral, and I think the time's come to release the documents. I want to know what you think before I do it.'

'You know what will happen if you do?'

'I know, and that's why I'm asking you first. But I'm beginning to wonder if, well you never know, there's nothing in it for George now to see us two off, despite what he said to you after Mick died.'

'I think he still means it, he's so bloody vindictive.'

'Well, what about you having a think about it for a couple of days. I won't be able to get the ad in the paper for this Wednesday, so it will have to be the week after. What I'm saying is that you, we, don't have to make our minds up right here and now. I'm ready to do it now, whatever, and to be honest I think we owe it to the others.'

Mavis agreed to think it over and after a bit of chit-chat I put the phone down. I was all prepared, so there was nothing to do now except wait to see if George had taken the bait.

Two days later, nothing had happened so I phoned Mavis again. She agreed it was worth the risk. Once it was agreed, we chatted about old times. It was the reminiscing of two old friends condemned to die. It was a joyous celebration of trivial but life justifying moments. It was also distressingly painful to know that we might never share such moments again. We talked, gossiped really, for more than two hours and we were still reluctant to let go when I finally put the phone down. Two hours later, George called.

'Hello Ronnie, it's George.'

'George? George? I thought you were dead!'

'No you didn't, Ronnie, you know as well as I do that I visited Mrs. Tibbets after the sad death of her husband Michael.'

'Oh yes, I'd already forgotten about that. Old age you know. Anyway, I'm glad you rang George because I'd like to have a word with you, a face-to-face meeting again, here at my place, before I do something perhaps I shouldn't.'

'Well why don't we talk about it now?'

'It's not the same is it, not the same as talking face-to-face? Things never get sorted out over the phone as well as they do when you actually meet up.'

'Well, I am rather busy right now Ronnie, I've moved several rungs up the ladder since we last met. I'm only involved with your case now when something comes up that I ought to know about. This is just a call to see how things are going with you. I could get someone else to see you if you like but, remember, re-negotiation of the contract is not a possibility.'

'Well that's that then. It would have been nice to have met up with you again George. Anyway, c'est la vie. Bye.'

I replaced the phone on the hook.

The phone rang again almost immediately.

'Hello, Ronnie Wheeler.'

'Hello Ronnie, it's me again, George. What's so important that you need to actually meet up with me?'

'Well, I'm not going to tell you over the phone, am I George? Not with half a dozen of your lackeys listening in and recording every word we say. You wouldn't want that either. You know as well as I do that you never discussed our business in the company of any of your lot. It's a confidential matter, just between us two.' I could almost hear George's mind turning over, considering what to do. 'It could be to your advantage, might even move you up the ladder another rung or two.'

'Bit late for that now Ronnie, anyway, just bear with me for a moment.' I heard the turning of pages. 'I could give you two hours or so on Thursday p.m. starting at, say, two-thirty?'

'Fine with me, I'm not going anywhere. Best to allow for three hours or more though, there's quite a lot I want to get through.'

'OK, two-thirty prompt, Thursday the seventeenth, but this had better be worthwhile Ronnie and not another of your little games.'

If George did answer it was eliminated by the dial tone of a dead line.

'Still the same bastard George,' I thought to myself. I was almost pleased that he was.

A Postscript.

17 May, 2001.

I have to write this very quickly. If things go as I expect, I will be dead within the next two to three hours. I hope Mavis will be allowed to live but in view of what I've done, I very much doubt if she will.

⌘　⌘　⌘　⌘　⌘　⌘　⌘

The doorbell rang at two-thirty precisely. I knew it would be George and, as I was alone in the house, I opened the door for him myself. An elderly bloke with gold-rimmed glasses and silver grey hair stood at the entrance. Black suit, black coat and trilby. Surely not?

'George?'

The old bloke smiled. 'Yes, it's me Ronnie. How are you?' I could tell it was George as soon as he spoke, like a bloody talking income tax form.

'Bloody hell, I'd have never recognised you in a million years George.'

'Not even in forty it seems, Ronnie. We all get older you know and, remember, we actually only met face-to-face for just a few days all those years ago. Well, are you going to invite me in?'

'Yes, of course, sorry George. I know it's daft but I was expecting a much younger bloke. Come in, come in.'

George stepped into the hallway

'Shall I take your coat?' I asked.

'No thanks Ronnie, I'm afraid the old bones can't handle the cold like they used to.'

'You tell me! And I've got ten to fifteen years on you remember.'

Once inside, George looked around. 'Nice place you've got yourself Ronnie, you've been very successful in the transport business I hear.' I knew that George would have been kept fully informed about my every move since the deal. This thought helped me to see him again as the ultimate bastard.

'Was, I've been retired some years now, which you probably already know. But what about you, still working for the bad guys catching bad guys?'

'I wouldn't put it quite like that, but yes, although now it's more in semi-retirement. I still oversee two or three cases that I was particularly involved in, and yours is one of them. The firm like to maintain continuity whenever possible you know.'

'And are you going to give me a clue as to what your other 'cases' might be?'

'Some things never change, Ronnie, and my silence on such matters is one of them.' And we both chortle in the way old blokes do over bugger all.

This was not going the way I wanted. I hadn't expected George to have turned into some apparently harmless genial old grandad. This was not the arrogant young bastard I swore to do for all those years ago.

'I'll give you a quick tour round the place if you like George before we get down to business.'

'Why not?' he replies. 'If you can't mix a bit of pleasure in with a bit of business at our age, when can you?'

We chortle again.

'Well, with that sort of attitude, I propose that we accompany our tour with a couple of large brandies.'

'And why not?' he says.

We go into the lounge and I pour out two good measures of brandy. George takes my glass and gives me the one I had earmarked for him.

'Cheers,' he said with a knowing look. 'Habit of a lifetime.'

'So be it, still you took the one I wanted you to have.'

George almost spat into his glass. I winked and smiled.

'Just one of my little games George, just to get you going.' He realised he'd been wound up and we both laughed aloud. We clinked glasses and began our tour of the house chatting away like old mates.

He's impressed with my library, the snooker room, the oak landing with its leaded windows, even the bleeding kitchen gets him going.

'I'm beginning to think I went into the wrong business Ronnie.'

'One of those things we never know until it's too late, George, anyway I suppose we ought to get down to business. I'd been thinking about this for some time and Mick's funeral finally made my mind up. Let's go into my study, I've got some documents you might like to see, perhaps even to keep as a gift from me, for old time's sake.'

We walked down the hall to my study which is at the back of the house. 'Here we are, we can look at them in here.' I opened the door and George stepped into the room but, before he could react to what he saw, I forcefully shoved him forwards, closed the door and pointed a gun at him. George was clearly startled. He looked around the room in much bewilderment. Every wall, every window and every inch of the ceiling was covered with aluminium baking foil. Everywhere he looked he could see hundreds of reflections of himself, and of me, pointing a gun at him. He realised immediately that he was in extreme danger and reached inside his coat. I was expecting the move. 'I wouldn't if I were you, George.' I said pointing a gun at him. 'You'd never make it.'

He stopped mid-movement, his hand motionless within his coat. He began to take in the room. It was empty apart from a small oak table, a very sturdy high-backed wooden chair and three unusually short large ratchet lorry straps on the floor behind it. But as he looked around the foil clad walls the room appeared to be packed to overflowing. There were hundreds of chairs and tables and Georges and Ronnies as the walls and ceilings endlessly reflected distorted images of each other on the mirror-like foil.

'Did you get this idea from a funfair Ronnie? Roll up, roll up to see the 'Haunted House of Mirrors'.' He mimicked a fair ground barker drumming up a crowd and smiled at me in that same contemptuous way he had used all those years ago.

'Well not exactly, George. You see, while I appreciate your appreciation of the visual effects of my handiwork, the real purpose of the foil is to prevent any radio waves from either leaving or entering this room. An old trick I learned in the Signals. It's acoustically pretty water-tight too'. George's arrogance took a visible dive. 'The point is

George, that now we're in here, if I have to shoot you, your jokers outside won't even hear the shot. Not even through the mike you have hidden about your body somewhere. You know that this room reminds me of the night me and the lads took over Guernsey. I have cut you off totally from the outside world and, when I take your gun, you will have no effective means of defence or attack.'

George was now beginning to look decidedly worried. 'So the gun please George. Take it out slowly and carefully, finger tips only, and put it down ever-so gently on the table there.' George withdrew a small hand-gun and placed it on the table.

'There's a good lad. Now take off that coat of yours and put that on the table too. Again, nice and slow, no sudden movements, you don't want me to panic when I'm pointing a loaded gun at you.' George took off his coat and placed it on the table by the gun. His arrogance had disappeared. He was scared, and rightly so.

'Now sit down.' He sat down on the chair. As he did so I looped one of the ratchet tie-down straps around him and levered it until it bound him tightly to the chair.

'There's no need for all of this Ronnie, I came to talk with you, not to terminate our agreement.'

'Then why two guns?' I asked as I took another small pistol from the inner lining of his coat.

'Just a precaution in case you decided to do anything silly. You're not going to do anything silly are you Ronnie? Not after all of this time?'

'Would I ever George?' I replied and looped another two straps at equal spacing around his chest, ratcheting them until they were as tight as the first. I had cut the webbing straps short so that they were now down to about six feet long. This made them easy to use and manipulate. The webbing straps were four inches wide. With only one inch between them they encased George's chest from his neck to his navel. I had lengthened the ratchet levers on two of them by welding an extra length of steel bar to them. I slotted a bar into the third. This was the one I had used first to bind George. Initially maximum leverage was not essential but now it was and the bar gave it the same leverage power of the other two. I had extended the ratchet levers to about two feet long and so with very little effort they could exert a force of several tons.

'There we are, all nicely tucked in. Do you still admire my gall, Georgie boy?'

'What's this all about Ronnie? You know my men will have orders to come in as soon as they lose radio contact with me.'

It's very good for the ego when it's confirmed that you have sussed an opponent's game plan to the letter.

'That's what all the tour of the house and brandies guff was about Georgie. To anaesthetise your goons listening in somewhere in the undergrowth outside. They'll be thinking that we're getting on like a house on fire. They lose contact for a time, so what? Do they go in when there's no need and bugger everything up. Phew. More than their job's worth they'll be thinking.'

'They will only do that for a few minutes.'

'Yes, you could be right George,' I said. 'I'd best reinstate radio contact then.'

I patted his jacket and found the radio equipment, a microphone under the lapel and a transmitter unit sewn into the lining under the armpit. I carried the coat with the radio links intact into the kitchen talking loudly as I went. 'It looks as if we're going to get it sorted then, George. I'll get us another couple of brandies and a pot of tea, and we can have a drink while we sift through the stuff.' I clattered about in the kitchen as if boiling a kettle and getting cups and saucers ready. 'Are you sure you don't want me to take your coat, George?' Pause for ruffling of coat. 'Bloody hell, George, what have you got in here. Don't bother, two gun George, one aimed at me and another in reserve. You haven't changed have you? I'll put it over here for now.' I chatted on as if George was with me and as if he had decided all was going so well that he could dispense with the needs for emergency back-up. I placed the coat next to a radio which was tuned into the light programme. I estimated it was loud enough for George's 'hidden' microphone to pick up the sound and so over-ride any others. I returned to the room.

The chair had moved a little towards the table. At least George was still a trier, I'll give him that.

'Right George, now where were we? Ah yes, your men. I think they won't be interrupting us for a few hours. How long depends I suppose on when you told them to come in with guns blazing no matter what.

We said three hours for the meeting so that's probably our time-scale. By then we should have concluded our business.'

'I don't know what you're planning Ronnie, but, whatever it is, you know that I've played fair with you from the start.' George was beginning to realise that, perhaps for the first time ever, he was the one in deep shit.

'Fair, George, what's fair? Was it 'fair' for Barney and Ikey? Was it 'fair' for Stan and Bertie? They weren't even about when the copper and Mordant were killed, so they wouldn't even have been done as accomplices to murder. And why did they die? Because two of them went to watch a bloody cup-final together and the other two had a night out together. You knew they had wives and families, young kids, did you care a toss about them? I wonder if they'd say it was 'fair' of you to have them murdered just for going out with a mate?'

'I didn't murder them Ronnie, and you know it!'

I tightened the ratchets on each of the straps by two notches. George winced. The straps were beginning to bite. 'Don't play word games with me Georgie, I'm a bad loser.' I tried to mimic the way George had said those same words to me all those years ago. I went on.

'You may not have pulled the trigger, George, or stuck in the knife, or used the needle, but it was you that gave the order for them to be killed. As far as I'm concerned, you are responsible.' I pulled in another notch on the straps.

'I wasn't responsible Ronnie, I was just doing my job.' George was finding it harder to breathe now and an element of pleading had entered his wavering voice. 'I have a family, too, you know.' I ignore the family bit, I have to stay focused, avoid emotional involvement, stick to the plan.

'Only doing your job? Only doing your duty? Didn't half the Nazi war bastards at Nuremberg say that, George? Only doing your duty in killing four innocent fun-loving blokes who never killed anybody?' I tightened the ratchets another two notches. They were getting very tight now and George was having to breath in short rapid gulps as his lungs were constricted.

'And then there's Spider. You let your blokes stand by and watch while he was slowly tortured to death. The Hammonds cut his fingers off, gouged his eyes out, while your blokes stood by watching, hoping that it might get them a bit of useful information. Because of you, they let Percy blow Thelma's brains out while Tony, poor bastard, was watching a few feet away tied to a chair waiting to be tortured to death. Did you know he ended up in a fucking looney bin and cut his own throat? And you say, 'I was only doing my job Ronnie'. Funny sort of job wouldn't you say George, funny sort of fucking job?'

'I was only following orders, I had no alternative,' he panted at me. 'You remember I had to keep checking with my superiors when we were making the deal, I hadn't got the authority to do it on my own.'

I tightened each of the straps by one notch. I felt and heard a bone break in his left arm. George would have been in extreme agony but for the splinting effect of the strapping.

'Only following orders? That's the excuse the other half of the Nazi bastards used at Nuremberg. Keitel; Jodl; they tried to use it, how does that make you feel Georgie to know that you are using the same fucking feeble excuses as those bastards?'

I stood back and took out a note pad. 'Have you heard of the Nuremberg Principles George? Just nod if you are finding it difficult to speak.' He nodded. 'Well this is the fourth of those Principles. I'm going to read it to make sure that I get it absolutely right. This is not a time to make mistakes is it George? Here we go.'

I stepped back from him and read aloud. ' "The fact that a person acted pursuant to the order of his Government or of a superior does not relieve him from responsibility under international law, provided", note this George, "a moral choice was in fact possible to him". Now would you say that you didn't have a moral choice George? Would you say that you could not have refused? You had a moral choice George, and you ducked it. What have you got to say to that?'

'For God's sake Ronnie.' He panted for breath between each word.

'So God's come into it as well now has he? I thought it wouldn't be long before he poked his nose in. Would you tell me, George, what part did God play when you killed my mates?' I pulled in another notch on all three straps. More bones broke. 'Did he tell you to do it?' George did not have sufficient breath to reply or scream.

'And where was this God when you were protecting the guilty British establishment bastards, and some of the most despicable bastards ever to walk the face of the earth, to escape justice? You had copies of enough evidence, George, to hang, draw and quarter the lot of them, but you and your bosses choose to do nothing with it. It was you mob who allowed top Nazi bastards to live, to live free, to live the good life for years after they should have been done for. Why? Protecting your own maybe?' George's hands and face were deep blue and his eyes strained in their sockets. I leant down and spoke into his ear. 'And where was this God of yours when you told us you greatly looked forward to receiving orders to kill us one by one, was that just 'following orders?' Sorry George, it won't wash, not with me anyway.'

I stood back so that I could look him straight in the eyes. 'Now what I want to know is quite simple, George. Was it, is it, Her fucking Majesty's Government that's responsible for all of this, or is it some clandestine bunch of aristocrats and plutocrats who have been, and still are, pulling all the strings?' George shook his head in desperation. One thousand reflections of his own agony racked body and exploding face stared back at him, as if waiting for him to die. 'Loyal to the end, eh George? Well, some good it will do you. Do you think they will care a toss about you?' George could only look back at me from bloodshot eyes ballooning out from his swollen blue face.

'At Mick's funeral Mavis said to me that you had 'squeezed the life out of Mick, out of the rest of us and out of what we did'. For that, George, or whatever your fucking name is, and for the murder of some of my mates, and probably dozens of other poor sods I don't even know of, and for enabling Nazi criminals and British traitors and collaborators to avoid their due punishment, and now quite probably for the deaths of Mavis and me, Ronald Wheeler, I hereby sentence you to death in a manner appropriate to your crime.'

When I pronounced my solemn verdict, I was looking directly into his eyes. With that, I heaved on each of the ratchet levers in turn. The second strap suddenly lurched two notches and the back of the chair frame collapsed and, along with it, George's chest. Before I could move to tighten the last strap, the life had been squeezed out of George and he was dead. He died silently. Even the pleading sounds of agony depend upon the movement of air. I learned that in the Signals too.

I returned to the kitchen and clattered about engaging in imaginary chat and making tea again. After serving this extra dose of anaesthetic for George's goons outside, I returned to my study to write this unscheduled post-script. And so I have finished it. I have told our story. Always one to plan ahead and have an alternative hand ready to play, I had a telephone link via a friend's main line which George and his eavesdroppers were never aware of. Mick had one linked up too, and we used it a lot in recent years to keep in touch, particularly since computers and E-Mail came in. The wonders of this modern technology mean that with one click on my computer I can send our story through the electronic ether to a dozen or more friends and associates in the hope that at least one of them will have the guts to broadcast it to the world. Once I make that play there will be little to do but wait. But before I do, my final thoughts on my life, a life that began in the slums of Birmingham.

⌘   ⌘   ⌘   ⌘   ⌘   ⌘   ⌘

I am sitting in my deep red leather Chesterfield chair and drinking a large measure of Richard Hennessy cognac, the best there is, from a fine hand-cut crystal brandy bowl. I am smoking a large hand-rolled Romeo Y Julieta Churchill Cuban cigar. I am remembering the good times in my life and the good friends I have known and I am embraced by a cocktail of relief, melancholy and happiness. When George's hoodlums come to settle up I will have no regrets, and few will regret my passing.

But remember this, we all live and we all die, every last jackass fool of us, but few ever know what it is to be alive. To know life, you must have known death. And if, from having known death, you have known what it is to be really alive, truly alive, albeit if only for a fleeting moment, you will know that death, nor nothing else, can ever take that moment of supreme life away from you. My own moment was when we were riding with the tide towards the Cartaret beaches at sun-rise that day in June, 1954. It was when we were Vikings.

'Gert' parked in the grounds of Wullford Hall.

The 'Pill Box' at Saints Bay.

'Or let my lamp at the midnight hour,
Be seen in some high lonely tower.'

John Milton (Il Penseroso 1631)

Editor's Post-Script.

Ronnie Wheeler sent me his story on the seventeenth of May 2001 but, unfortunately, I did not look at it until the eighteenth. When I telephoned him but there was no answer. I rang his two helpers, an old couple called Janet and David Paseley. They told me that Ronnie had died in a fire at his home only the day before. The whole house had been totally destroyed but sufficient bits of Ronnie were found to conclude that he had died in the fire. A joint police and fire brigade investigation later concluded that Ronnie had been drinking heavily and had fallen asleep while smoking a cigar which set fire to him and the furniture. Two days later, the 'Deaths and Births' column of the Birmingham Evening Mail recorded the death of Mavis Tibbets from natural causes. Despite strenuous efforts on my part, I was unable to find any obituary I could link to the mysterious George.

If the documents were ever found or released they, nor the names of those Nazi traitors and collaborators inside the British establishment identified in them, have ever been revealed to the British public. When I was finally able to get to Ronnie's burnt out home, I collected some ashes from the room where he had written his last thoughts. I'll never know for sure if they contained any particle of Ronnie's remains, but I scattered them on the waters off Saints Bay, on the anniversary of Mick's death, in the hope that they did.

Ron Dawson

Ronnie picnicking above Saints Bay

The Police Station (Now Law Chambers).

The Radio Station (Now a private residence).

Acknowledgements

I wonder if anyone could ever write a first novel without the help, support, advice and encouragement of many, many, other people. I would like, therefore, to acknowledge and thank all those of my friends and acquaintances who have contributed, wittingly or unwittingly, to this, my first, novel. Firstly, my unreserved and warmest thanks to my wife Tricia, for her immeasurable contributions throughout the whole painful process. Without her support I would never have started it, let alone finish it! My deep gratitude and particular thanks then go to two good friends, Michelle and Ken Barker, for their invaluable advice and diligent proof reading. To Jackie Upton, Mike Ford and Roger and Deborah Merry, again good friends all, for their specialist input and welcome encouragement, Paul Brooks for his advice on DUKWs, and Tony Brassell for factual corrections to Guernsey details. Thanks too, to those of my friends in Winterborne Stickland and Pickering who put up with me during thpains of writing it. And finally, my warm thanks to Big Mick, Tony, and Spider; JD and JC; Bertie, Stan, Dave, Barry, Ernie, Ikey, Barney and Ray, and Brum itself, for they know what, and why!

The Harbour Master's Office, St Peter Port

The Telephone Exchange.

The Price Albert Pier Slipway, St Peter Port.

Editor's Notes

1) The Letters DUKW were used by General Motors to designate the year and type of the vehicle :

'D' for is the GMC (the makers) designation for 1942, first year of production.

'U' stands for 'utility' and amphibious

'K' denotes that the front wheels were driven.

'W' indicates that the four rear wheels were also driven via a tandem axle.

2) What Ronnie described as a German Pill Box at Saints Bay is in fact a Martello Tower built during the Napoleonic wars although it may have been used by German forces during their occupation of the island.

3) 'Rock Around the Clock' was written by Jimmy De Knight and Max. C. Freedman and recorded by Sunny Dae in 1952. Bill Haley recorded his different version in April 1954 with Decca Records (Myers Music). It became arguably the first 'Rock and Roll' anthem.

4) The original 'Shake, Rattle and Roll' was recorded by Big Joe Turner in December 1953. Bill Haley released his 'cleaned up', and most well known, version at the beginning of 1954 with Atlantic Records. It was written by Charles Calhoun (Unichappell Music Inc.).

5) The image of a DUKW on inside frontispiece is a modified image by Chicago Ducks, with kind permission. (www.chicagoducks.com).

6) 'Rock Around the Clock' was written by Jimmy De Knight and Max. C. Freedman and recorded by Sunny Dae in 1952. Bill Haley recorded his different version in April 1954 with Decca Records (Myers Music). It arguably became the first 'Rock and Roll' anthemn.

7) The original 'Shake, Rattle and Roll' was recorded by Big Joe Turner in December 1953. Bill Haley released his 'cleaned up', and most well known, version at the beginning of 1954 with Atlantic Records. It was written by Charles Calhoun (Unichappell Music Inc.).

The Worm that Flies in the Night
A Diary of Incestuous Love and Serial Murder

A multiple killer stalks the streets of a city. He kills young innocent women. He attacks and kills them randomly without pity or remorse. But he kills men too, any that might stand between him and his ultimate destiny. And what drives this monster to kill is an ageless, powerful and potentially destructive, force: a son's love for his mother.

'A brilliant exploration of the criminal psyche. A gripping and unnervingly accurate portrait of an obsessive and psychopathic killer.'

Dr Roger Merry, Cognitive Psychologist.

'Breaks the mould for crime thrillers. 'Who dunnit?' is turned on its head to become 'Why did he do it?' The distorted reality of a sociopath presented in all its horror. A must read'.

Mike Ford, Detective Sergeant (Ret) Crime Squad.

' A modern Greek tragedy inspired by the most ancient of sexual taboos and an informed understanding of behavioural and emotional maladjustment. '

Peter Penrose, Consultant Psychologist and Expert Witness.

ISBN : 978-0-9561732-0-1

The Amazing Adventures of
Scary Bones the Skeleton

In complete contrast to his adult novels, Ron has written the first in our 'Magical Stories for Children' series. Reviews by children, parents and teachers show that he has created a character who is loved by children and adults alike. In the first of the adventures, *The Lost Dog and Bone*, Scary Bones, his two friends Sasha and Ben, and a mysterious piece of red string, save a town's kidnapped dogs and find an important lost bone. In the second adventure, Scary Bones and his friends meet the Pirates of Brownsea Island. Aided by the island's famous red squirrels, the brave trio save the wonders of Captain Grow Bags treasures for us all to enjoy

These are traditional style stories for reading to younger children and non-readers and as a time and time again reading book for older readers. (up to 11-12 years). A loveable character and original heart warming tales destined to become future classics.

ISBNs : First **978-0-9561732-1-8** ; Second **978-0-9561732-2-5**

MTBooks
Mulberry Tree Books
Mulberry House
Winterborne Stickland
Dorset DT11 0NT

www.mulberrytreebooks.co.uk